the Steam Magnate

the Steam Magnate

DANA COPITHORNE

Aio Publishing Company, LLC

Published by Aio Publishing Company, LLC.

This book is printed on acid-free, recycled paper.

LIBRARY OF CONGRESS CATALOGING-IN-PUBLICATION DATA
Copithorne, Dana, 1980-
  The steam magnate / Dana Copithorne
    p. cm.
  ISBN 1-933083-08-5 (acid-free paper)
  I. Title.

PR9199.4.C667S74 2006
813'.6--dc22

    2006014952

Printed and bound in the United States of America.

To my family, near and far, for a lifetime of support,
especially my mother and father.

To my friends and mentors, especially Lauren
who encouraged me to write.

To the many people who've helped me
in innumerable ways.

book one

the meteor tower

Kyra arrived late at night, on a crowded, rattling steam engine, at an ancient place they called the 'City of Mirrors' or the 'Broken Glass City', depending on the language used. The city earns these names from stained glass that has been superimposed onto the exteriors of the walls and walkways, as though glass were shattered and thrown about into patterns, some random, others deliberate. The murky stone beneath dilutes the clarity of the glass and creates the illusion of hidden texture inside the walls, as when the stones beneath a river are visible under shallow water.

Despite the awesomeness of the place, apparent even under the dimness of night, Kyra felt gripped by a cold and powerful fear, as she had been sent here as a vassal to one whose mind was contorted toward revenge. The one who had sent her cared little if Kyra returned. She was to find a certain person in this city, to stay out of the sight of anyone of importance, and to rest assured that those who were making her a part of their scheme considered her quite worthless. The man she was seeking, whom she knew by the name of Eson, had likely arrived some days earlier and with a great deal more opulence than her own arrival had occasioned. There was mention of a contract or deed of some kind that she was to try to obtain from him through her innocuous and seemingly guileless manner, and through deception and over an extended period if need be. It would not be an instantaneous thievery, and perhaps not thievery at all, as the contract was said to be at least half the property of her employer. So was her task set before her, a vast pool of darkness into which she must step. She would be prompted with further instructions as progress was made.

But she had no proof he was in the city yet, and as she later lay in her narrow hostel bed absently listening to the sibilant plotting of more leisurely travelers, she had no choice but to imagine her entire venture would be in vain, a folly of lost days and a rapid return to inconsequence. She had been supplied with a meager ration of information, and otherwise left to figure out on her own how she would accomplish the deed before her.

But soon she slept, and just before dawn, she caught a glimpse of him in a dream. He disappeared around a corner in a streetcar terminal, and she inhaled vividly a fragrance, soft and northern, of a coat of silken wool. The metallic complaint of an iron gate was the dream's last impression, and it evolved into the waking world of the hostel. It became the sound of a bed frame as the person ensconced in the bed directly above her own dislodged herself mightily and swung over the edge of her bed, with all the grace of a drunken mountain goat.

Attempting stealth on the descent, the heavy-hoofed traveler managed to kick Kyra's bed only once before gaining a foothold on the floorboards. Kyra silently congratulated the mountain goat and pretended to sleep for several more moments to alleviate any of the goat's worries of having woken her. It was yet early, and companions who awoke together lowed quietly and slipped out with small commotions. Stealth was her own area of expertise and her sole claim to achievement, so she could hardly begrudge others for lacking it.

Decisively, she stretched her legs and sat up into the light of morning to make sense of the coming day. The air in the hostel was clean and bore overtones of clay, being made of the light stone that fashioned this city. She met the glance of another guest walking past her dorm bed, who had the fierce, lionhearted face of an optimist and a golden-red mane that brought to mind flowering, sun-soaked valleys. Her expression made Kyra wonder if the day ahead could harbor something beyond her own skeptical forecast.

The flow of days during her interlude in that place did indeed take on a quality beyond her woeful prognostications. The odd resonance with strangers and a near miss with the Man in Question (as Veridi, the esteemed Heiress who had sent her here, affectionately called him), in addition to the blurring of hours and the intimately basic level on which she came to know the inner marrow of the courtyards, walkways and nightspots, all gave it the cast of a fated landscape in which she was to learn something, but would never know exactly when she had done so. And the odd friendships besides would make her marvel that it had only been a few short days in her life. When she finally left the city, it was into circumstances so strange that even this interlude would reorient itself as the more familiar and comforting world.

Today she met the fierce, glowing-haired optimist at breakfast, drawn to her as a shadow that can only exist in the path of the sun. Her name was Neriv, and she came from the overgrown, vine-covered estuary land on the southern coast. Neriv belted out an almost growling laughter at the dry bread and watery brew served as breakfast, and she and Kyra agreed to forage out in the market for something heartier. They took a liking to each other, with the openness and lack of suspicion that is the unique, random prescience of those who meet on the road—yet Kyra had been lectured roundly in advance of her journey about things such as fostering friendships while under the oath of the assignment, and though she cared little for authority, that of the Heiress or otherwise, she did hold a natural regard for confidentiality and resolved to keep a solid mask over the true nature of her sojourn.

Together she and Neriv found a soup shop in the market that vended a rich broth with meat and spices and peppery local vegetables. They had it with a light, sweet kind of tea and a square of the region's hallmark dessert, which was slippery of texture and sharp of taste.

They sat for a minute after breakfast on the edge of a fountain in the crowded market. Neriv shared a bit of her story with Kyra between enthusiastic mouthfuls. "I grew up a long, long way away. Down in the river country. We have such a beautiful river near our house, my family and I. But I need to see some other kind of place, you know? So I've taken up a job up in the north country." She shuddered lightly and paused, as though the chill air of the north wound about her already, and as though the choice had not really been one of her own making. "These days here, they're my enjoying ones. I have to make my way up north later in the week." She spoke quietly yet with emotion.

"But watch out here, watch out for yourself. Don't lose yourself in this place. I don't really trust it here." Neriv looked intently at her, as one does who has found agreement with one branch of another's mind, and hopes to trace the branch back into an network of agreement in the roots of the other's thoughts.

Kyra took a sip of spiced tea. "People don't quite seem real here... they're masked, in a way," she offered in a companionable semblance of agreement, though she had thought little of it. She watched the figures drifting past on their invisible trajectories, people moving as elements in the landscape—very few of them meeting her eyes with their own, a wall of anonymity surrounding every person or small group who passed by. The market scene seemed a modernist composition of shape and movement. People seemed oddly veiled from communication in a way that she also distrusted instinctively, but to her it was no different from most cities. In Kyra's rustic place of origin, a stark transparency of motive and a sense of honesty had been the custom, but she had grown familiar with urban places in her few years away from home. This city was only one step further along that continuum, being the largest city she had yet visited. She had volunteered little information about her own place of birth, and Neriv did not ask.

Even so, this was no vast metropolis, and the two travelers relaxed in the morning market. The sky was hazy above, and the ambient quality of the light stone and glass encased them both in a glow of impermeability; they became as glassy and masked as the city dwellers themselves. Kyra felt insulated from her earlier fears, the intimidating figure of Veridi diminishing in her mind.

The southerner watched swirling marketgoers for a moment without speaking, then rummaged in her pack and soon began flipping through a worn guidebook, with a list of names crossed out down the inside of the first page. "Here's me, right at the end." Neriv pointed to the last on the list of the book's owners. Here and there were notes, watermarks, the odd drawing, as more than one of the owners had had a penchant for leaving caricatures speckled around the pictures. "This is my grandfather," she added, indicating a leonine caricature of a young fellow haggling at the same market they sat in now, which appeared to have changed little since his times. "He also rode on horseback across the desert between here and the south lands!" she said with pride, as she turned to another caricature of her adventuresome relative. He was shown this time on a galloping steed, clouds of desert dust kicking up behind the horse's hooves. The worn parchment pages of the book evoked an old world of chivalric deeds and heroic expeditions.

No such personalization decorated the grim dossier that served as Kyra's guidebook on her mission to the city. Neriv rifled through her book with ardor and talked Kyra into going up the hill in the middle of the city to its ancient meteor tower, rumored to have been built of melted glass fallen from space. She gestured beyond the market toward the warm, stone hillside. At its crest an entirely glass and metal structure could be seen pressing gauntly upward at the sky as though a storm of geometric shards had frozen there in an instance of divine intervention, or as though people had tried to intervene in the divine.

A bit of sightseeing would pose no threat to the already dubious success of her mission, Kyra decided. Now that she had a companion in this foreign place, she felt even less pull toward the burden of her solitary duty. The scant information with which she had been entrusted gave the impression that most of her tracking should occur in the later hours of the day.

The thought still did give her pause. Who *was* this ill-loved man she was supposed to be seeking? The Heiress reviled him, and Kyra had no reason to believe he was worthy of anything else. She really knew only a bare minimum, and felt distanced from the pattern of events in which she had been engulfed.

She set aside her nagging fear of the one who had set her on this mission. The anonymous, glass-coated city promised her a world beyond dossiers and grim duties.

They made their way upward along stone walkways like riverbeds with shining glass intermixed in the sand-colored stonework. Houses were stacked one on top of the other as though they had grown, the way coral grows in warm seas, from some original homes now buried deep beneath them. Glass windows scattered over the carved stone walls and stained glass held together by iron frames covered whole rooms or roofs with clear-colored patterns. Indoor gardens like glass aquariums or museum cases were visible within, and their botanical denizens looked out over courtyards and stairwells. Certain stairways had been encroached upon by the expanding buildings and were too narrow to serve as anything more than garden terraces, providing angular views into other courtyards and stairwells. Trams lunged along ancient trackways cut into the matrix of the town, and electric wires craned precariously over the narrow roads. They were in the elegant old quarter of the city where culture, though decadent and beyond its moment of cosmopolitan glory, wrapped itself with a pretty sort of vengeance around every streetlight and cobblestone.

Enjoying the sound of her companion's voice, Kyra asked her more about the places she'd come from, and Neriv spoke both fondly and with pride of her homeland. She would always overlay Neriv's flowing voice over this landscape, no matter how often she returned.

As they ascended the hill, the landscape sank below them, gaining depth and distance. The world appeared to be made of sand sculpted into architecture, and further beyond, a flat patchwork sea of grasses stretched into the distance. Industrial and poverty-stricken areas and bland suburbs recently hewn out of unsuspecting ground were set into perspective. Kyra casually formed a map in her mind, as she would have to seek out the quarry's wide-ranging haunts later on.

But by midday, she had been led far from thinking about her search, the man in the dossier or the map. It was due to a kind of recklessness in her character that she had even become enmeshed in the cursed scheme, and that same recklessness pushed away her obligations like a marble that rolls to the lowest point on a floor. The glass floor slid past beneath her and she was lost in the moment of escape and ascension that drives the pilgrim and the wanderer alike.

Breathless but fueled by curiosity, they reached the structure at the top of the hill and after passing coins through a trough under a window and being collected into a small herd, they were led into the structure. A guide with sweeping gestures and an echoing voice led them upward through the tower. Through portals in the melded meteoric glass and metal the hilltop air flowed as though music was alive within the walls, and each place within the structure had a pitch of its own. Echoing strains of conversation sieved through, rocketing around in the constant, resonating undertone of the place. Though a relatively modern construction, the place created a primordial music and was the city's monument to the living sense of change that flowed through its streets.

Kyra fell further and further away from any notion of searching. The man named Eson was only then a photograph and a few sheets of paper, an obsession of the overly possessive heiress who had sent her to this city. She knew only of his fashions, his odd line of business, his supposed, vague wronging of the Heiress. Kyra had never been riveted by politics or business, and he interested her as little as the international money exchange columns that stretched across the pages of the morning news. An obscure steam power magnate from the closed lands to the north of the border, he might as well have been a cardboard cutout, young though he looked in his file's picture, and rich though he must be. He wore a styled suit in the photo and sported an ostentatious hairstyle of the kind much admired in places of consequence the world over. Kyra didn't consider herself materialistic, having little use for power or overt wealth, and an instinctive pride set her apart from the elite class to which the Heiress belonged.

She was vaguely fascinated by the lands of the north, but knew no one who had gone there, and had no clear image of the place in her mind. She had heard only vague, unnerving stories of the north, or the Steam Territories, as they were sometimes called. Her idea of the north contrasted darkly with the vision of the City of Glass, which increasingly distracted her as she submerged in its aura. The deeply layered town below her was all she needed for the intense moment in which she lived.

The guide was speaking of other meanings in the glass structure, of nomads in the arid lands nearby, of cultures clashing, and of glass being carried up the hill and piled skyward. Kyra could have found it very interesting if she were in a more tranquil frame of mind. She listened, then didn't, and with Neriv drifted away without meaning to as Neriv struck up a conversation with some other people. Throughout the day, they grew into a band of myriad and exotic wanderers which took on its own life, rolling down from the hilltop and into the city. The pack was alive with an electric excitement and they surged through the city like a wave of wild creatures.

Evening fell upon them and they descended by tram into the lower regions of the town. The stone walls and paths glowed faintly under soft streetlights, and when they got off the tram, they were on a maze of narrow streets lit by paper lanterns where droves of people, in every grade from the blandly handsome to the strange and transient, gathered and wandered by cafés and nightclubs. Roiling and thick as the crowds were, Kyra clasped the arm of one of her own crowd to avoid being separated from her group in the sea of random subcultures.

She was suddenly struck by curiosity as she passed by the sign of one nightclub café, tacked above a narrow door propped open in a flaking wooden façade. The name boiled up into her mind as a place she had been told to search in her dossier. It didn't look like much more than a down-market dive, but people were streaming in and out of the narrow doorway, a dim, rosy light escaping with each movement of the door. The inward-streaming crowd hinted that the entry led somewhere infinitely more impressive than seemed possible from the disintegrating exterior. It must have been once a classy enterprise, to be graced with a wooden exterior in this dry plains city. The façade was faded to darkest forest hues, and only absorbed the light from surrounding lanterns.

She chose to take the club's sudden looming presence as a sign that her life's events ran along a predetermined course, and must be reacted to and played out according to that course. She felt the sudden sense that a law of uncanny balance had led her there, and that the law of fate was best not ignored. This same law of fate had often served her well when seized by sudden whims, as it seemed to append her own small, individual will onto the collective, deep desire of the universe. With little thought and sudden fervor—her usual method of action before the things that were soon to take place—she made a decision.

She made a brief excuse to her group, who cooed and doted before releasing her to the night. She felt a wrench of unease at being alone again, but an image of the Heiress boiled up in her mind, and she knew action must be taken to escape retribution. Pretending to head back to the tram station, she circled around the block and turned in to the café's door. It was an immense place inside but warmly lit, like a cave taken over by fireflies. Though its exterior had consisted only of a shabby, decaying wall and a sign with a chip missing, the interior was nearly extravagant, set on three tiers with a stage at one end on the main level and flimsy staircases leading to upper terraces on all sides. The paper lanterns were in profusion, and a jazz band was warming up to play to a crowded room. People jostled everywhere and bar maids and waiters swam about the crowds, surfacing and ducking though the guests as efficiently as dolphins navigating a choppy ocean. She swam through as well, circling the perimeter of the main floor, surveying the terraces. And there on the third floor, in a distant corner, was the man she had been told was her mark, though a quarry dangerous and unpredictable. The silken coat that had made its sly way into her subconscious was slung over his chair. He wore a styled suit and sported an ostentatious hairstyle of the kind much admired in places of consequence the world over. He sipped a martini pensively, and seemed, even in stillness, to calculate and weigh options with eyes darkened in the dim light of the terrace.

It could not have been any easier. She nearly laughed in victory at how her instinct had led her so well! She had found him, now she had only to barge her way through a fluid multitude of partygoers and up two frail staircases. The Heiress and her agents had led her to believe it would be difficult!

Her first obstacle was a heavy knot of young people far gone with drinking, and as she tried to sidestep them they expanded their circle outward to meet the wall. The music had started up in full force and people began to jostle all the more. She managed to get through the gauntlet of the first group only to nearly collide with a waiter and an overstacked tray. Beyond this was a knot of dancers, thick as the interwoven figures carved into a temple wall, but living and radiating life as no wall could. "If they were statues, I could climb over them," thought Kyra and nearly laughed again as she submerged into the crowd, a detached sense of play descending on her. She heard a hiss of air as someone nearby activated their levitation platform and rose above the crowd, finding their footing again on the second level terrace. He climbed casually over the railing to meet some friends at a table that nearly upended with the weight of an extra hand. Kyra watched with envy from the sea of the first floor.

It was a good five minutes before she successfully wove her way through this group to the bottom of the lantern-lit stairwell,

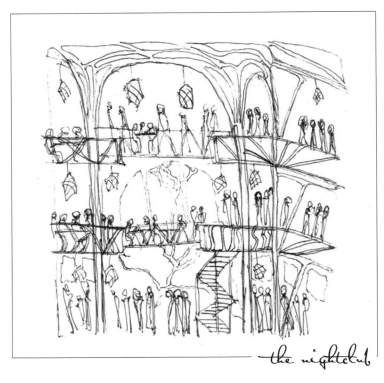

the nightclub

where there appeared to be a dam composed of those attempting to move between floors. The weak structure of the staircase listed under too much weight, and she feared that it would collapse altogether while she was in transit. Gaining the second floor, she felt a dizzying sense of altitude and a change in the air as the heat of the dance floor dissipated but the smell of smoke from those lounging at tables filled the air. Quickly rounding the terrace to the next staircase she anxiously realized she had let the man called Eson out of sight for several minutes. She dashed up the staircase to the dimly lit and significantly emptier third floor, into an atmosphere of dark tables and dubious transactions. The music was still lively and the party still happening, but she felt a lurch of despair as she saw the table empty and devoid of person or object but for a small envelope and an empty martini glass. She inhaled deeply and caught only the slightest strain of a fur coat, from someone at another table. She exhaled just as deeply and slouched into the seat closest the envelope. She chose to assume, by the same rule of fate that had led her into the club, that it had been left for her. She lifted the unsealed edge, but got no further as she was addressed by a voice, low but female and tinged with an acrid tone.

"You've been remiss." The voice paused, and Kyra put away the letter. The voice did not ask to see it. The woman attached to the voice was tiny but sharp-eyed and sharp-clawed, and wore a charcoal-colored suit. The voice was her most definitive characteristic and it continued, cutting through the white noise of the club.

"The Heiress did not intend for you to dally with other young fools. Do you really think you can shirk your responsibilities so blatantly and face no consequences? You found him by chance, yes, but you arrived too late, too distracted and feckless to follow through with our commands. Whatever miraculous power of intuition you think is at your disposal is a false compass. You must be as incisive as an arrow, and as quick. We are watching you, and don't let this remote location lull you into thinking you're on vacation. Young mercenaries like you are as expendable as martini glasses." For emphasis, her claws lifted the martini glass off the table and released it delicately over the floor, where it shattered daintily. A waitress behind the bar bristled visibly. The voice spoke once more:

"Your luggage has been moved from the hostel to a hotel close to this café. I will escort you there myself."

With that, Kyra was ferried through a back exit on the third floor, down an outside staircase of the kind appended conveniently to certain buildings—was it the escape route used by the elusive man so important to Veridi? They passed through the narrow, lantern-lit streets into a quieter area of desolate courtyards and closed shutters, then through one last courtyard, which seemed to emanate a ghostly whiteness from its stone floor and walls. The claws authoritatively opened a set of doors at the end of the courtyard, inlaid with colored glass in fan-shaped patterns, then directed Kyra to another door. She left Kyra with this warm goodnight:

"Don't let the appearance of luxury deceive you into thinking you are being rewarded. Confidentiality is of the utmost importance, and you can consider this solitary confinement. We shall expect you to take up active seeking tomorrow. Understood?" Without waiting for an answer, she whisked herself away across the courtyard, disappearing into the white stones around a bend in a passageway. It was Kyra's sole live encounter with this abrupt apparition.

"Of course." She answered into the darkness, and turned into the doorway as the voice had indicated, closing the door softly behind her and turning the latch.

The room was small and sparse but clean and possessed the cool, arid feel of the desert at night. All things were the blue of night-vision, and she did not bother to turn on any lights and reveal the room's daylight colors. Her thin traveling case awaited her, unopened on the bed, and the envelope, also unopened in her coat pocket, awaited her investigation. She changed into the comfort of nightwear and opened the letter to read by moonlight.

The suave penmanship of the message altered the portrait she had so far of the man in question:

Sarah,

Forgive my absence at this, our first and possibly most vital

rendezvous. I was forced to remove myself quickly. My lungs
are weak, and sought desperately the night air. Please come
tomorrow instead, to the third arch of the monument at the
Hour of Birds.

   I wait in hope,

   Eson

There was something touchingly ingenuous about this message, which the intended 'Sarah' would never receive. It appeared
to be written by one in a position of leisure and confidence, to one
who would have little choice but to accept the new summons.

She felt both a relief at how easy this would make tomorrow's
search, and a developing unease as she gained a sense of a person
beyond the dossier. In sleep she hoped to slough away the weight
of sordid and helpless involvement in the affairs of other people.

Despite the turmoil plaguing her to the moment of oblivion
she slept well that night, in the room that was like the night desert. She put the evening's trouble out of her head and dreamt
only of a dust storm enveloping rooms, people, and monuments.
When she awoke and looked out a small window onto the street
below, there was indeed a haze over everything, beyond the dust
of ages that had coated every stone already. Every piece of glass
was dulled to the luster of minerals. The breeze was imbued with
the sensation of chalk. She was little surprised to see a dream turn
to reality, though she had never had the experience before.

She shielded her eyes against the unaccustomed glare, and
turned back into the room. A type of breakfast, as well as a slip
of paper that said simply *Pretend to be Sarah*, had appeared just inside the door to the room, and seeing as there was no table, she
carried it back to the bed to eat the way she imagined both Eson

and her own Heiress took their breakfasts. She imagined further that they had done this together in intimacy at some point, and that therein lay the reason for her own inclusion in a scheme that was part revenge and part subterfuge. The strange codes of honor binding the aristocracy created the necessity for elaborate plans and the delegation of impure tasks to underlings like her. She would not have chosen to aid in the bizarre machinations of the absurdly wealthy and under-occupied, but she'd had little choice in the matter.

The truth was this: she had been caught in the storehouses of the Heiress's illustrious house while working there as an itinerant servant. She had been caught perfectly by chance, as her ability to avoid detection had allowed her to sneak into these same storerooms on many occasions before. She had taken, as gifts to a dear friend back in the hinterlands of her home place, only a selection of the smallest and least valuable things, such as a watch that had stopped working but could be fixed with the right form of expertise. Her friend valued such things beyond any reasonable amount, and expressed such a fascination at each object Kyra brought that she continued to risk the thievery.

Those who caught her were themselves servants who had little reason to be in such a place so they showed little outrage, but only a cool sort of self-congratulation, as those who have discovered a windfall and stand to profit by it. They smirked to one another and all but ignored her as they pushed her through the old wooden corridors leading up to the Heiress's incongruously modern conference room, with its intimidating, simple pine doors. With trepidation, one of the captors pushed lightly on the door and shoved her into the dreaded chamber ahead of them, remaining himself on the doorstep.

"We caught this one lurking in the vaults," he muttered with a mixture of fear and slovenly righteousness. As the Lady of the House only looked up cynically from her papers and offered no word of encouragement, the two shrank back through the door as if pulled on a leash, leaving Kyra to face the Heiress's bored and unyielding glare alone. She was older than Kyra but still a young woman, a recent inheritor of a massive estate, with an icy cast to her sharp features that bespoke an ancient lineage of overlords. Kyra stood at the bottom end of the room, hoping to appear solid, though tempted to lean on the door.

"If you needed money, you need only have asked," the Heiress said in a sardonic tone of voice that implied more the opposite of her words, and let Kyra know exactly on what lower ground she stood. (Though she already knew this, let no mistake be made.)

"But since you obviously have ambitions toward earning it the hard way, I propose to you a task." This time her tone made clear there was no choice in whether Kyra accepted this task. "It will involve traveling away from here, and if you do not return after completing it to my satisfaction, you will receive no payment. If you fall under the power of forces other than our own, we will cut you off from all the benefits accrued by your position in our esteemed network. And we will ensure difficulty in your later endeavors such as they may be. You have brought your head up from under the sand, and now you must prove your worth to us or lose everything you have achieved so far." Kyra contained a sigh brought on by a sense of relief on one hand, and an abyssal sense of dread on the other.

The Heiress paused, then concluded abruptly, "A lower agent will inform you of the necessary details." Kyra heard the door behind her open, and the same leash reflex pulled her backward into the company of her still waiting captors. They looked at her questioningly, and she nodded to them as though nothing were out of the ordinary. They stood and watched after her incredulously while she walked away, seemingly as free as they themselves. She managed to hide from them completely her sense of confusion and dread at the odd form of punishment she had been offered.

The ghost-white courtyard looked even more unreal under the new haze of dust in the morning. She had several hours before the Hour of Birds. She felt a doubled unease within herself, as there was no way of rehearsing or predicting the outcome of the meeting. Eson's letter informed her just enough of the situation that she felt she might be able to swing the necessary deception.

She quelled her doubts and rode the tram to the market, half-hoping to meet Neriv again, as though nothing had interrupted their night on the town.

But explanations would be required where none were possible, and in any case, her friend had spoken of leaving very soon, and had perhaps left early that morning, awaking to the dust and deciding to give the slip to this city. The Broken Glass City did seem emptier and somewhat calmed, though the market still pulsed with life, and the local foods smelled as appetizing as they had the previous morning. Kyra tried a kind of hot bread stuffed with mushrooms and savory sauce, with more of the aromatic local tea to follow it. She enjoyed a satisfaction in the rich food and calming tea.

She browsed through hanging bolts of fabric, and felt that no matter what became of the quest, the chance to travel to this city, many hours train-ride from her own, would be a worthwhile trade. The fabric seller spoke another language, as beautiful in its unknown sounds as the materials were in their exotic textures and patterns. They held a broken conversation in the bits of language they had in common, but soon gave up, ending the transaction with universal shrugs and head-shakings. She bought a small woven cloth piece for a friend back in her home territories as a promise to herself that she would return someday, though she had no wish for it to be soon.

In this part of the city few people were local, and many had traveled some distance for an interlude in this place that had been the ancient capital of the surrounding country. Though considered a backwater by some, the place seemed to hold a unique sway over others. Kyra decided to take a winding route toward her ultimate destination, the ancient stone monument. Her way passed through an area of light warehouses and machinery, many of which had been converted into artisan's studios in a recent trend toward bohemianism. The dust thinned perceptibly as she came to the top of a hill, and she looked out over a landscape of cluttered scrap yards and extinct forms of machinery. Some dark forms were firing glass over a flame in one enclosure, while in another, people sorted industriously through panels from old vehicles. Tracts of dust obscured other tableaus, and she breathed thankfully of the clear hilltop air before descending once more. Beyond another low area, she could see a tram careening on its narrow trackway around a hillside, and above, the craggy heights of the monument, which she recognized from photographs, though in books it usually took a second place behind the starkly modern glass monument she had seen yesterday. This monument was older, on a smaller hill, and smoothed into the surrounding lines of the city by centuries. It stood as a silent tribute to the contemplative endurance of the city.

She was in a strange state of mind as she passed through the final low streets before reaching the monument. The buildings had once again become the narrow and ancient structures she had seen in the old quarter. People stepped out onto their enclosed balconies in the uncommonly dull midday air. As people do who find themselves in odd circumstances, Kyra naturally projected her own sense of the moment onto the people she saw, and assumed the city was in the midst of a universal, significant occurrence. She felt a heightened sense of purpose. The end of the street disappeared in the dust and she fell into step with someone who murmured their concern about the coming days, half for her ears, and half as if questioning the dusty air itself about its intentions. Her throat took on a dry feeling from walking and from dust, and she stopped in at a very small tea shop. In the center of one wall a rather opaque etched window looked out onto the street.

Cool tea had rarely tasted so good, as she looked out into the half-obscured sky.

She was addressed suddenly while she drank. "Of course, you know what this is all about, right?" said the tea shop's clerk, a brooding young man whose low, husky voice barely cut through the sound of the air purifier plugged in on the counter. She was stirred from her thoughts.

"No. What's what all about?" she replied.

"The haze that's blowing over everything today. You know, the dust." He gestured to the window and the outside world, from which they two were insulated under the whirring air purifier's powerful effect. "They say it's because of a massive storm over the eastern ocean right now, that's pushing the dust from the desert into this part of the continent. It's supposed to become impossible to navigate within the next two days. Anybody who can is packing up and leaving. It's unreal." He indicated the small air machine beside him. "I got this as a present last year from a paranoid relative, but it may be my ticket in the coming week. I'm thinking of putting a sign out in the road, letting people know they can come in here for a breath of fresh air and a cool drink."

Kyra looked around the shop, empty but for the two of them. On the countertops around him were pieces of small machinery, half-built projects, and some delicate tools. The walls were adorned with maps, set out in an order from ancient to modern. She looked more closely at them and realized that many were maps of possible futures. The nations and autonomous territories,

stone and glass buildings; tea shop

the disputed regions, were remapped in patterns alternately plausible and unlikely, terrifying and assuring. There were geographical maps, including one that showed their region subsumed under a rising ocean. A political map made one hundred years ago predicted they would be under the sway of the northern empire by the present day. The maps disconcerted her but at the same time made her curious.

She remarked on one of the maps, then asked him about his take on the nature of the world. "In a city of ancient things, you surround yourself with prophetic visions of the future, and with technology. Do you think future technologies will save us from the world, or destroy it?" She spoke in a way that was natural and unpresuming.

He looked surprised, but replied with interest, "I look to the future, and to technologies, because I think technology can protects us from forces rooted in the past. I can't do anything about the past, but the future is ours to adapt."

Kyra's next thought was gently cynical. "We use technology to protect ourselves from nature, and hope that we can call on nature to protect us from our technology."

"I agree that the way technology is used now damages the natural world. I think the two can be integrated, though, so that technology works in keeping with nature."

Kyra nodded. She felt pleased to find someone with whom she could have this kind of discussion. In the halls of the Heiress's house, there had been little to engage the mind beyond daily concerns—and while the city here was rich with promise, losing track of her friends had left her unanchored. Finding a new ally gave her solid ground again, and shook her from the apprehension she felt about her impending meeting at the monument.

He was asking her name, telling her he was called Jado. She asked him what he had meant by forces rooted in the past. Did he mean old kingdoms or old beliefs? He only shook his head, said it would take too long to explain, and that these forces were like old gods, but posed as humans. They were mortal, yes, but held powers that put them above other mortals.

She would have asked him more about his cryptic remarks, but she looked at her watch and realized she was in danger of being late for her meeting. "Is there a fast way to get up to the monument from here?" She spoke too abruptly, conscious of breaking the bond between them with her relatively mundane question.

"There is a bus, but it doesn't run very often. It's best just to walk, I'd say." He sounded a bit detached, as if veiling himself from her now that he knew their conversation was at an end.

"Thanks for your... conversation. I have to go now, but I'll come back here another time."

"Bring some friends when you come back!" he called after her, as if to solidify the agreement that they would meet again. She smiled back to him, then took a deep breath and darted out into the street. She wondered if she would ever see him again.

But she had to think only of what lay ahead of her. Sarah had been late last night, and she didn't want to follow suit. She had no way to know what she was risking, and no reason to believe she would have a second chance at meeting her quarry.

She arrived late that day, when we at last were able to meet.
I remember her, out of breath and coated lightly with the dust
that had swept over everyone and everything that day. I deserved
to be kept waiting after my weakness of the night before. I was
not used to the dry air of this city, and felt unable to go through
with the meeting in that crowded and smoky place. Once on the
hilltop the air around me became clear, and it was with gratitude
that I accepted a warm towel for my face from the owner of a
drinks counter near the monument. I made my way to the third
arch, where there is a comfortable place to sit and relax in relative secrecy. I had bought us two cool drinks, but didn't have the
patience to wait before beginning mine. I hadn't realized how dry
my throat had become, and my eyes as well felt slowed. I had kept
my coat with me, despite its odd appearance in the mild climate
here. I am told I carry the cold with me when I leave the North,
and cannot be really comfortable without its presence. Though

it seems eccentric to some, it's a solid tradition of the northern mountains, not one I am about to give up for a difference in fashion sense. I pushed my hair out of my eyes, and it too was brittle from dust. *I must leave here* was my most urgent thought, an impulse from inside, an instinctive fear of this attack by nature on me and on the city. I am used to exacting control over my surroundings, gearing them for comfort, and taking that leisurely ability in my stride. Now I coughed and headed for shelter, as though I were one of the nameless people around me.

I have always loved this city. Even on my first trip here several years ago, I sat in this spot and bought a drink from the same counter, admired the same view. You can look up into the higher arches of the monument and see carvings in the stone that tell of both ancient myths and the history of the country, from its beginnings until the most recent years, as several stone panels are left blank and a new carving is commissioned every decade.

The famous meteor glass tower is nearby as well, a unique monument to the city's history. Earlier in this century, nomads who subsist in the dry plains and deserts south of the city found great pieces of silvery glass, as if a giant marble had fallen from space and shattered on the surface of the desert. The hill areas on which the central city is built had once been the grounds of the nomads' great riding competitions and endurance quests, a site they'd never relinquished their claim to, and leaders of the tribes had come riding into the city's old governing center brandishing pieces of the glass and calling for a symbolic architectural structure rising toward the heavens that had disgorged the glass— along with a repatriation of the hill-site that had been theirs.

Somewhat miraculously the city had agreed, and laboriously, the people had hauled large pieces of the glass up to the top of a hill in the middle of town and had secured them together with a metal structure, to create the current architectural concatenation.

A symbolic confluence between the city people and the wild nomads, its mystic passages were said to guide the pilgrim toward heaven. Visible in the great distance, it served as a compass for the nomads, an orientation to the heavens. An inscription on its south side reads, in a desert language, "At upward angles walking, our faces are in view of god." They claim this lettering catches the sun's blaze and is visible from miles away, but I think it may be fanciful desert talk.

They didn't used to charge people to walk around in it, either. But now it's so mucked about with tourists there isn't any choice. The desert people protested the fee being implemented, and there was an unpleasantness at the site about twenty years ago. The government wanted to keep this unpleasantness under wraps and so appeased the nomads' demands with a token treaty right: if you can prove you hold desert ancestry, you may walk the passages for free. Though I respect their courage and ancestral rights, I'd dishonor my own clan if I claimed relation to another tribe, and simply paid the couple of beads at the entry counter. Though my feet have been wetted in a privileged stream since my birth, I've not become a party to every advantage in these lands!

I could see the meteor tower from my spot at the older monument. In design, the glassworks relates to some astronomical system of one of the nomadic groups, and casts an unruly sense of disorder over the delicate, somehow vulnerable city at its feet. I know I have a prejudice, having been brought up with my ancestors' rigid codes of belief, but the glassworks vexes me nonetheless. I always feel much more comfortable under the ancient and venerated curvatures of the monument in which I sat.

My study of history began in this city, and when I earned my fortune I set up a second residence here, where I do work in the early part of each day. I don't mind being away from my home in the north as long as I know I can easily return there and tend to my family's spring. Wherever there is freedom I am home, and the political unrest boiling over in the northern capital has an unpleasant way of spilling over into everyday life, so I am glad of the occasional respite. In fact I had planned to stay here much longer than I now anticipated.

My personal life has been a bit of a wasteland these days, I have to admit. I have a bad habit of forming my friendships from a light, weak substance and so have a wide but shallow band of acquaintances, all with busy lives conducted in far-flung places. It's the unfortunate way my life has panned out, so I'm alone most of the time, though I am well connected in a variety of circles.

My last encounter with a woman turned out so badly that I regretted ever having gotten involved. With most I have a degree of success, and even a feeling of having come away with something, be it a piece of another's soul, or a more concrete souvenir. But this woman was of so inhuman a caliber, and of such a robotic nature, that I could gain no sort of ground or closeness, and almost lost myself in the end. I concluded that one powerful being cannot effectively form a union with another without one or the other being eclipsed, and eventually consumed. I have been months in recovering. Work heals me, and my place in the world makes sense again. I'm bored of solitude once more.

What I hope for from Sarah is an experience of redemption. From her letters I can see her so clearly that I feel safe in resting my hopes on her. In short, the weight of the life I live can't be supported alone, and I need another to take up the edges of the sailcloth, and be a part of all that is to take place.

I contemplated the meeting that was to occur, and wondered at how much I could expect from it. Would Sarah as well be willing to travel away and escape the dust as I was anxious to do, or would she need time to establish trust in my purposes? I could not stand many more days in the city with the impending storm.

But I hadn't even met her yet. She had no idea yet of any of this, or of the future I envision for us.

When she arrived he had been waiting for her, and they met in a purity of gaze that transcended any prior thoughts of either. They met for only a short time, and under the smooth arches of the monument all voices turned to echo, and all identities to a wordless code.

Only this would be apparent to the outside observer: a very young woman and a man also youthful briefly shared a bench, in a shaded alcove just aside from the swirling and fishlike movement of people visiting the monument. Neither was remarkably beautiful in the conventional sense, but in the short course of their conversation, they each palpably took notice of the other. The young woman was a stealthy slip of a creature dressed in ordinary jeans and a jacket, an unsurprising figure in the urban scenery. Her dark hair fell in blades across a round, slightly stoical face, and her deep-set eyes were intense pools of reflection. He was angular and slightly delicate though not effeminate, and his style endowed him with a disarming charisma, which was more a totality than any one striking feature. His eyes were steady and directed on her throughout their brief meeting. The surface behind them was a dark clear pane of glass over stone, like the surface of deep water. They appeared relieved, as those do who have been anticipating their meeting with a fear of failing to come to the same place.

They appeared to discuss something with great intensity, and to reach an agreement, or a pact, though with obvious trepidation on the part of both. He had a light cough, half nervous and half from dust, while she continually swept her hair back from her face, and drank the cool tea he had bought for her, the first of many gifts. It seemed as brief and easy a meeting as any, with people aimlessly darting past all the while, oblivious to the

the monument

strangeness of the transaction. He never once doubted that she was who she presented herself to be—or possibly he did, but found the distinction to be of little importance—and she seemed equally unquestioning of him, as though they had known each other already.

It was with seeming abruptness that he looked at his watch and reluctantly stood to go. They clasped hands for an instant, then he gave her a small envelope and turned to disappear around a bend in the structure, then descend into the cloudbank enfolding the hill. She watched him go, her eyes resting on the spot where he had disappeared, and sat still for a moment. She didn't yet look at the envelope, but watched the circling mass of people flow past. The same slightly dust-coated people circled by many times over, unaware of their destination, though in a definite order, the way bees swarm in concentric patterns within the hive. She was as though invisible, and no one looked at her for more than a second. She opened the envelope, and looked over its contents for a long while before standing up from the bench and joining the orbit of those around her. She found a stairway leading through the upper levels of the monument, and looked at each stone carving and water-like piece of glass with the searching look of one who has been caught off guard and seeks to regain a sense of proportion, as if within the carved history of the city there were hints to a new puzzle it had offered her.

She descended once more into the city and retired to her hotel room, walking, like those around her, as though she were under the power of the surrounding haze. Light was tossed off particles of dust, coming from all angles instead of from a distant sun, and life in the city was thrown off its axis.

That evening, she met him again in the nightclub café, this time going in with him through a side entrance on the upper floor, the same she had left through in the long gone realm of the night before. They sat close together at a small table, leaning closer to speak through the echoing noise of music and voices. From the high vantage point of the gallery, they observed the dance floor far below, as if through a warm sea of glowing lanterns. Decorative drinks arrived, their aqueous colors an intoxicant. "Drinks of the desert!" he told her. "You can contain an oasis within you in drinking this."

"Everyone has an oasis inside," she replied enigmatically.

He smiled and made a sound of affirmation, staring momentarily into the depth of the liquid, an antidote to the dry air that had besieged their eyes that day. Looking up at her again, he asked that she keep with her the envelope he had given to her, and she assured him it was in an inner pocket of her own coat.

At this point, he and she were joined by two men claiming to be old friends of his, who loudly insinuated themselves into the conversation, and made the already cramped table appear yet smaller. Moving further around the table to accommodate them, her angle of vision was altered, and deep in the crowd of the first floor she caught sight of her lost friends from her first day at the hostel. She took the opportunity to slip out from the table with a murmur of explanation to his curious look. The other two expressed little surprise at either her presence or her leaving.

She retraced her course of the earlier night, winding back down the narrow terraces and flimsy staircases, slipping through crowds, past obstacles and waiters festooned with trays. She did this with an uncommon level of ease, as those around her collided with each other, and ran aground against walls or tables. They fetched up in one place and remained there, marooned but in high spirits, and never without a drink from one of the agile waiters and waitresses.

Like a specter, she materialized in the presence of her friends, who pulled her into their dance as if she had never left their company. The music spun out of control and she was tossed around by the tumult of the crowd, until eventually she reached the side again, and glanced upward to see her companion, still in his coat, leaning over the railing above and watching her in his casual but calculated manner. (Another watched them both from yet a different view, but neither was aware.) He was alone again, and looked—perhaps was trying to look—forlorn in a lofty refuge.

The crowd was so loud that she could only mime a farewell to her friends, who were at that point concerned about little beyond the intensity of the music and drinks. Once more she darted through the party, up the first staircase and past a row of scattered chairs and high tables. She was almost around to the second staircase when she met a solid obstacle and could go no further.

Her roadblock took the form of two people, a man and a woman, towering and steadfast in their refusal to let her pass. They sported venomous attitudes and jackets with sharp points and spikes. The man boomed downward in a voice like rocks cascading down a muddy slope, "We don't know who you're in league with, but you'd better have a good reason for impersonating a member of our circle. We don't take kindly to those who interfere with our plans."

The woman had a rough, metallic smoker's voice. "Our dealings with the northern countries are tenuous at best, and to have our careful liaisons rent asunder by outsiders leaves us in a difficult position."

The man spoke again, "We suggest, *strongly*, that you vacate this part of the country, and forget that you ever heard of anyone named Sarah, or took part in anything else of a similar nature. Hm?" The last noise was sharp and guttural, accompanied by an aggressive, bullish toss of the head.

She only feigned ignorance, shaking her head and stepping back. She evaded a chair and managed to rest her hand on the railing of the terrace, with relief catching Eson's eye. He had descended to the second level and was approaching the two thugs with a quick but strong stride. She heard him direct a sharp and impolite word in a northern dialect at them, at which they retreated, though stubbornly and with a look of resentment. He reached Kyra and made a kind of wall around her with his coat, to be spirited away up the staircase and out onto the back landing.

In seeing their reaction to him—surprising given their physical stature—she couldn't doubt that he had a certain kind of power over people around him. In a few short hours she had become bound to him already, though she did not usually give her emotions to others in such short order. She felt safety in his aura and something was kindled within her heart: her honest admiration subtly woven together with awareness of his being. Their discussion moments ago about history, cultures and foreign countries had been much more than she had expected; he had seemed to be inviting her into a shared inner life.

Once under safe cover of the night air, they stood on the narrow landing and he spoke to her. "Sarah, I have to leave, and return to my home in the mountains. I can't stand the oppressive atmosphere of this gathering dust storm, and I have reason to distrust several of the people I've encountered here, including those two who were just now accosting you. I apologize, because I know they would not have bothered you if you hadn't been with me. This town's changed. It used to be a place where you could trust those around you... but anyway, I can speak of that another time." He paused, seemed to gather strength, then spoke very directly. "Will you leave here with me, and come to the place in the mountains where I usually live? Though we haven't spent much time together, I want you to join me there, for a short time. Your letters speak more than any words could."

He spoke with a kind of certainty that was both disconcerting and tempting, as though it were the way things must be, and she had only to give her word to make the world follow a perfect order. Though to accept was to go beyond the parameters set out by the Heiress or her agent, and though her inner instinct was to quietly gather her case and take the earliest train of the morning back to her own land, she nodded calmly, as the undead would nod if given reason. The welcoming obscurity of her home, her friends awaiting her return, and a grand career of service and thievery in the works, all were eclipsed by a magnetic sense of being pulled under his spell. The envelope he had given her that afternoon possessed the intensity of an incantation, and now she was powerless to refuse his words. His lean hand around her shoulder offered a monumental comfort and the sense of being carried upward into a life that would otherwise be impossibly out of reach. Even the dust in the air seemed to be cut through within the aura of his coat. The fact that she was not actually Sarah figured little in her decision. She wouldn't later remember exactly what she said, but at her word they were woven together by a supernatural thread.

He looked genuinely relieved but coolly unsurprised by her agreement, and he accompanied her back through the sleeping streets to the pale courtyard and her desert room, at the door of which they made plans. He would return in the early evening of the following day, and they would go to the station, to catch an overnight train across the flat land and into the northern mountains. He swept a blade of hair back from her forehead and placed his mouth lightly above her brow before turning away into the night.

The dust neither thickened nor thinned overnight. On her last day in the city, she again sought the friends she had encountered on both her first and third day in the city. She wandered once more to the tea shop in the old area of town, and to the market where she wove between temporary shops and food counters and stood with other ephemerally gathered people as they watched street performers: harlequins, charlatans and contortionists. She only once encountered one of the companions she had seen at the nightclub, who said only that her friend from the south had moved on that morning, leaving nothing other than well wishes. She saw no sign of the rough characters she had encountered the night before, or of any others she could identify as being in their 'circle'.

She stayed for a long time at the tea shop where she had taken refuge on the first day of the dust. It had by this point settled into a thin film over the city, with forecasts still predicting a worsening in the coming days. She spoke easily with the shop clerk, Jado, confiding in him that she was in a situation of uncertainty and was wondering if she should rethink a decision made too quickly. His humble advice was to take whatever path led away from everyday tedium and toward the promise of new experience. This set her at ease, and the rest of the day passed by in a kind of peace.

The specter of the Heiress again receded, and Eson's image grew to fill in the space where the Heiress had loomed. She found peace in a situation of complete instability. She told Jado she was leaving the city after only a few days, and he looked at her with what could have been envy, or simply interest. When she realized it was time to leave, she felt a slight wrench to be leaving one of the only familiarities she had found in the city. She noted again that Jado seemed to withdraw when she told him she had to leave the tea shop. This time he asked for no promise that she return, and she was unsure if she could have given it. She retraced her steps back to the room by the courtyard after wishing him well with the projects strewn about the shop's counter.

She received a phone call in her hotel room in the late afternoon, and recognized the voice of the agent who had brought her to the hotel. "You have been warned. If you accept the conditions set out by his agreement with you, you will step beyond our ability to protect you. You could have convinced him to stay in this city, where we could keep a close watch over you, but instead, you will risk following him to his own territory! If you succeed on your own terms, we will of course reimburse you fully, but if you encounter trouble, our help will be impossible to attain."

The call ended as suddenly as it had begun. She had little time to think, as there was a knock at her door, and then her life changed forever.

The train gathered momentum, and as night fell, escaped from the cover of dust. It carried them along under the black sky and its patterns of salt-white stars. A child waking for a moment in one of the cars imagined the stars to be the lights of other cities, a distant land mirroring the surface of this one. There were arid farms on both sides for the first hours of the journey, then small trees and greener fields. Kyra slept a bit, but awoke frequently from the movement of the train, catching fleeting images of the landscape. Soon there were rock faces: iridescent and supernatural in the dim starlight. The trees became heartier, but did not develop into thick forest.

In the early light of morning they passed a border check-point, and all awoke to give proof of their right to passage. Huddled within the folds of Eson's dark coat she felt sudden worry, but he only waved a card at the border patrollers and they asked no questions.

There were other passengers in the sleeping car, all returning through the mountains either to their remote homes, or to larger places. Though the passengers were not great in number, the car was crammed to the edges by billowing silk-wool coats, as though a soft, clean animal slumbered. The animal awoke into several people, all of whom bore the same cool demeanor as Eson who had been asleep beside her, looking innocent as a forest creature. No one noticed her huddled in the dark sea of lustrous wool, and as she breathed in the heady air, it was as if she were waking in a great den of foxes. Perhaps she had a sense of foreboding at that moment, waking into a cold landscape among unknown people.

The clear window of the car framed a still clearer mountain-side, fresh with snow and sparingly populated by stocky, bushy evergreens. Steam welled up from hot springs beneath the snow and dispersed in the slate-colored sky above.

The train pulled toward a structure of wood and steel on a train platform, behind which there at first appeared to be nothing. As the train neared the platform, it became clear there was a covered glass passage heading upward, apparently also into nothing, on the hillside behind the platform. Stone outcroppings and burly trees obscured all else.

She had never been to this part of the country, and she seemed, to those who took notice, enthralled. Coats stirred and voices called to each other in sharp accents as the train cars aligned with the platform and sighed into stillness.

It didn't take long for her to fall further under the spell cast by her host and by the enchantments he offered. They stood together on the enclosed glass platform with the other travelers, waiting for luggage to be shoveled forth from the baggage cars. A box was handed out to him, which he asked her to open there. She lifted out the long coat he had had bought for her and swung it around her shoulders, becoming the fox-wife he had waited for this moment to create. Although warm enough from the steam heat that radiated from the walls and floor, the coat made her real and solid, and coated her in the likeness of those around her now bustling for boxes and cases. With quick feet, the fox-people began disappearing into the passage, an overland tunnel into their modern, alpine lair.

They moved with the fleet crowd up the passageway into other walkways that led between houses and other buildings in the hillside. They branched off at one passageway and came to a sleek polished wooden door, with high windows on the mountainside above it. Others disappeared into the doorways around them, until the enclosed footbridges and walkways were empty.

Inside was a high, uncluttered room, the curtains drawn over windows that spanned the entire wall, floor to towering ceiling. Morning light was visible through the translucent material, and the room appeared to be in slumber awaiting its master. Up another staircase he led her, almost absently, to a guest bedroom before disappearing on a winding, narrow stair to his own room, apparently distracted by something urgent to attend to. She placed her suitcase in an empty corner of the dim room and closed the door behind her softly, then rested her head on a pillow atop the capacious bed, for she had slept little on the journey.

Everything here is run by steam. Steam billows out from the roofs of buildings, and steel pipes run along the lines of the buildings which are high, like those in the glass city, but made of a darker kind of stone.

47

We are the lucky that can live high up, near the water's sources, before it is piped downhill to the power stations. We're all wealthy because of the steam sources, and so we are largely immune to outside forces. We are few in number, and all have inherited at least some wealth from our ancestors' positions as guardians of the original springs. Many, I among them, have been able to increase our wealth greatly through private dealings with myriad and secret persons. I have my own spring that flows next to my home into a pool surrounded by rocks, mine and now Sarah's to enjoy.

Steam heats our narrow houses and the enclosed walkways running between them. The entire town is built into the hillside, and from a distance it looks only like a wall of windows and dark beams set into the slope. The twisted evergreens insinuate themselves anywhere there is a slight chance for survival, their branches pressed against our windows like spiky green hands. Rivers of evergreens run along the valley below, and the train tracks continue toward the lights of our vast and hideous capital.

Her decision to follow Eson there had been made rapidly, and in its aftermath, both felt they must step carefully. They had got in over their heads, and didn't quite know what to do. For some days, he left her mostly on her own. She would spend long hours in the hot waters of the rocky pool or watching obscure northern video programs that held the fascination of novelty, and each day, they would spend a little longer together in the evenings, before he inevitably went out on a midnight errand of some kind. It was always he who broke the connection, who suddenly walled up a distance between them. She never asked him what he did on his late-night excursions; he trusted her in his domain. He would speak to her so passionately of fascinating and cultured things, and listen intently when she spoke her mind. He would lead the conversation toward love and the great and unnerving feelings that were within him while they relaxed together on his cool, modern sofa.

It was only after he had evaporated into the night that her head cleared enough to remember her obligations to others, and while the Heiress and her assignment now seemed distant, so much was left unanswered that she felt a chasm of uncertainty take shape beneath her. Yet, she was drawn to him as to no one else before. When he spoke to her of the distant cities he would take her to, she felt that it would be impossible now to betray him. But the nagging doubt kept at her, even after they had taken to sharing his large bed on the highest floor, and had become so closely entwined that distance was clouded over by embraces and knowing looks.

Guests came frequently over the few weeks that Kyra stayed in the mountains, both local and from afar. They were men and sometimes women, filmmakers, entrepreneurs, and bureaucrats, all of them strange and filled with exotic notions, doomsday prophecies, and political grievances. They ensured a flow of interesting ideas and conversation in the otherwise remote location of the mountain house. They treated her, if not quite as an equal, as a passable accessory to their circle.

She was fascinated especially by the personality of a filmmaker and her actor husband who made movies in the northern city against the conformist and autocratic pull of the government there. Their status allowed them to do so, as Eson was allowed to travel and maintain foreign business contacts. "We're the only ones who can keep a voice of dissent murmuring in the northern capital!" the filmmaker told her, with passion. "But we are often watched, and to come out here to this sanctuary gives us the respite we need." Drinks flowed freely in the mountain refuge, and the discussions and movie viewings ran deep into the night. Kyra once slept for a few minutes on the couch, and awoke to see what looked like a candlelit séance happening in the room before her, an intent look on the faces of Eson, the actor, and the filmmaker. They stared into the space above the low table, shadows gathered around them at every angle. She glimpsed this only momentarily before sleeping again, and didn't mention it the next day when all awoke in the places they had been sitting in the night before.

The filmmaker left a stack of video capsules with Kyra, and she watched them over again, talking with Eson about them, learning the northern patois. It differed only a bit from that of the central plains and forests to the south of the mountains in technical construction but was very different in character, suffused with an undertone of steel and steam. Eson switched easily between the two modes of voice, but his acquaintances spoke solidly in the heavy northern tone.

She was curious about the capital of the steam lands, which were different than the world she knew. When Eson asked her once about her own past she gave cryptic responses, which he seemed to accept. For a common person involved with an aristocrat, there is frequently a sense of humility on the part of the former. Eson no doubt assumed this was the case with Kyra, so asked her little more about it. That there were other reasons she avoided disclosing her life before the Glass City never became an issue of conversation between them. Similiarly, the guests only asked her about things removed from the subject of her own life, as they sought to avoid an awkward impasse on the topic of class. They pretended there was no discernable difference between themselves and her, though she knew this was not the case.

I can tell I have brought her a long way out of her element. I have given her a gift of a long coat of her own, that she might join the foxes' life that we enact here. It's true that the atmosphere is much different than in the southern cities; that there is a tension brought on by the turmoil happening in our government. At least up here we are guarded from most dangers, and are within throwing distance of the border. I have asked her if she likes it here, but her answers are roundabout and cryptic. About other things, she is so much more forthright, and I have even been shocked sometimes by her blunt appraisals of the world and its workings. She is something of a cynic, but I sense she puts that aside when she thinks of me and of our recently blossomed affair. In all, I am becoming attached to her mysterious character, her face and expressive eyes.

I'm still a young man, and have little need for marriage, or even for love, but the dust of success has settled around me in patterns of remoteness and alienation. My bedroom is high and the ceiling distant. The walls are of smoky red and blue colors, and the light is low. To see the satin ocean of my bed covers reshaped to enclose her form perfects this otherwise uninhabited sanctuary.

I say it is uninhabited because I am so often away. I am always in connection with a variety of far-away people and traverse the continent to meet with them. If she proves lasting, I am hoping to have a visa made for her by one of my friends ensconced deep in the nation's bureaucratic networks. She could accompany me on these journeys.

But for now, I must keep her hidden away in my mountain vault, where only visitors to my home, and the people who live with me in this borderland outpost, will see her. Those who live around me are mostly of a like-minded nature and unlikely to fault me for taking advantage of our lofty remoteness. (I know for a fact that many of them house illegal servants and not all are treated so well as my own guest. There is a pact of secrecy about this sort of thing. Authority's radar wanes in the hinterlands.) When I inform my visitors that she is the one that I was for so long writing letters with, they are awestruck that I have made her mine. She is my prize.

My life is easy. I forget about the problems of my country for days at a time, now that she is with me. I regret that I will have to leave again soon. I have been called to the capital to help with a minor problem with the energy supply. I hate these ventures into the sprawling mess of the practical distribution of steam power. Is it my problem if some minor official in the bureaucracy is siphoning power for his own district? I received the call to duty the morning after we had some particularly wild guests. My head was in no shape to come to grips with it.

Until I must leave, we continue to sleep late, eat well, and spend long hours in my hot springs. Though the air outside is cold, we are always warm. My guests arrive in awe, and leave in envy.

Sarah and I also spend afternoons reading aloud to each other the letters we once wrote to each other. I am winning her over, so that she may never want to leave my embrace, my universe. The business of the other before her has almost disappeared from my mind.

The days passed in a cloud outside of regular time, and though she rarely left the confines of the house and the rocky spring beside it, Kyra felt as if her earlier life had been a trap, while her current enclosure was a new kind of freedom. Eson would brush the hair back from her face while they embraced in the spring and kiss her deeply amid the steam and dark rocks. The evergreen trees tapped their branches on the rocks as though they wished to join the entanglement.

And then, with little warning, he was gone.

She awoke. The bed was empty beside her. There was a letter. She reached across the satin ocean of the cover and gathered the letter close.

bedroom in the mountain house

It echoed the poetic tones of his other letters to Sarah, which he had read to her from his draft copies, but it seemed to be written in haste, much like the note he had left on the table of the nightclub.

> *Dear Sarah,*
>
> *I have been called away from your side. I am nearby, in the city that you can see distantly from here. I will return so swiftly that you will have barely enough time to be lonely. I didn't want to bore you with the details of my business, nor set us up for the prospect of a difficult goodbye. Please don't be angry that I have chosen this way. I will be in contact within the day.*
>
> *Eson*

She got up slowly, sitting up in bed before leaving its protective shell. Was this to be the result of her journey, to be alone, completely, in a place foreign and without connection to the outside world? She had not realized how dependent she had become on Eson's constant presence. All was the same as before, but somehow, the spell she had been living under thinned in the air and she saw only a foreign house around her, warm, but offering no guarantee of her safety. She felt suddenly aware of how vulnerable she was, alone here with no proper identification allowing her to reside in this closed province. He had left her no way of contacting him. She felt a spreading chill.

She was alone in the fox's den, and there were other foxes in dens around her. She could feel echoes of their cool laughter as she aimlessly scoured the house for a number she could reach Eson with, or a document that might prove her existence as a legal visitor in this country, though she knew none existed. She consoled herself, as she knew she had no reason to worry; he would be back soon, would call that very day.

So she waited for him to call, restless, and with little appetite to read from his library. She listened to simple but intense music, letting it serve as a backdrop for a calm-surfaced but internally uneasy frame of mind. But around mid-afternoon, she heard a sound at the front door, and was drawn to investigate it. A card had been dropped through the letter slot, and the name on the envelope was not his, but hers, her real name!

The front of the card was revoltingly sentimental. It showed a couple running in a sunlit meadow, and in gold lettering said *Con-*

gratulations on your Engagement. Inside the card were written these words, unsigned, and in an erratic script:

> *We can get you safe passage back across the border if you will bring to us the evidence that we need to release our group from a binding pact, made under the threat of blackmail. You will find our letter in his house under a stone square, along with a document sealing your own fate. Take your time. Make the decision more wisely than your earlier ones. You have one week to take action, when our person stationed at the border will finish his tour of duty.*
>
> *P.S. Sarah wishes you well.*

Feeling like the target of a cruel joke, and puzzling over who had sent the card, she felt tempted to consider searching for the purported document. With the other half of her heart, she wanted to tell Eson about this and have him smooth it over with his fluid, conjurer's words. He existed in a place high above, and could see things invisible to those who walked the ordinary ground. She wanted him to weave a yarn about how all would soon be wonderful, and how he would take her to the sandy coast and to green islands and to dizzyingly high places. She had resolved to forego her original mission as if it were a troublesome stone in her path, favoring instead the deep emotional state that he offered her.

She knew he kept his papers in an innocuous study on the second floor.

She brewed a fresh pot of tea in the seldom-used kitchen, the note in front of her. She needed to muster her resolve before launching what felt like an attack on the study, a room she had not yet entered. She had been shaken twice already that day, by his absence, and by the absurd note. With a terrible need for answers, she rushed headlong toward the third and final quake.

The mountain sun palely illuminated the room, set below the great bedroom and beside the guest room where she had first stayed. In that room, itself stacked between the bedroom above and the ground floor below, were stacked boxes, shelves, trunks; everything that did not fit the sleek character of the rest of the house. Why was she searching there, in that previously most uninteresting room of her lover's house? She asked herself this again and again. Could she really cast doubt on him, on the scant basis of an errant note through the door? Though he had never told her that she was not to enter the room, nor had she been invited to do so, and she felt she must justify the trespass to herself. She told herself she was compelled by a need to find out more about him, to deepen their relations. She realized she had become so attached to him that she was cast into despair by his absence. She had grown so that she wanted nothing else than to be near him, not caring about the otherwise empty nature of her days, or about anything besides what he spoke to her of, so deep was the enchantment. She felt vines around her heart, and only wanted them to wind tighter. She determined that to merely explore the room was not a betrayal, but an act of concern for their love.

A paperweight in the form of a solid stone square grounded an airy, disorderly stack of papers on the worn surface of a square table. Was it in these weightless filaments that her future was to be determined?

She lifted the stone for only a moment and pulled out the first set of sheets, bound in a leather cord. These were the precious letters between him and Sarah, and she spent some minutes poring over them again, feeling that it was she who was being dishonest, that she must somehow make amends to him on his return. When they read the letters together, she acted the part of Sarah, and with Eson's attentive gaze felt she was the woman whose words fascinated him. Reading them in isolation, she felt like a third party witnessing an exchange deeper than she felt capable of comprehending. The resulting spark of jealousy, and the almost possessive desire to be at the center of such intimacy made her feel it would be impossible to betray Eson in favor of the Heiress's task. No remuneration could approach such a deep sense of being alive.

She wondered again who had sent the absurd card. The gloating tone echoed that of the hooligans she seen in the café, and remembering them and how her lover had come to her defense, she felt another surge of remorse.

But in light of what else she found in the small room, she felt torn between turning away from him or abandoning all that was sane and stable in the world. She set the letters down gently, and though she willed herself not to, picked up the next bound packet of papers. After the solace of reading over the letters, she was reluctant to release these papers from the solid weight of the stone. There were two, and the first one cast a chill over her soul.

She recalled what she'd read in the Heiress's dossier regarding what she could now scarcely believe had been her 'task.' The contract the Heiress had wanted her to regain was not an ordinary parchment, nor did it concern any mundane business engagements. It was a type of deed that while not exactly an enchantment, was binding in ways deeper than the law written by political states. Deeds of this type were written and signed by people who had an uncanny control over the universe around them. This deed bore the name and heraldic crest of an ancient clan, Eson's ancestral lineage. Eson's flowing signature was inscribed liquidly at the bottom of the page. In flowering, entwining and subtle language, the deed signed the rights to another person's life, mind and wellbeing over to Eson. Somebody had signed it, though in a slurred, unsure hand. She could barely make out the name, beyond the fact that it began with a W. The soul in question was named midway through the document, penned in once more by the slurred hand: Sarah. An additional phrase added in smaller print beside this name ...*or one who acts on behalf of or in the guise of the above-mentioned Sarah*, and was initialed by both who had signed.

Kyra spent a minute filtering what she had found. Eson and another person, this W., had made an agreement in relation to Sarah. She was to be under Eson's control according to the agreement—but Sarah had not appeared at the agreed meeting time in the Glass City, and so could not possibly be enfettered to Eson as the deed specified. Kyra thought for another moment, realizing *she* was the person acting in the guise of Sarah for whom the small print made provision. Was she then subject to the deed's power?

It was an ancient power Eson held. Its vine-like bonds could grow around any tree that set itself within the confines of his written deeds. She had not even signed the contract! But then, neither had Sarah, it appeared. Could anyone sign over the rights to another? She felt perhaps she was leaping to conclusions, that the deed meant nothing, and she was not being indentured to any such powers.

Although... Eson had not doubted her identity, had never needed proof that she had written the letters.

But it was unthinkable. She couldn't believe it, not yet. She couldn't betray him by thinking these things.

She thought of the card again. Whoever had sent the card was not concerned with her life, but with their own suspect machinations. And the mention of Sarah only served to muddy the waters in an already deceptive current. Whatever they thought she was part of, and whatever these papers meant, she would ask him when he returned from his business. Her own deception of identity rested deep in her mind, so deep that she need not disturb its dormancy, at least not until the moment was right.

She looked to the other sheet in the packet, also signed by both Eson and the other slurred hand, which swirled in deep and drunken curves. This contract declared not the life of one person, but all of the monetary profits and successes of a circle of people, all of whom were named, to be the property of her lover. Were these the people who had sent the note? And how had one person signed over rights to so many others?

Kyra thought back to her original mistress, the Heiress. Almost by unwilled movement, she unpacked further pages, each one detailing the coercion of a person or group for Eson's benefit. Some were pacts regarding electricity or the smuggling of goods through the border, even through ocean ports. No wonder the border guards at the rustic mountain crossing had turned a blind eye to her passage!

At last she found the deed detailing the woes of her mistress. Knowing the Heiress's wealth was guarded by ancestral pacts and long-held rights of immunity, she wondered how Eson had circumvented those deep-rooted talismans.

The deed said simply that the wealthy Heiress would live in a state of deepest emotional opprobrium unless she was able to destroy the contract with her own hands. It was signed crisply with the woman's own name. Kyra shook her head in disbelief as she contemplated the paper. The weight of her task came rushing back to her. She held in her hands the piece of evidence so important to her erstwhile employer.

She felt the weight of warring loyalties as she restacked the grim papers and edged out of the room, pulling the door closed behind her. She retreated to the hot spring to settle her mind. Snow fell lightly from the darkening sky, and dissolved to form a cool surface on the pool while her body was insulated by the warm water below. She let snow melt on her face, and cooled her mind in the mountain air. It was only a short while ago that dry dust had covered her and clouded her thoughts. She wanted nothing more now than to return to the anonymous safety of the city, to the tea shop and nightclub, to find the friends she had lost, who were not part of the welter of chaotic forces boiling around her.

After Eson at last called her, she returned to the springs, which exuded a sense of peace over their surroundings. She had been unable to keep a note of unease from her voice while speaking to him. He sounded weighted by his own problems in dealing with the capital, had spoken of "the corruption of the bureaucracy that insiduously confounds the free citizen," and she had felt unwilling to bring up the small matter of the stack of deeds. "I will return to you," he'd promised. "You're the only stable branch I can rely on, my anchor of reason in a corrupt world." Though disquieting, his words pulled her further into the whirlpool of devotion.

Lying once more in the springs against the smooth stones and closing her eyes, she could understand the connection Eson had said he felt with the springs.

Within moments, she heard a sound of impact nearby and felt a small stone brush against her leg before rolling deeper into the water. She opened her eyes at the sensation, and saw movement beyond the translucent door leading into the house. She felt a bolt of emotion, thinking for a moment that he had returned. But the shifting silhouette in the house was much smaller, moved in more halting and hesitant way, industrious but without vigor. It was a servant, pale and gray-eyed, who came into the house on a sporadic schedule in which Kyra could perceive no logic. The servant had never spoken to Kyra and kept eyes averted from her, and Kyra hadn't ever tried to engage her in conversation, as it seemed improper within the domain of this encoded house to interrupt another's tasks. The servant was a part of the domestic realm in the suspended mountain enclave, and may even have been some kind of simulacra. There were rumors, always, of unfathomable technologies existing in the northern country.

Kyra closed her eyes again, and decided she would simply

wait until the servant had left to go back inside. Steam escaped into the air above her, kilojoules of potential energy released into the gathering dark, as it had done for millennia. This particular spring had been left untapped, not diverted into power generators but enclosed as ecological property within Eson's inherited tract.

She looked up again when she heard the smooth sound of the door sliding open. The servant looked at her with no contempt, admiration or query; her expression simply bespoke reciprocal pity, a servant whose tasks were simple observing one whose tasks were not. The servant vaguely resembled Eson in her northern cast of features, but her face was weighted by service. For the first time she spoke to Kyra, and her voice was low but strong.

"You don't know what you have entered into here. You shouldn't wait to find out. You are balanced on the net of your illusions."

Kyra listened, and felt she was being haunted by a presence beyond simple humanity. Vapors separated her from the servant, who was slight as a forest sylph, dressed in gray, illuminated in the half-light reflected from the rock walls surrounding the pool. Kyra nodded respectfully, as to an equal, waiting to hear something that would make sense of this haunting.

"You will never become one of them. They don't take in any others. Things are of use to them or not, of value or not, worth keeping or not."

Kyra felt less patient, disquieted, and turned away slightly, attempting to restore the unspoken veil that kept them from looking or speaking to each other. The gray servant continued to talk, but softly, stepping backward into the cavernous room and dimming her own radiance to a duller hue.

"Their ancestors took hold of the power that emanated from the underground springs in the mountains, and now they live as though their own blood flowed with power from the planet's heart. They are ruthless, and care little for those beyond their coven. But the one you are enamored with is said to be the worst, even by his kindred. They won't have any entanglements with him anymore. They say he is being so careless in his dealings that he makes enemies on all sides, and that to deal with him is to fly in the path of a devastating electrical storm." The servant bowed out of the doorway entirely, closing it softly.

Kyra remained in the spring for a few minutes to ensure the servant had left, and to forcibly bury herself in its absolving waters, away from the outside world. The house that had felt dormant and watchful earlier now seemed a kind of shapeless hologram, too modern for the ancient clan that owned it and reflecting half-truths from all its surfaces. She recalled Eson saying it had been completely redesigned in the last years. He said he couldn't stand to be surrounded by the old walls and furniture, the old spirits.

Kyra reentered the house with caution, fearing unknown variables, and looked into each room, ending up in the lofty bedroom. The high window in this room was the only vantage point that looked out over the square forms of the mountain dwellings, connected by enclosed walkways, suspended above the ground where the mountain slope was steep. The distant city in the north was a coruscation of lights and steam.

The only perceptible change that had taken place in the high room was in the statue of a bird resting on the low table placed under the window. It had always been there, a metal statue polished to a shine with black-tipped feathers and closed eyes, simply a beautiful object, but now, though still obviously cast in metal, it appeared to pulse with a life that was more organic than machine. The bird appeared to sleep, if only because it was now capable of being awake. Kyra crouched before it, and the bird's eyes opened into sentient black orbs.

As the eyes opened, a curved black rock beside the bird, which Kyra had earlier dismissed as a paperweight, began to change. On the rock's surface appeared a curved, moving vision of herself and the tall room behind her. The bird statue was a seeing device and the rock showed its keeper anything the bird saw!

Had the servant activated this machine for her? The bird watched her with its still eyes. She wondered if it could move, looked around for a book or guide, and was amused to see her own image in the rock as the bird watched her. She sat back out of the bird's field of view, watching it. She had a sense it was there to help her, but suspected that it was also a continuation of the haunting she had been through in the pool.

She absently began to move the beads on an old-fashioned counting machine that rested on another table. Had she placed it there earlier, or was it the servant at work again? As she moved the beads, the robotic statue stretched its wings out with a sound of small metal plates unfolding. A different bead's movement caused the bird to turn its head, and changed the view that appeared on the rock. She had found the meaning she was seeking.

She practiced controlling the vision bird for many hours into the night until she could successfully guide it around the perimeter of the room, and control its head movements. It flew tirelessly and without error, unless she herself miscalculated. Eventually, she guided it back to the low table and it slept once more, its eyes closed in serene beauty.

Kyra ordered food by phone as she and Eson did most evenings, and it was delivered shortly by a fox-grinned, vaguely mocking teenager who could easily have been Eson's brother, or the pale servant's, but was dressed in the pristinely sloppy manner of an indulged youth. The delivery job was likely only a means for him to expand his coffers of pocket money, Kyra thought.

She slept for the few remaining hours before dawn, and upon waking, set the bird on some practice circles of the room before opening the tall window of the bedroom and sending it out into the sky for a turn around the vicinity. She was struck by how cold the alpine air felt. She was wary of the windows of other houses nearby, not wanting to give any of the neighboring inhabitants reason to become suspicious of her actions. Many people had seen her get off the train when she arrived, and in a small community, one set of eyes could mean many mouths.

Once she felt adept at piloting the vision bird without having it in her field of view, she brought it back for a rest before sending it on what she knew would be a longer journey. Its presence was an antidote to her loneliness, but she was curious about the city she could see in the distance, and would be traveling with the bird in her ability to see through its eyes.

I sense my pretty dove has been spying. I could hear a knot of conflict in her voice when I called today from the capital. Here in this gray city, they accuse me of collaborating with anarchists in the south, and withholding hidden stores of steam power. Others are blatantly thieving from the steam power business, but because of my isolated position in the borderlands, I am targeted as a defector. I detest these conferences and wish to escape to my ancestral refuge, and to the one who now shares my days.

I imagined she would find the papers within hours of my leaving her alone. Of course there is no way for her to undo the deed that binds her or those that bind others while she is on this side of the border. It matters little with whom she is in league. She will realize that with me lies eternal comfort and shelter from the sharp lower teeth of the world's callous jaws. How she reacts to her discovery will be the true test. The world will be hers as it is mine, if she chooses it.

The vision bird flew above houses, past steam power generators, down the slope of the mountain. It passed over the rugged, stocky pine trees, and leveled out into the alpine valley with its low grasses, and continued toward the northern city. Steam pipelines traced the valley floor, crossing over rivers and through forests without interruption, toward farming towns and then the great city.

The first aspects of the metropolis to loom into view were its factories and its temple complexes, the largest features of the outskirts of the city. The vision bird by midday was flying over the outer districts. The outskirts were a welter of industrial and religious architecture, with dwellings, markets and parks all humbled at the feet of the monoliths. There was little that looked modern outside the dome. The squalor of ghettos and clouds of intermingled steam and factory smog alternated with itinerant camps of nomads in places that had not been cleared of pine trees or stones. The temples were wild stone masses, populated with gods and monsters, stone waterfalls and whirlwinds, and the air seemed dulled by cold. Campfires were lit here and there.

The city center was enclosed under a clear dome, inside which was a convoluted network of connected buildings. These were both ancient like the Broken Glass City and sleekly modern like the refuge in the mountains. Where the Glass City had seemed to possess a median standard of life for most of its citizens, though, this city was clearly divided between the land inside the dome and the land without. The bird approached the dome, which bore the clarity of a drop of water in contrast to its sprawling, clouded environs. Inside were clean grounds, orderly patches of flora and imposing structures. The bird flew high up, so individual people were only abstractions in its vista. Kyra saw all of this in the curving surface of the stone on the table in Eson's room back in the high room in the mountains. She was seeing for the first time a place she had heard much about, but had never really contemplated as a reality. Spoken of with horror and awe by those further west and south, the northern country represented the dangerous potential of industry and religion fused together.

She landed the bird on the smooth, curved roof of the dome. She now saw interlocking tiled pathways and stairs. Sleek trams ran smoothly on magnetic tracks.

Only one building met the roof of the dome, connecting into it and leading to a satellite dish and a turning radio tower, as well as some weather apparatus. She had heard that magnetic fields in this region made for frequent, dangerous storms; while the earth below provided clean, safe electricity, the sky above provided it sporadically and disastrously. The factories and the dome were designed to repel lightning, but the decorated tops of the temples were hit every year during the rainy season.

Eson had relayed a wry joke about those who follow the new god of industry being preserved by their service, while those who followed the old gods were sent to meet their gods rapidly. He had gone on to say that in truth, it depended more on whether the lightning hit on a workday or a rest day. Kyra hadn't laughed but had told him it was a grim remark, considering that all his business in the capital was conducted under the safety of the dome. He'd replied that it was only a proverb, repeated mostly by those to whom it referred, and that in any case, he had his own old gods to serve, so he would wish no ill on others who did so as well.

His old gods were very different from those of the people who went to temples, and belonged exclusively to the small cohort of families of which Eson was part. She had been reluctant to ask him about these gods, as she feared what they might mean for her involvement with him. Thinking back to the servant's warning, she was again made uneasy by her ambiguous position.

Seeing the northern places for the first time, even contained

steam capital dome

within the small orb she had placed on the table before her, she felt a new awareness of the country she had so easily agreed to visit. The Glass City surged up in her mind as a place of comfort and fascination, contrasted against the alien environment she witnessed in the orb. She hoped they would go traveling together soon, to the anonymity of cities and free countries.

At any rate, the mountain home was likely as safe as the inside of the capital's dome, however safe that might be.

As she wanted to bring the bird home before navigation became difficult at night, she set it into flight again, this time away from the dome, southward to her. As night fell she closed the curtains against the eyes of the houses around her.

The bird returned, its wings untiring and its eye keeping an unending watch on its path.

I've been here two days only, and have already been reminded of how this place taxes me. I'm dogged by the echo of serious feet on marble floors, imperious silhouettes stoked with self-importance traversing the government hallways. I am watched by my enemies' sycophants, and by my once-friends, who now smirk with betrayal as I pass by. There is only one bureaucrat who sticks by me here, and it is because his position is weak and he cannot afford to lose even an unpopular ally like me. My friends are out on trips to their movie set, and so I can't confide in them now, though I am staying the night alone in their city home. Even one of the bureaucrats who visited me so recently in the mountains now betrays me; he ignored me when I spoke to him outside the council room.

I am driven toward forfeiting this corrupt empire completely and making my way of life elsewhere. There would be a way to keep the electricity revenues flowing to me. I keep a crisp stack of parchment and a bottle of indelible ink in my case, waiting for a situation to arise.

It would cause me grief to abandon my house in the mountains, though, with its underground springs. My ancestors came here hundreds of years ago, and by their own zealous sense of elation in their quest found the springs hidden high in these rugged hills. They had come across the eastern sea, spurred on by a vision in one of the ancient pools of divination nestled in the moss gardens of the sacred homelands. An older religious sect who saw my ancestors' ways as a blasphemous threat to their own theocracy provided them with brutal persuasion to leave the comfort of their home. Despite the impassioned protests from those who felt the journey to be an act of madness, nearly half of the original group came across the ocean to this cold land, which was even then a hotbed of instability. The land was settled, and always had been, but this state had never achieved the even level of liberty of those below the chain of mountains. This nation was much more like those of the imprisoned islands of the west.

My ancestors arrived in this country nevertheless, and were largely ignored because of their insulating wealth. They were to make an exploratory pilgrimage into the mountains, they told anybody who inquired about the seemingly unreasonable voyage. The dome hadn't yet been built, but there was already a marked disparity between wealthy and common folk. The country then practiced an ineffective brand of socialism, to which my ancestors were granted immunity. They journeyed into the mountains in search of their spiritual succor, taking with them a bevy of guides and pack animals, as well as technology brought from beyond the sea. (The other continent strove ahead of this one with its machinery in those days, though the opposite is now true).

The mountains rest on a fault zone where two continental plates crush together. This allows the springs to exist in one remote place. My ancestors found the springs and built the first shrine to our saints, who had guided them here. They built the first of the opulent houses present today and lived in a monastic solitude, their lives given over to adoration of the springs. The next generation had more of a flair for the entrepreneurial, and began constructing power generators to harness the geothermal power and sell it to the government of the region. How did they manage to escape the tight economic grip of this country's rulers, and keep their rights to the steam power? That is a matter of our dynasty's talent for charismatic persuasion, brought with us across the sea, and of the enhanced personal energy that we gain from these springs. There are stacks of deeds in the family vault that date back centuries before my time.

Over the generations, of course, we've separated into sub-families, each holding dominion over a set of sacred springs. I'm the last of my line, and so everyone is set to destroy me, subsuming my power into their vaults. This holds true both for my fellow heirs inhabiting the mountains and for the government bodies here in the capital, who are eager to drive a wedge into the power of the heirs. The ancestors earned rights to these springs through their spiritual vigilance, and as their descendants we must honor them by defending the rights to this power. As such, I would much rather see my springs in the hands of other heirs than those of the corrupt government. If the springs were only a few miles further south, they would be within the territories held by the Glass City, and all of our family's current troubles would be remedied. The line of the border was drawn, though, long before any of my ancestors graced the surface of this continent. Bound by the caprices of long dead surveyors, my family became citizens of the northern empire.

There is a conspiracy at work around me. The bureaucrats have not even had the decency to fabricate a subtle deception. In the high council yesterday, my former allies stood one by one and addressed the director at his high seat before the great window. Mottled patterns of fast-moving clouds alternately shadowed and illuminated the hall through the window panes, as if to reinforce the arbitrary and changeable nature of the council. Each petty official spoke of the need to oust undeserving private citizens from their positions of wealth, referring to outmoded gods, arrogant lassitude and unworthy heirs. They spoke also of a need to keep the tight reins of central control over energy resources. As though I had not helped in the implementation of accessible power to the outer districts!

The minor dust storm I endured in the City of Glass seems like a captivating pipe dream in comparison to this treachery and surveillance. The time may have come when I must break from the past, and rely on my own merits to brave an uncontrollable world.

There is another meeting of the council tomorrow, and I fear it will not go well. I may have only tonight to secure even the barest chance of keeping my house and springs. I sat this afternoon on a marble bench inside one of the terraced concourses within the dome and shook up the inherited bottle of ink that I would employ in my evening's plan. I intended to use the weak bureaucrat as my agent, sending him with some seemingly innocuous documents to be signed by key members of the council. They would hardly be aware of what they were really signing. I imagined this bottle of ink spilling onto the striated gray checkerboard of the polished marble floor, engulfing the hall, the council, and the dome that surrounds it. A petty council will not defeat the ancient majesty of the divining pools and sacred springs!

He called her again the day after the vision bird returned. It would have been his third day in the capital. His voice sounded upset, and he didn't make her any promises. "The situation here in the capital has escalated, and I fear I'm no longer safe. The territory's council is sending its agents up the mountain road to search my house, though they don't know of your presence there, I assure you."

Kyra replied calmly, keeping a stable tone of voice. "What does that mean for you, or for me?"

He too made an effort to calm his voice. "I'm sorry, Kyra, that I've done this to you." And with purpose: "You must, unfortunately, leave very quickly and cross back over the border. Go back to the security of the Glass City."

Her heart began to beat faster. "And you?"

"I'll meet you there in a few days. Really, don't worry for me. I have help. I always do. And so do you, now." He was speaking now in short bursts. "The border guards will let you through, without doubt. You must be assured of that."

"They won't capture you?"

"No. Certainly not." He hesitated. "But there's something I'm afraid I must ask of you. I've already asked so much, I know... but this is important."

She still held to a rational tone of voice. "What is it?"

"There are some papers in my study on the second floor. They are of key significance. The steam government must not be allowed to confiscate them."

"You'd like me to carry them with me when I go back to the Glass City?"

"Yes. That's exactly what I need you to do. Can you take them? Do you know the ones I mean?"

"I do. I can put them in my luggage easily. It's no trouble."

This left him wordless for a moment, though she felt he must have intended for her to find the papers. She still felt unresolved about the disconcerting evidence she'd found in the parchments, but saw cooperation as the only way of freedom for them both in the present moment.

"You are so good and calm," he said. "Now, there's a train ticket and a key to my city apartment in a cabinet on the top floor of the house. Take those and go as soon as you can."

"I'll leave as soon as we—hang up." Her voice caught in her throat. They'd soon each be alone and out of contact for at least a few days, during which anything might occur.

He seemed to register the difficulty in her voice and spoke soothingly, his voice regaining its usual calm. "We'll both be safe by tomorrow morning. If the situation is worse than we expect, we can always fly further afield, to one of the coasts or somewhere far from here."

"You're right. We aren't that far away from the free territories." Still, right then they felt very far away indeed.

"You must feel I've put you in great danger. I apologize—though I know fear can't be undone with promises." He paused, and she was about to reply when he added, "Ah, I'm afraid I must ask something else of you."

What else can there be? Rationality was wearing thin. "Tell me."

"I would only entrust this to someone of great integrity. It involves a family heirloom, of sorts."

She murmured encouragement, though it sounded weak to her ears, and waited.

"Above the springs where we relax, there's another spring, smaller, that feeds the larger one. Look up to the top of the waterfall."

She tried to look from her position inside the house, but could only see swirling steam.

"The stone that anchors the parchments to my desk must be placed in a stone alcove above the upper spring. It's very important; we may lose everything if the spring is not properly safeguarded. You can easily climb up the wall beside the pool, where it is least steep. The spring is directly above, and its water feeds the larger pool."

"Don't worry. I know it's important," she reassured him, relieved the favor was so simple.

"Can you do it before you catch the train?"

"I'll do it right now. Don't worry."

She thought she heard a sigh. "Yes, of course. I've kept you too long. Go and be safe in the Glass City. I'll see you as soon as I can."

She looked out at the deepening sky of the snowy afternoon

twilight after he hung up. She must catch an evening train. She had begun to see the mountain house as a kind of enclosure, and felt relieved at the prospect of returning to the city, though the journey would be risky. A wealthy political exile makes a dangerous lover, and she as well would be a renegade for as long as she surfed in the wake of Eson's affairs. If she made it across the border into the southern lands, those who looked for him might be searching for her with as much fervor. She'd be carrying the contracts that ruled their lives, and so would be a target. He had made all this clear to her, and from her current position she could do little else than help him. It should have terrified her, the prospect of collusion with such an unstable man, but the chain reactions of loyalty and affection had already taken her beyond the point of objectivity. The amazing human ability to adapt had allowed her perspective to swing and see this as a normal way of life. She feared for his safety on the journey.

Acting quickly, she ascended to the sanctuary of the third floor, the vision bird a reassuring prescence—a vigilant seer and protector—and searching through the cabinet for the key, found it and beside it a train ticket. She quickly placed her meager complement of clothes and personal things into her case, shut the long curtains over the towering windows, and took a small pack out of the cabinet, gently wrapping the bird in a pillowcase with its viewing orb and the control device, and placing all three into the case. She looked back over the silent, moody room, then, before stepping down to the second floor and collecting the packet of papers. They felt as though they were burning her hands with the power encoded into them. She buried them in her luggage, and hid the stone inside a pocket of her coat.

The wall beside the pool did not look difficult to climb. She dug her hands into nooks in the rock and made her way up the wall with little trouble, pushing up onto a ledge where she could look down into the pool. She had never climbed up to this second, higher spring. It was gentle, too small to bathe in and fed only by underground vents. Contorted low-lying pines framed it, bending inward to warm their branches over the waters, and above the pond was Eson's ancestral shrine. It was simple, consisting only of a hollowed portion of the rock wall, with words inscribed in the alcove, and a small dish for offerings.

The spring anointed her with its steam as she leaned over the water to place the rock on the dish. It glowed a brilliant gold hue that illuminated the hollow and allowed her to read the inscription, a prayer to the restful sleep of the ancestors and an invocation of the powerful forces that ran through their bloodline. Kyra paused as she read the words midway through the passage:

> *To those who live with the planet's wellspring within them, the legacy will be written into all actions. This spring is the life source for the ancient family that watches over it. Those who act in the family's service will know the legacy, but will never possess it as their own. They will be given over completely to the service of the legacy.*

She shook her head softly as she contemplated this, remembering the servant's words.

A cool draft heralded the onslaught of evening, and she backed away from the shrine, climbing over the edge of the rock face and stepping back down into the house. The words in the hollow made her once again aware of the old house hidden beneath the walls of the new, and of the old laws that governed the life she had entered. She had begun her relationship as the observer, as one who seeks, and she had become an adjunct now to the plans of another.

With the feigned attitude of a northerner who has just ended a vacation in a mountain retreat, she closed up and left the house where she had fallen so deeply under Eson's power, and ventured once more into the maelstrom of the outer world. Walking past a neighboring house, she saw the pale servant, who did not look up, though Kyra passed very closely in front of her. She quickened her pace in the enclosed corridors, and then stepped once more onto a train that would journey by night.

It was a much different person who boarded the train to the Glass City than had arrived in the mountains weeks earlier. She would only realize how different when she once again began to interact with the outer world.

They had been unsuccessful in their many attempts to contact her. She had disappeared over the border under the guise of Sarah, and they had lost both their connection to him and to her. The final card had gotten through, by plain luck and by whim of the border guards. If she could be made to realize that her fate bore the same mark of disaster as theirs, she could be swayed toward their cause. Though cynical and wrapped in cruel jokes, the card had been a plea for help.

"She'll help us escape his grip," they assured one another. They met in a dim room in the industrial depths of the city and knocked back dark bottles of drink, betting away their cash before it disappeared from their lives and resurfaced in Eson's, then walked home in the dark of night, drowned in seas of lost hope.

Only one member of the circle stayed away from the others. He worked in a small tea shop in the old quarter near the monument. He awaited nothing more than the return of the girl who had come out of the dust storm.

Kyra kept her head low as the train slowed to a halt at the border station. She presented Eson's contracts to the guard who asked for her identification. On seeing the deed, the guard inhaled sharply and tersely said, "That's good enough," moving hastily on to the next passenger and avoiding her eyes, as she avoided his. Other passengers, the same breed of aristocrats who had surrounded her in a thick miasma on the trip north, observed her archly from behind hand-held reading screens. She detected their subtle aversion, as if traveling alone under Eson's seal she had become a threat to their ways. She felt uneasy to think of the house she had just left being searched, and about Eson's journey. She didn't know how he would be making the journey, or how safe he was. He could be caught before he could escape across the border.

She slept only sporadically during the trip, and watched the sky and mountains pass by, relieved to once more be in free territory. She intuited a new sense of power in relation to her surroundings. The stack of deeds kept safely under her coat was at once a record of her bond to Eson and an icon of her own nascent power. She saw constellations in the black sky as maps of the soul. She dreamt of transformation, of being a constellation that drifted and reconfigured at great speed as though time were quickened, unsure whether the transformation was an evolution or a growing dependency. She enjoyed the prospect of power, but wondered at what cost it would be gained, or if Eson were even capable of granting it to her. The bird sleeping calmly in its case acted as a familiar and comforted her with its presence. The dreams were twisted then by other visions, of Eson being kept prisoner by his government, of the house being taken away, with all the power that came with the ancestral property. She feared she was powerless to help him, and was running away in cowardice.

Nevertheless, near morning she felt a flash of elation as the train left the mountains and the Glass City came into view on the rolling plains of the horizon. Morning sun caught on its walls and roofs, setting them ablaze.

Kyra reentered its landscape once again not knowing what it was she envisioned for her sojourn in the city.

Weary, I have finally returned from the north to the relative peace of the Glass City. It was no easy journey, as I had to travel by a steam-driven convoy through the rough, old winding roads in the mountains, my driver unknowing of the depth of the situation. The day in the capital was disastrous beyond belief, and I fear I may have given Sarah the fright of her life in instructing her to smuggle my papers across the border. I have had few comforts on my journey, and worries over the fate of my position in the world, as well as Sarah's wellbeing, have torn away at my inner core. I've been haunted continually by the image of my ancestors' spring, maddened to think of the government stepping onto our ancestors' territory, desecrating it with their presence. I have been wracked by guilt at the thought that I didn't return to the spring, stand before it and defend the wellspring with the fierceness of a zealot. Such delusions of bravery I had while cowering under a crate in the musty wooden caravan! In truth, I was deathly afraid of imprisonment, of having all of my connections to prosperity destroyed. I knew that my weak-minded helper in the capital's bureaucracy had succeeded in the creation of a new deed, with the signatures of certain, strategic officials on them. Still, I felt I was losing much more than I had achieved by this forced flight from my country. I gained a second's reassurance at the new deeds, which were hidden safely in my coat. They had thought they were signing petitions! I almost laughed in the musty enclosure of the caravan, but my lungs caught on the dust that cloyed the air in the outmoded vehicle. I thirsted for the fresh water I knew was harbored within the mountains we wound through, but I could afford few requests of my driver.

When dropped at the side of a country road to trudge anonymously to a far-out tram station, I felt that my luck had turned away from me completely; I would lead a broken life from this point on. My only hope was that Sarah had carried out my wish and done what was necessary to ensure the safekeeping of the spring. I felt guilt at having asked too much of her.

It is only on returning to my small sanctuary in the Glass City that I feel like myself again. My tiny apartment here is in the upper level of a sandstone complex, and looks out over a courtyard from a small glass room that would house a garden if I had the inclination to keep one. The windows in the apartment are small and of stained glass; the air within is warm, clean and cast through with the colors of the windows. With relief I see signs that Sarah has already arrived here, though she is not in now. She has thought to bring with her the vision bird, though I don't remember having left it in an active mode. She must have discovered it on her own, among other things.

I think the journey will have been good for her. In the act of crossing the border alone, she must have felt a surge of power. I have kept her in the mountain refuge too long. Here she can live again, and will help me to rebuild what I may have lost in my disaster at the capital. I will need to enlist further help for my plans.

It's time I tell her of the moss gardens and the divining pools. She must be told of the past, and of the role she will play in the future. I know who she is, and it hardly matters that she has deceived me. Our identities are built not on our individual natures but on the courses of action we choose. In choosing to be Sarah, she has chosen to live out a role that will survive beyond either of us. The patterns were set deep in the past. We continue them.

The light filtering in above the table was clear, as they had opened the stained glass portal to let in the evening air. Kyra had returned some time after Eson arrived, bringing with her some food, and they passed several minutes silently, respectful of each other's presence, neither favoring a sentimental reunion. They sat across from each other at a small table covered by a tablecloth of an abstract pattern that could have been silver thorns, or jeweled, sharp teeth.

She spoke first, began saying at last what needed to be said. "Eson, there's… I don't know how to say this." She paused, then stated it blandly. "I'm not Sarah. My name is Kyra, and I've never met Sarah. I've been dishonest—but I feel a connection to you that's real, and I've done everything you asked me to do in the steam territorites. The stone is in its place above the spring."

Eson registered little surprise, and even smiled as though proud they had come to the point of speaking directly. The reflecting surfaces of their mutual deception had finally been set into a clearer alignment. "I don't know who you were before you met me, but I know who sent you and who you are now. I also know that you are building your own strength, which is connected at its most basic root to mine. Who you have become matters more than whether you were ever Sarah or not. That you care for me genuinely, and I for you, is all."

She spoke with care in return. "I could very easily have taken the deed to my... to the Heiress."

Eson sat back slightly.

"I wasn't able to betray you, but I don't know if I can accept what it means to be part of your world. Even now I feel I should walk out and leave you to your deeds." She hadn't thought it until she said it, but the possibility of leaving seemed real to her in that instant. Emotions were cavalier things that demanded strong actions.

He waited a moment, and answered in a way that deflected what she had said, bringing to light his need for her. "In illuminating the shrine above my family's spring, you have proven yourself to the memory of my ancestors. You've helped me more than you can know. There's no question of betrayal between you and me." His next words were spoken with difficulty, but ended decisively. "You may leave if you want, but if you stay, there's something I'd like you to have."

He brought out a small box ornamented with endless, interweaving vines that seemed to move as he passed the box over the table to her. She pressed on a corner, and it opened to reveal a small bottle, an ink pen, and a roll of delicate parchments. She felt her eyes widen, and took her hand away from it.

Already he was closing the box, moving it backward to the center of the table.

"Even if you decide you can't stay with me, please stay this evening, until I return. I have to visit someone for a short while. If you like, send the vision bird out over this city at dusk. You'll be amazed to see the glass, blazing like shells on a rocky beach." He stood and she stood as well, and they embraced for a short, intense minute.

"There is a legend, passed down through many ages, from the old world that I have never seen, but have heard about since I was young," he said. "I want to tell you the legend, and I want you to be part of it, Kyra."

The light in the window darkened, and Eson glanced up, as if noting the deepening of evening with surprise. The sun set later in this city, though it was only a few hours to the south of the mountainous country. Such was the world they lived in, that one place varied so dramatically from another. People changed as they moved across the coordinates and interstices of the world map, liquid shadows with unknown potentials.

Eson pressed his hand to her heart and looked at her deeply. She did not answer him in words, but brought his hand to her face before he moved toward the door.

She sat again and looked into the pattern of vines before her on the lid of the box. They branched in ever dividing possibilities, but were locked into place by the idiosyncrasies of their entangled patterns. She opened the delicate box with the curious, guarded air of someone who is on the edge of a decision.

book two

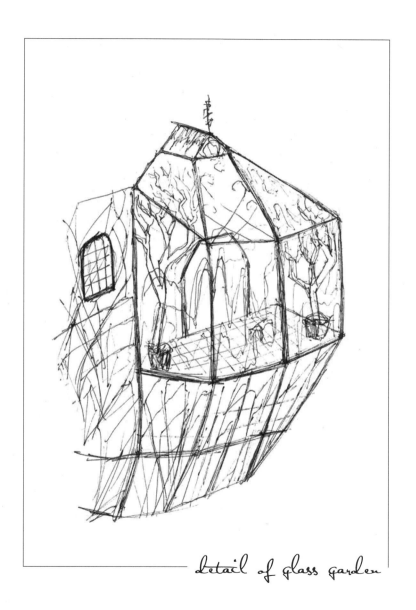

detail of glass garden

Jado had spent his entire life in the City of Broken Glass. Its streets were the landscape of his past and were part of him in a much more heightened way than they were for those who traveled briefly through the city. Even the girl who had come from the dust storm, though he had seen in her a perceptive eye, open to the nuances of the environment, was essentially a visitor. While he knew she could see things he couldn't see from his embedded perspective, she had no way of knowing the accumulated details of the city. These were the details Jado had been steeped in over the course of his whole life.

Even most people who lived in the city didn't see these particular details either, not the way Jado and the people in his interconnected community saw them. He was of the tenth generation of refugees from the western islands, and they called themselves Niyali, which means 'island people'. His culture was one of the more recent to make a home in the Glass City. They had arrived in a land already delineated and built upon by others. They had little physical property, but took ownership of the land by way of naming the city's places in their own language.

Niyali inhabited courtyards and the sheltered angles beside outlying walls until houses were granted by a phase shift in the city's government. The houses were meager and set in low, crowded spaces, but they had electricity, were safe and were owned by the Niyali in a way that couldn't easily be revoked by the next shift in government. They felt they had come at a lucky time in the city's life. They kept a record of the lives and stories of all their relations, and entwined these stories around unassuming landmarks in the urban tableau.

They had a gift for the design and construction of machines, among other things, and took up the design of clocks, engines, water purifiers and air-circulating devices. They found a special significance in the patterns of glass that covered the walls of the city. They had moved from an island landscape to a landlocked region, and many of them now had never seen the ocean in their lives. Both Niyali and others say that the glass remind them of the ocean they had been forced to leave behind.

From his earliest memories Jado had framed his existence around the places he played in and the stories surrounding them. His family's house had opened onto a sand-colored courtyard whose name can be translated as Five Gardens Meet Above a Square. The gardens were indoor rooms belonging to people living on the upper floors, and though their house had no garden of its own, Jado looked up at the gardens every time he left his house. He felt he owned five gardens, as he spun slowly in a circle naming them each in turn.

His meeting point with friends, and a trading post for cards, beads and urban legends was at The Staircase Narrows. Festivals were held every year at a courtyard called Glass in the Pattern of a Celestial Calendar. He was not allowed to venture beyond Vines

Creep Along a Wall, and had been warned to walk quickly past Sunlight Appears Only at Dusk.

The world of his childhood was one of daylight, festivals and stories. He had loved the stories of Yakim, who built machines in the age before the Niyali had left the islands. He thought of her inventions when he passed by the wall at Glass Spells a Name. This place was a curving walkway, and in its patterns of glass could be read the name of every hero spoken of by the tales. He learned to build, as many of his relatives did, but always built more unusual machines than the others did, and always thought more of the future than of the present. He grew up this way, and every year he was a celebrity for a few days when he helped put on a fireworks display at the summer festival. He spoke both the Niyali language and the lingua franca of the Glass City with ease. The Niyali community expected a type of cleverness from him, and he didn't mind this expectation. Then he became an adult, and people expected more than cleverness from him.

Some months after Jado finished the school that had been his prison in adolescence, an elder in the Niyali community visited his family. She was a genteel merchant with a slow and lyrical voice. A translucent holograph of the Celestial Calendar floated behind her as she moved, and settled slowly around her as she sat, imbuing her with its regal light. She spoke to his parents and older brother of Jado's abilities, of the community's strength and its growing identity in its younger generations. She told them there was a chance that some money could be compiled to help send Jado to a scientific conservatory to study. His parents were proud beyond measure, and called him into their capsular front room after the elder had left them. He listened to his parents, but a haze fell over him at the thought of enduring more years of school, from which he had so recently broken free. He explained to his parents that he didn't feel right using the community's money for something he did not even want to do. And besides, how would the difference in cost be made up? The community wasn't that wealthy, he knew.

In the end, Jado simply couldn't bring himself to take the actions that would have set him on a course for the conservatory. Instead, he drifted through his own patterns, and those of his friends, both Niyali and of other cultures. He contemplated moving out, and stayed often with friends who lived in feral packs on the eastern edge of the neighborhood. They had jobs of one kind or another, and used their earnings to buy virtual gaming gear and mid-range narcotics. By unspoken agreement, they didn't ask him about the practical aspects of his life.

One or two of his friends had disappeared to the university, and Jado occasionally crossed the city on a tram to visit them in their dwellings. He felt no envy for them as they conducted noxious experiments and solved tedious equations, though he did join them in drinking to assuage their woes.

He eventually tried an apprenticeship that was offered him in The Cragulin's timepiece workshops at Courtyard Lit by Reflections. The workshop was an amorphous series of warren-like rooms gradually phasing into other buildings connected to it within its depths, and was like a machine, with clock technology built into the walls and precise mechanisms governing the ebb and flow of its days. The light was artificial and bright within stone chambers that were usually lit softly in homes and most shops.

Jado was given a tour on his first day, with two other new apprentices. They were shown the chemical room, where the time-sensitive reactions of certain chemicals served as a check for the timed workings of the machines. Statues stood as sentinels in the corners of the room, which was otherwise devoid of decoration, their eyes mobile, constantly scanning the room, serving as security devices. They were uncanny representations of the gods who ruled over the timepiece families of Cragulin. Tampering with the chemicals could throw off the calculations and working rhythm of the shop, the apprentices were told. "It was punishable by banishment into the desert in the old days," a clerk assured them, robustly.

The trainer, Lurs, gave the apprentices an inspirational lecture as they watched the chemicals converge and react. He was in fact not a member of the shop's lineage, but a hired personnel instigator, fresh from the training institute in the bland suburbs of a southwestern technology town. His voice was reamed with the sneering jargon of a petty tyrant eager to stretch his claws. "You neophytes will become as precise as these chemicals. Your future here depends on it. You're going to be our next team of razor-sharp technicians. We're counting on you, and if you can't make the Standard, you're out. Kegat, what's the first rule of building a Cragulin Standard Timepiece?"

Kegat, who was the favored apprentice and properly devoid of individuality, snapped up the bait. "Always watch the clock! Never to see when you are going home, but to keep your work flow in tune."

"Good, Kegat. Somebody here's listening. You guys are going to have to keep each other on track, okay? If one member of the team is weak, you all go down." He passed his eyes over Jado as he said it, though Jado had given him little reason to doubt his capabilities.

So the apprenticeship began.

Jado built machines well as he always had, but could never make the same device more than once. Always an improvisation would occur, a veering off from the Cragulin Standard, toward a more visionary form of technology. His mother and father were proud of his inventiveness as they always had been, but his overseer was frustrated by the unpredictable nature of his creations, and saw them as a waste of materials.

Jado complained that clocks confined him to the present moment and to linear time. Months passed, and he realized he wanted to build things that would affect the future, and so built a small clock that ran on the power of the sun. The shop overseer, after consulting with the foreign technology trainer, cast him out, saying he could build whatever he liked, but not while taking up an apprentice's position at his workshop.

Kegat and the other apprentice worked without looking up, but obviously heard Jado take his leave. They mouthed the letters "CST" as they worked, an incantation to Cragulin Standard Time. The shop chant had infiltrated his head, and had whispered CST to him in odd moments outside the shop, thoroughly against his will. His sole thought as he entered the outside world was that he would at last banish the work chant from his mind!

He returned home to his neighborhood, which had taken on the aura of a sanctuary since he had started at the workshop. The world of the Niyali community breathed with a life that the gray workshop lacked. He waved to friends who sat during their lunch break outside the neighborhood shops. He bowed his head deferentially as he passed the mercantile outlet of his would-be benefactor. He felt a mixture of defeat and relief that made for an odd brew in his mind.

He returned to his family, who were not really upset. His parents, being unusually resourceful, began immediately to seek out other options for him. That very night they were able to produce a solution so they would not face the embarrassment of explaining to the community why their son had left his apprenticeship.

Jado's older brother's wife had a tea shop near the monument, and she was looking for someone to take care of the shop while she left for a time to take care of her children. He was able to wake up the morning after the end of his apprenticeship and leave for the tea shop as though he were heading to the workshop. Nobody asked any awkward questions of him or his family, and the wayward son had time to continue his machine-building projects.

Jado's sister-in-law had a fondness for maps, and the interior of the tea shop was adorned with them. The varied smells of the tea combined into a rustic, organic scent, and Jado gladly took to spending his days in the shop. Maps moved him beyond the confines of the present moment, into the past and future. There was a map of the Niyali islands as they had looked before the Takeover, when his ancestors had lived in a state of freedom. He couldn't easily imagine the islands, which were now closed off from outside media and visitors. He could imagine, sometimes, a future where the islands were free again and his group would be able to return to meet those who had stayed.

If the sea floor were to rise, though, as some predicted it would, the islands would disappear entirely, and his family's homeland would be submerged. Even the Broken Glass City would then be an island in a shallow sea, bound on two sides by chains of mountain islands as it had been in prior millennia.

Faced with these maps and the worlds they presented, Jado could not keep his mind focused on the intricate close-knit world in which he had grown up. His mind turned outward to other places and opportunities. He enjoyed speaking with the people who came into the tea shop, who told him of places they had seen. Some of them lied, he knew, but he nonetheless enjoyed their stories. He felt, after a short time, only relief at having left his apprenticeship. After the tribulations of the workshop, he enjoyed the freedom of having little expected of him.

His one remaining regret was in choosing the friends he had been involved with for a time after school, before his apprenticeship began. He had met them through one of his old friends as they cruised a bar in another part of town. Only Jado bothered to meet with them again. They were tough, mostly older than him, and had vaguely anarchistic leanings, though they didn't appear to act on them in any visible way.

He had stopped bothering to visit them after he realized that he had been weighed down by a strange sense of aimlessness since he met them. One of them had borrowed some money from him and had still not returned it several months later. There was some shady business they were associated with, and Jado felt they were not worth the trouble they were causing him.

Soon, the only person from that circle he saw was Sarah, a young woman who occasionally visited his shop, and was not like the others in the group. He didn't know much about her, but felt that she was looking out for him, as though she knew something about him he didn't know about himself. She spoke of many things, of futures and of plans, of power and justice. Her visits kept him wondering about the world beyond his city and his past. When he told her about his ideas for creating power generators fueled by the sun and wind, she mentioned she was corresponding with a man who owned a steam power fortune in the northern mountains. Jado asked if he and she could ever hope to collaborate with him, and Sarah's answer had surprised him, as she usually spoke of people without any harsh judgment: "No, he's terrifying. If I could, I'd like to see all his power taken away. I won't even meet him in person." She looked chilled by the thought of him, and Jado offered her more hot tea. He didn't ask her any more about the man, and they talked of many other things until she left.

He had been at the shop several months when the dust storm came, and with it the other young woman he thought about, waited for, and imagined spending further hours with.

It was weeks after the storm that he had another visitor who would keep him wondering about the possibilities of his future in the broader world.

It was in the dim hour of evening that the young man entered the tea shop. He gave the impression of great stature, though he wasn't tall, and the impression of authority, though he was young. He seemed to draw the air in around him like a star in its late stages. He brought the cold in with him, too, though his complexion was healthy and his movements lively. Jado nodded to him, and left him to decide on a kind of tea. When no decision was made after a few moments, Jado looked up again, and saw that the man was looking not at the list of drinks, but at the maps on the wall above. This was not unusual in itself, but the purposeful air of the man's gaze seemed unlike that of a casual visitor who has found something interesting on the walls of a shop.

He studied one map that showed the Glass City and its region being annexed to the northern empire, and he remarked to Jado that he was disturbed by the world proposed by the map. Jado agreed it was a disturbing idea, as everything that he knew of the country beyond the mountains had led him to view it with fear.

The young man was looking over the other maps, the machines on Jado's counter and, surreptitiously, Jado himself. He had an appraising look, and, like Sarah, gave an air of knowing something about Jado. Jado wondered what he had really come here for, but at the same time felt an instinctual admiration for him. There was such an exactness of purpose and calm sense of entitlement to the man. Rather than feeling invaded, Jado saw someone he wished to emulate.

The man's steely eyes rested on a map of the west coast of the continent that showed its unique tidal patterns and rock formations. "How much do you know about the countries on the coast?"

Jado replied that he knew some things, knew that the coast was out of reach to people like him who had little money. "Why do you ask?"

The man shrugged, and gave a circuitous answer. "I came from the northern country, and know that it's corrupt there. This city is politically a free realm, but it's old-fashioned and not conducive to creating opportunities. It relies on tourists for its lifeblood. I believe the coast is even freer than here, and is a place a person can truly make something of himself."

Before he could reply, the young man asked him another question. "What kinds of machines can you construct?"

Jado gave him an easy smile instead, feeling a slight reserve. "Who are you, can I ask?"

"My name's Eson." It was said plainly and without pretension.

So this was the man with the steam power fortune! He couldn't fathom how it was that Sarah had formed such a different impression of Eson than he had. This man was not terrifying; on the contrary, he felt at ease sitting here listening to him speak of freedom, the ability to fashion one's own destiny.

He told him about his small machines and his visions for a future with natural power sources, and declared an interest in Eson's steam power legacy. Eson replied that it was his own vision to help people through his position in the energy hierarchy. He added, rather cryptically, that if there were others who couldn't face the strength of his actions, it was they who were weak and misguided.

"I once put a project in motion that brought free power to one of the north's worst districts. I was opposed by a lot of people, but I had to put personal loyalties aside and do what was important. You can get so mired in the workings of the bureaucracy that you forget what you wanted at the beginning. Is it important for you to do the things you really want to do? Then you can understand me. Doesn't it get dull here, day after day, your machines not serving any purpose, your dreams no closer than they ever were? I would like to turn my efforts toward better things, and I think you're a person who wants to do the same."

The man sitting in his shop told him of the ancient springs in the mountains and of their power, of the steam and the living stone from which it arose. He explained that plates of rock colliding had created the springs, and went on to say that as people anchored to the floating plates of the planet's surface, to keep in constant motion was to create power. To move, collide and interact was to follow in the pattern of powerful forces of change that released electric potential from the earth.

Jado was fascinated. He intuited the planet seething beneath the streets of the city. The place called Glass in the Pattern of a Celestial Calendar was said to work as a conduit for the energy that lay under the rock foundations of the city. The festivals and smaller rituals held there brought the community a sense of strength. Though the patterns had been set in the stone many years before Jado's family arrived, it was they who had read the meaning in the patterns. In moving to the city, and perceiving power within it, they had claimed power for themselves. Jado had an intuitive understanding of Eson's ideas, and added them to his own store of beliefs as easily as he could add another brew of tea to the shelves around him.

He felt inspired to action by the iconic newness of Eson and his ideas, which came from beyond anything he had known in his life. It was as though a musician had passed by and enchanted him into taking part in a concert: a curtain had been lifted by the ideas Eson brought to him, and he felt he was a performer on the same stage as his masterful visitor. He at first felt that an unknown hand, perhaps the planet itself, had composed the music he and Eson would perform on this stage. He then conjectured that it was Sarah who had written the score. He soon abandoned that notion, though, as it became clear that the man before him was in charge of what he was orchestrating, whether his power stemmed from the planet beneath them or not.

The score they played was the music of promise, which would lead Jado beyond the named places he knew and enable him to throw himself into a drama of choices and sudden, satisfying action. He'd see other places and learn their names. His machines would serve a purpose, and he would be out of view of his home community, which had begun once more to oppress him with its smallness. He had spent his life on set courses between points prescribed to him by his culture and, though he knew these places as part of himself, he wanted to grow beyond them. He would raise the glass canopy to allow for larger trees in the garden of his mind. The enchanter and his music beckoned him to take flight, to climb higher in the world's trees and play reckless music in their highest branches.

Did he think about the nature of the enchanter himself, or wonder if the stage might really be a puppet theater, or a conjurer's rigged set? Jado passed these thoughts through his mind, but they seemed inconsequential. It grew dark in the shop, but neither moved toward an electric light. Jado communicated with a densely drawn silhouette.

Eson spoke as a sharer of secrets, and as a prophet. Jado was invited to partake of a future that branched upward and westward. Eson was convinced that moving to the west coast would put them in touch with planetary and social powers. There was an imperceptible switch in the conversation, after which Eson spoke of the plans as being both of theirs to imagine. Jado was pulled along by the enchanter's music, and even as he listened devised machines that could help him to realize the ideas that Eson's words relayed to him.

When Eson finally stood to leave, his silhouette took on the gravity of a vision in the spectral light that diffused dimly through the shop's windows. The structure of the shop around him became a framework of thin lines, inside which he was the only solid figure that Jado could see. It was as if they stood inside a shell or a time capsule, and the enchanter was preparing to leave him in some alien time zone he had himself designed.

"I'll return here tomorrow night. Stay here until I arrive, even if it is very late. I should attend to someone I've been neglecting lately." Cryptic though the man's leave-taking was, Jado felt he had been admitted into an intimate sphere of collusion, and simply nodded in agreement and farewell. The square door opened into a block of pale light before engulfing the visitor and shutting once again into an inert shape on the wall.

Jado stretched and realized he had been sitting absolutely still throughout the visit. He prepared to go home. He knew that the world he walked into would be new to his eyes now that Eson's hand was conducting the concert. Independent by nature, Jado had never so immediately been drawn into another's world as he had into Eson's that night. He was not a naïve person, but felt that Eson was an exception to rules that would have made him cautious of most people. As he walked in his home city, each place became a fresh sight to him from that night onward.

The places Jado knew had been the settings of stories he had heard all his life. When he was a child, the stories were of heroes and thieves, ghosts and angels. As he got older he was told other stories that changed his view of each spatial reference point. Sunlight Appears Only at Dusk was at first a ghost tale, a place where one must be fearful for his soul when walking past. Later, Jado learned it was also a place where some of his past relatives had been arrested and taken away on false grounds a hundred years earlier. So the place took on a different meaning, and his sense of identity sharpened.

He had always known that Vines Creep along a Wall marked a boundary he was not to pass, but it was only as a youth who was old enough to cross the boundary alone that he learned it had

wall where glass spells a name

been the site of a violent brawl between someone of his culture and another person who claimed territorial rights over the city streets.

He knew that the names of saints were written in the walls of Glass Spells a Name, but he didn't know of how those who were in trouble walked its length in search of answers. He was told this only when he came across a problem of his own in adolescence. He had been told if he walked the curved lane at dusk, he would see in the wall something that would aid him. He saw first the name of Yakim who built machines, as he always had. But beyond this, he also read words that had never appeared to him before, and which helped him, in a subtle and indirect way, solve his problem.

Glass in the Pattern of a Celestial Calendar, the place where they held their festivals, had been discovered when his people first came to the city. It was said to be a mirror image of a celestial calendar that had existed in one of their temples on the old island, one that had been decimated during the Takeover. Jado knew this because his parents had told him when he was very young, after he had asked them about the meaning of the calendar and the festival. The Takeover was only rarely spoken of in the community, and for the most part the festivals were wild days of exotic foods, frenetic music, and dancing in the lantern-lined streets.

As he came to know more about the city around him, he was constantly reminded of who he was, of what had happened in the past, and of how much he owed to those that had gone before. The streets that had been his playground became also his way of defining himself and his culture. He still took a joy in the landscape, and found fresh angles in it with each passing day. While he felt deeply attached to his home and family and to the community that had always surrounded him, he was ready for the future, and ready to cross boundaries to meet with it. When Eson returned to his shop the next night, Jado was waiting calmly, with the lamps lit, and a ceramic pot brewing strong tea to offer to his guest.

I've just enjoyed a rich and enlivening brew of fine Cascaradian tea, served to me by a host whose combination of youth and maturity leads me to treat him as a confidant, though I have only met him twice. The tea builds fire in your soul, and you are inspired to great things when drinking it.

Being in the Glass City again is a relief, though a double-edged one. My new plans are being brought into focus with a rapidity and clarity I could never have achieved in the confines of the northern domain. When I leave for the western coast, I will have the help I need. I'm kept busy with drawing up these plans, and my life has purpose again! As to the one who has become a large part of my purpose, I have learned her original name. She is called Kyra, and she is also Sarah in my eyes. She is many things, and she knows this.

Kyra will remain here for a time after I leave for the coast with my freshly minted apprentice. Jado has an incredible gift for building small devices. In their ingenuity, his machines approach those we once used on the other continent, before we forsook our material encumbrances and came here to find the hidden springs. My vision bird is but a last vestige of those sublime, antique technologies. We used to have stores of them, lovingly polished, but few remain. To see the young man creating such things reawakened in me a fascination for finely-tuned mechanical treasures.

I wouldn't have thought that enlisting help from the pool of names I keep in my deeds would yield such talent! Jado is one bead on the large string of ten debtors I was able to secure from the careless gambling of an inebriated low-order businessman. I simply won a game, and with it won the fortunes of an entire circle of this city's fine citizens. I have made casual forays to this circle's usual haunts in the hopes of turning up someone of value, but the group that met regularly was largely devoid of fresh life or vigor. When two of them approached Kyra in the nightclub during my earlier sojourn here, I was surprised they had even managed to take that much action.

Sarah is one of their number, but of course I don't include her in my harsh appraisal of her peers. The question of where she has really been, while I half-believed she was with me, is still open to conjecture. Jado as well differs from the group, as I've found since visiting him in his map-laden burrow. Whether he knows he is named in my deeds is immaterial. He will abandon the mediocre and embrace the new, whether he is bonded to me on paper or not. I suspect already that he has loyalties besides those to me, but he will learn in time that those are no longer viable in his new life.

The maps in that hole-in-the-wall shop fascinate me almost as much as the machines. Though he claims the maps are not his, he says he has spent many hours looking over them and imagining possible futures. His obsession with the maps informs me of his dream to venture through unknown places. My sudden appearance in his life must be like a flash of lightning on the horizon of a calm sky.

I've told Kyra about those futuristic maps, because they captured my imagination. She gave me one of her intent, searching looks, and answered by telling me of her own visions of the future, about her own wish to map the city around her here. She has become a more complicated companion since we've returned to the city. The quest she had when she originally sought me has been eclipsed from her mind, I think. Yet, there is again something she isn't telling me, hidden beneath the words she meters out. I grasp hints of it in her questions to me, and in her pointed interest in the things I tell her about my past and future. It matters little, however. I will let her play about with her ideas, invent her own games and exercise a level of control over our shared world.

I have told her of all the myths she will live out as my both my lover and my psychic reflection. Since I have told her about the distant past that shaped my identity, she has grown more aware of her quests here. Her responses to the history I present to her are ambiguous, but she must believe what I tell her, as she has seen the strength that this history yields. I care even more for her now that she has developed into a person of her own means. But I have let her know that all she has gained is still bound by my powers. She is foremost an actor in the legend I am living, and secondly the director of her own life story.

Though I have been the one to give her the power she has, I still don't know what she is thinking. We've been staying here together in the Glass City, and she recently told me that she is gaining the ability to read people as I do. It was the first time she had been direct with me about her knowledge of even my abilities, and I was taken by surprise. If she was afraid of me before, she no longer is, and our situations even seem to have reversed in some way. She sometimes takes the box of parchments I gave her, along with the vision bird, and goes into the city. The bird has become allied to her, with the odd loyalty that machines of a certain sort are capable of expressing. She records its flights onto black orbs, saving them, watching them while I am out, or sometimes while I am home. I don't know what she does besides this, when she is drifting free in the city. The constraints that our kind of power comes with haven't yet encircled her as they have me.

The other night while I walked back from a late-night meeting, I was struck by an unnerving sensation as I traversed a walkway in the old city. The walls were lit with the ghostly reflective quality the city takes on after dark, and the desert breeze was faint from the south. I stopped when I noted a change in the feel of the air around me, such as I only notice when someone nearby has attention focused on me. There was no one around that I could see, but the feeling persisted as I altered my route to avoid a place that might harbor those who would harm me. I stepped into a shadow to see who would pass by, and a figure appeared briefly from around a corner before perceiving me and quickly stepping back into a passage. I caught only the barest glimpse, enough to form the impression of a person quite small but not delicate of movement or subtle of intent. Once they'd stepped back, I felt the energy that had been impinging on my own being reeled back as if in defense.

The night air became once more the usual zephyr of the desert, but my suspicions were set on alert by then, and I hurried through the streets, not slowing to enjoy the cool calm of night. I know not if the person I saw was affiliated with the woman I dislike in particular, Kyra's own tormentor, but I was set on guard nonetheless.

It occurs to me oddly that I have Veridi to thank for having sent Kyra into my life. Such odd gifts may be bestowed by one's enemies!

I know Kyra doesn't yet intuit this kind of threat in the city, as she asked me directly the other day why the people who had been seeking the deeds from us weren't now following us or trying to take them away.

We were reclining in the deep glow of evening, inside the glass-walled garden enclosure at one end of my suite. My garden resembles a desert more than a paradise, because I am so rarely here that keeping plants as prisoners would be pointless. By way of answering her question, I explained to her that we were kept under the radar by our ability to keep ourselves within certain undetectable domains of space. I told her the truth, as simply as I could, about these domains of space. "By keeping to the proper energy trails within a place, you can ensure that your own energy trace won't be broadcast outward. This apartment, the club we visited, and the monument where we met, are all aligned along a set of coordinates that form a net over the city. The dossier you originally had listed many places in the city, but only the club was really relevant to your search. You had a special prescience that allowed you to find me. Most are not so open to the hidden currents that govern the spaces we walk in. That's how I came to know you were the right one. It doesn't matter if you wrote the letters to me or not. You found me. You are being rewarded for your gift of perception. Others are not so skilled, and they can't find us, unless we are careless in our wanderings. I can't go back to that nightclub now; too many people know about my connection to it. You shouldn't go there either. I don't think it's safe for you anymore."

I knew it was an autocratic demand, but I had her safety in mind. I didn't know if she had any intention of going to the nightclub, but didn't want to leave that risk open. Kyra had an orb in her hand while she listened to me, and she watched it present an aerial voyage of the squalid industrial quarter that marred the southeastern corner of the city.

"Why did you record that?" I asked her after a few seconds

had passed and she had made no reply to my explanation.

"I recorded it because I really want to live in this place and so can't be confined to the beauty of the Old City. I want to experience a true sense of being situated here, including the contrasts. Especially after viewing the capital in your country, where a dome separates those who are given the advantages of technology and wealth from those who aren't." She paused, switching tracks with her next comment. "I can see why you want to cut your ties with that city."

I nodded. "You want to collect the city into your being, by recording it all. I would like to do the same, but by branching out into other places besides this city and the Steam Territories."

I waited for a moment, knowing she had mixed emotions about my wish to branch outward.

"I do want to cut my ties with the capital in the north, but my house in the mountains is different from the polluted capital city. The spring and the house, together as a gift from my history, must not be allowed to disappear from our lives. Did I ever tell you the true value of your final actions there the day I called you from the capital? I will always be grateful to you for that."

Kyra shook her head, and I don't know if she meant I hadn't told her, or if she was denying any need for gratitude.

"The stone you placed into the shrine guards the house in much the same way that it guarded my deeds, except that its radius of protection is increased by being in the shrine. Soon after it is placed, it builds a field around it and its environs. Any person who enters the house—except for you or me, of course—begins to feel dizzy, and soon leaves."

"How does your servant keep herself from being affected by the stone's power?"

I looked at her in surprise, because I assumed she knew about the servant's nature as an example of the steam country's technology. "She's not an organic entity. Fields like that don't have an effect on her."

I didn't want to say more. The simulacra made me uneasy. I feel a gulf of emptiness around incarnations who don't exude the warmth and pulse of the living. But simulacra are inherited by groups of our families, and are the only servants we can trust. They are like holograms, and outlive us, seeing our patterns played out over generations instead of being reincarnated, as we natural creatures are.

Kyra nodded, not disturbed by my answer. I wondered if she and the servant had ever spoken to each other. There is little that shocks her now that she has seen the country beyond the mountains. She leaned her head on my arm, and we watched the evening deepen over the city. The bird, which Kyra kept shined to a metallic luster, was perched on a stone-dry branch that arced across the glass wall in front of us. It watched us with tiny, onyx eyes, and I was treated to a tiny image of myself with Kyra in the orb she held out in front of us. We looked like a sculpture of people, set as an icon into the geometric form of the glass room. The dry branches of trees that once survived in this garden formed a box around us, and I mused to myself that if we waited long enough, we would become as solid as these branches. We were like the statues of gods that exist beside fountains on the old continent. I thought of the mythic people that existed long ago, they of whom we were acting as manifestations. We were strong, and even such setbacks as the disastrous betrayal in the capital couldn't destroy us.

I had received word earlier in the day that my networks in the north were not totally to be undone. The deeds disguised as petitions the officials there had signed kept a hold over my business interests. The weak sycophant proved able to carry out the devious act that I would have defiled myself in performing. The whining dog now demands that I return the favor to him. It is a nuisance, but his use has been filled, and I have still my steam power shares. I will make it up to him, but must cut short any delusions he has of my obeying his tremulous, weak-spirited orders.

While I couldn't have such complete control of my electricity legacy as I did when able to live freely in the steam territory, the currents of trade are still set to filter benefits and profits in my direction. In my move to the coast, I will create a linked pathway of energy, like a fiber-optic cable, between the Steam Territories, the Broken Glass City, and a city in the tidal shelf region called Waters Rising. Kyra will be the link that secures the Broken Glass City in this chain. Jado will play out a similar course in the Waters Rising. His presence is vital to the realization of our intended future.

They are both bound to me, in ways they don't realize.

Since they had arrived back in the city, Kyra's relief at Eson's safe return had been tempered by a sense of doubt about the ethics of his mode of making a living. Her doubt had transformed into curiosity as he began to tell her about the deep history that was inscribed in the roots of his actions—and, he said, of hers. The doubt was never completely effaced, though, and Kyra balanced on the edge of disbelief while she listened to his account. Her mind was alive always with questions, and her agreement was never total or relaxed. Especially when he told her she was the embodiment of an ancestor creator-goddess who had formed the ancient landscape with her footsteps, Kyra held onto a measured sense of skepticism. She would help him to enact his visions, but she had a different mode of enacting her own. Yet she was fascinated by the myth, and as she traced the footpaths and streets of the city, she traced also the patterns of the old continent.

The stories told of the original pools that rested like bowls of water in the once-wild valleys of the old world. Thousands of years ago, there were no people inhabiting those lands. Cities didn't exist, machines were a distant dream, and people owned only what was in their minds and on the land around them. Vulnerable shoots of human enterprise began to pepper the landscape, arriving in boats from their origin place in the south. They brought their gods with them and birthed new ones as well. Settlement encircled the wild valleys but did not delve into them. The wind howled fiercely in its hollows, and no food could be grown in the erratic, sharpened earth. People and their tame gods, as Eson called them, were afraid of that land. The pools were not used for divination, and the moss-covered walls of the jagged hillsides were believed to exude poison. Sunlight avoided reflection on the deep, rough pools of the rugged valleys, and the animals were nocturnal and predatory. Eson's ancestors came to live by and divine from those pools, but only after a portentuous event disturbed the surface of the waters.

The uprising occurred one day during a storm that set the surfaces of the pools into a discord of warring wavelets, set in motion by opposing winds. In the deep heart of the storm, a whirlwind began to form above one of the pools, and from the whirlwind emerged a giant. She was a magnetic, composite, expanding being who incorporated everything she touched into her identity and under her dominion. While she began as stationary and water-bound, she eventually swept as a spinning whirlwind out from the deep pool and raged through the valleys, leveling the jagged hills and purifying the mossy hillsides. The dreaded animals, sharp stones, and deep waters all became part of her, and while she turned the rugged land into a place where humans could live, she also embodied the wild nature of the land, and infused this nature into the first group of people who appeared afterward: Eson's ancestors.

She was a rebel spirit, and her way was incorporated into them. She never took a human form, but she was understood as the first of the people who lived there. Eson's ancestors became different from the people around them, abandoning their tame gods for her, and moving into the fresh lands she had prepared for them. She served them and they served her, along with a retinue of lesser spirits that arose in her wake. Her spirit came to rest in a statue of two lovers that reclined beside the most revered of the pools in the moss valleys. The valleys became moss gardens, and they were a rich bed of food and shelter for the small group that dared to enter them. Her name in the old language sounded qute similar to 'Sarah,' perhaps explaining Eson's attachment to the name.

The people of Eson's family lineage were always characterized by the rebellious nature they had been given by the spirit. The philosophy set down by the earliest ancestors was encoded in an illuminated, color-plated book Kyra had paged through idly while staying in the mountains. The words were in a script she couldn't read, and only after hearing Eson's account of the beginning did she think back on the pictures of the book with understanding. He kept a copy of the ancient treatise in the city apartment as well, and Kyra glanced over it again in spare moments.

That Eson related her to the creator spirit was both a form of praise and a prescription. She felt a purpose was being created for her regardless of whether it conflicted with her view of the world. She believed there was a certain order to the world, such that to dream of a dust storm and then have it occur in reality wasn't a surprise. Yet, real deity worship had never been a part of her life. She didn't consider herself to be religious, and to be cast into a messianic role within another's religion struck her at an awkward angle.

She wrestled with trying to understand Eson's motivations. Perhaps, having lost a measure of stability in his world, he was struggling to reestablish order and meaning, she thought. She resolved to do only what she would do of her own volition, and if her actions overlapped with his myths and visions, then she would allow them to do so. She now understood the origin of his animistic ideas of obtaining power from the planet. If she could not embrace them herself, she could at least intuitively respect and make provisions for them.

After hearing his account of the myth, her objective remained that of learning about her surroundings, so she could build knowledge, power and meaning in her life. She also set herself the puzzle of trying to learn about the people who were named in the deeds, feeling they had answers for her that Eson couldn't give. Though she admitted it not even to herself, she wanted also to learn about Eson's intended actions, beyond what he was telling her.

The Glass City was perfect to her and to learn from it was to define what was right and wrong about cities as life-giving systems. Though young, she had wandered far from home, and in the Glass City she saw a place that could be for her a new kind of home beyond the oppressive house of the Heiress. Having seen the northern capital, she was further driven to find out why this city differed so much from it. She was haunted by that capital, and was as much afraid as Eson that the political agendas and corruption present there would expand outward into the free world. They were united by this congruency in their views.

But her fear rested at a deeper level than his, in her estimation. She knew that if the stratification she saw dividing the capital ever moved outward and enveloped other countries, she would decidedly be on the impoverished outer side of any dome created. In his near loss of fortune, Eson came to her to be much more real as a person, one who was also vulnerable to the powers of the greater world seething around them. While she had before felt an edge of resentment at his inalienable state of privilege, she now felt that he had suffered from the threat of loss, such as ordinary people do throughout their lives.

Despite doubting the obscure underpinnings and dubious

motives of his actions, she wanted to stand with him preserving and cultivating the power he had. This was especially so since she herself had begun to feel the energies he commanded empowering her own actions. Yet, she felt as well that there were things he was keeping from her, and that the simulacra servant's words couldn't be totally ignored. His immunity encased her, but she could only speculate at the solidity of it under invisible strictures that might be waiting in the future.

There seemed always to be something invisible hovering over them now, too, whether they walked in the city as a normal couple might do, or lay in the warm-colored square reflection created by the window of Eson's room. A glass skylight allowed clear sun rays and patches of starlight into the small room. The city dwelling was much humbler than his mountain house, and felt more neutral and innocent to her. The air was dry and clean, and though something was still always in the air around them, it was less foreboding than the miasma that suffused the mountain house. She watched the stars shift above them while he slept, cool and quiet, beside her. The coolness he exhaled didn't make him unpleasant to be near, it only made her aware of his presence in a way that was always renewing and fresh. He spoke to her before she slept, and she had the sensation of resting next to a fast-moving stream. When she awoke, he was often gone already into the curving channels of the city.

She at times suspected that he had worked an enchantment on her, to prevent her from awaking and following him in his outings. While she had on first meeting him wondered if he were really human, she felt now that he was not only human, but was something else as well. She would not concede to believing in the animistic tale he told her, but could also not deny there was more to him than the flesh and blood of most.

It was in her forays outward in the Glass City that it became obvious to her that she herself had changed into something quite different from her original being. People deferred to her in odd, everyday ways, at shopping bazaars, in public places like galleries and museums. Even in that most prosaic dance of the pedestrian who banks left and right to move out of the path of another who does the same, she sensed a submissive and apologetic air far beyond the usual. That she was able to obtain good prices for vegetables or jump queues at the tram stations was no indication of the supernatural, she knew, but it was in the very searching and almost supplicating looks given her by passersby that she sensed an underlying awe. She had once been invisible to those around her, but now felt like a beacon. She hadn't changed noticeably in her mirror reflection, but in something else, she had. She came home once with a pensive look, as she'd had a strange encounter with someone who tugged her arm in the street, soliciting a blessing or something else unknown. Eson had said softly, "You've started to notice it, haven't you?" At the time she'd said nothing about it, only smiled and raised her eyebrow at him in the way that was one of their shared jokes. They had fixed a light snack then, and he asked her more about what she'd seen in the city that day. He volunteered little information about his own day's activities, claiming they had been tedious. The night had passed much like any other.

Her usual habit, by day or sometimes by night, became mapping out courses through the city with the vision bird and then following them through on foot. The wheeling and diving path of the bird allowed her to see the city from a multitude of angles. It eluded gravity and ignored walls, while never faltering in its detail, or failing to navigate home. She felt a voyeuristic sense of omniscience in her observations of the city. Most people didn't recognize the bird as a machine, though a few pointed in amazement at the shining, fast creature that defied the behaviors usually expected of birds. Only once or twice had someone looked up at it with a knowing, incredulous gaze, watching it disappear over a wall, or standing up on a crate to look at it more closely. It never struck her as odd that she had never seen Eson roaming the city through the eyes of the bird. It was a large place, and he had told her that he kept to narrowly defined tracks to avoid detection by various parties.

She intently watched over a growing collection of orbs, setting them out roughly by city district in a back corner of the suite. When she ran out of orbs, Eson brought her more, before she even thought to ask. He was mysterious about his sources, and would only say that he made special trips to an old friend of his, who was delighted to see the rare old technology in use again. Indeed, some of the orbs were cracked or spotted, and some were faded to a steel gray color, or even blanked out periodically while she watched them. There were places in the city that eluded her mechanical eye, and though the bird navigated past with safety, the orbs refused to show them to her.

On occasion, she saw something taking place in the city that caused her to set down the orb quickly and rush out into the streets, hoping to catch an event before it ended. This happened once while she had been combing the streets of a nearby district. The usual crowds of the day were flowing all in one direction down a set of streets. They converged on a courtyard much like the one she had passed on her first night in the city long ago, but much larger, and filled that day with people, food-tables, musicians and performers. The orb provided her this scene silently, the movements of the people detached and small within it. She was brought suddenly back into the sense of longing for excitement and spontaneity she'd first had in the city. Expertly flipping beads along on the control device, she directed the vision bird to roost on the secluded rooftop of a nearby house and set the orb down in its place among those that kept her record of that part of the city.

She left a note for Eson, who was away at the time. She closed the windows and turned off the video screen in the living room. Within minutes she was darting toward the tram station nearest the apartment. People stepped aside for her as for an errant vehicle, though she was as small as she had always been in stature. She caught a tram, and hurtled with it through the streets, the voices of many others snaking around her.

"—won't happen this year—"

"—had a great disc-sounding with—"

"—and that's the least likely—"

Though random and disparate, Kyra realized she was hearing them all at once, and was following the conversations between speaker and receiver, as though all were speaking directly into her mind. Perhaps it was only her ear becoming sensitive after hours of silence with the orbs, but she was experiencing something unlike what she was used to. She realized with greater shock that one of the conversations wasn't even in her own language. Could she really be absorbing the city's cultures to a degree that allowed her to learn its many dialects by ambient diffusion?

She suspected it had to do both with her journey into the mountains and with Eson's constant presence. She felt disconcerted by the chords of dependence that ran through her now, even more deeply than when she had fallen under his initial enchantment. She recognized that first spark of emotion as an enchantment now that even more densely forged bonds had replaced it.

By the time she slipped off the tram, she had begun training her mind to listen carefully to her surroundings. This was input the vision bird couldn't supply, and she wondered if there might be a corresponding old-world machine that recorded sound as the bird recorded images. She made a note to press Eson further for the location of his orb dealer, and moved along the streets, conscious of the eyes upon her. She would also ask him more about the guarded paths he felt were safe to walk, as her own nascent abilities might soon force her to become restricted in the same way as he. How different she was from the free-wandering girl she had been when she first came to the Glass City!

Her path led her by a wall covered with thick, creeping vines that had escaped the confines of a walled garden, and pointed her onward around a corner into a wider street. She passed a place dark with shadows, light blocked out on all sides by a rampart of walls, and hurried along a curving walkway where glass scattered intricately on the walls. Was it really words that were spelled out there? She had never noticed before, though the bird had shown her this walkway more than once. Emerging into a courtyard ringed by staircases, she saw a knot of children holding a secret meeting on one of the narrowing, terraced stairs, trading beads with the seriousness of smugglers and money exchangers.

She could hear, now, the music she had seen being played silently within the orb, and she turned up another staircase, coming out into the courtyard the bird had shown her less than an hour before. The tune was rustic and brought to mind lurching caravans, open-air living, and finely tempered wooden instruments. The ticking of many clocks could also be heard, she realized, behind the walls of the courtyard. She could read the inside of houses vaguely, just as she had read the many conversations on the tram—which was happening again, though the music formed an audio barrier to her unintended eavesdropping.

The dominating feature of the courtyard, above the milling crowds and tents, was a sublime pattern in the glass. Here the glass shards were larger and set in a more deliberately evocative pattern than on most ordinary walls. It implied a cyclical turn of seasons and years, each piece leading to another as one day leads to the next. The geometries of the pattern induced a sense of order, peace and reason over its courtyard domain. The festival beneath was loud and fast-paced, but the calendar resting above it was still, serene and talismanic.

Having arrived at the festival, she felt an excitement renewed. She was a part of the life of the city! She simply circled the outer edges of the courtyard as many others were doing, and enjoyed the music, the welter of crowds, the smells of food. Most of the people around her looked like part of one cultural group. She felt a bit of an outsider, but no one took notice of her as such. Many looked similar to the young man she had met in the tea shop near the old monument. It was a free day; no one worked and the music carried the courtyard upward into the cloud-patched sky. A sudden shift in clouds put the courtyard into shade, the glass pattern darkening above it.

She bought a wrapped packet of food and sat down on a staircase, seeing an empty spot. Two young women sitting nearby leaned close to speak to each other, talking loudly to hear each other over the sound of the music. They included her in their conversation, touching her arm lightly as she ate her food. They wore huge golden earrings and flowing clothes. The woman closest to her told her about the music reverberating around them, moving in a rolling way that bordered on dance as she talked. The people here, Kyra thought, were very different from her original impression of the city's dwellers as aloof and hurried.

"This is a combination of the old music of our island countries and the music borrowed from the desert nomads. They borrowed our music as well. There was an alliance between our cultures during the difficult times that passed in earlier generations," the woman explained, gesturing to the space in front of them as though Kyra were to picture the past taking place right then. "They don't often come to our festivals now, but have their own, in the dry plains and desert near here. We're celebrating with them through our shared music."

She went back to speaking with her companion, switching over to that language with the ease of those who are bilingual from a young age. Kyra noted with relief that she was unable to follow the conversation. She nodded in answer, and felt moved by the music that was both a symbol of deserts and of islands in the sea, waves and dunes coming together through sounds. She closed her eyes, and drank in a freedom that was as immediate and fresh as the music. She was here in a free city, far from the house and burdens of the Heiress. Far away, too, were the Steam Territories, exotic and harsh.

She opened her eyes when she felt a nudge to her arm again.

The woman gestured subtly into the crowd. "There's a desert nomad," she said. Indeed there was a person, covered in layers of bright fabric; only a delicate, made-up face and two locks of hair were visible. Her eyes were lined in dark pencil, and swept alluringly around, theatrically eyeing the people who passed as she moved with a sidling, sweeping motion, causing the crowd to make way for her. She demanded audience, holding the edges of her robes out to either side like fanned wings. Gold plates draped over her clothing would have glowed in the sun if not for the clouds that still dulled its rays. Kyra realized then, observing the great height and angularity of the nomad, that she might actually be a man—but before she had time to observe further her attention was snapped away by another figure moving to the nomad's side.

Kyra studied the figure, trying to see if it was the young man from the tea shop or only a doppelgänger. It could be either, in this crowd of loosely knit kinsmen. A light rain had begun to fall, and the warm stones of the courtyard exhaled a fresh, earthen smell. Covers went up over the food-tables and the musicians, who never paused in their playing.

She knew rain was a relief and a good sign to the citizens of the Glass City, especially in light of the dust storm that had swept through so recently. A local had told her the deserts to the south threatened ever northward into the green plains that still filled the flats between the city and the mountains to the north. "Wasn't this year the driest yet?" was a common remark to overhear.

The women next to her put their hands to the air in the rain and sang in rich voices in their own language before rising to their feet and gravitating toward the dance area near the musicians. A look told her she was invited to follow, but she had already set her course for the figure who appeared to her as Jado.

On catching up with and speaking to him, though, she saw he was a bit older, taller, and stockier than Jado. She had already met his eyes, so she asked, "Do you know a man named Jado? He works at a tea shop in the streets below the monument."

"Well, Jado is a common name, but I happen to have a cousin named Jado who is looking after his sister-in-law's shop. That could be the one." His voice was easy and calm.

She smiled. "I think it may be."

"He rarely leaves that shop these days; it has become his hide-out. It's the best place to find him."

Still smiling, she thanked him and turned into the crowd, which quickly engulfed her in a wash of color, sound and humanity. In the multitude of people she was like anyone else, no longer a runaway or a thieving servant. There were many new identities to choose from now.

She thought suddenly of Neriv and the others she'd met during her earlier stay in the city. It had been easier to speak to people and make friends before her journey to the Steam Territories, she realized. She'd been open to the world, unfocused and in search of a purpose. Now she had a purpose, and though it still involved searching, she felt much more directed toward finding something of a specific nature. She decided she would revisit the tea shop, and as well, the nightclub where she had originally seen Eson. While she respected his word, she couldn't accept his restriction of her movements. She had come back to the city with the understanding that her physical restriction was not to continue as it had in the mountains. She knew instinctively that in going to the nightclub, she might find a sealed area of Eson's life, one she could not yet access, perhaps something he was keeping locked away from her.

But for that day, after she had enjoyed the festival and believed she had learned more about the city, she returned home to tell Eson about it, and to ask him if he knew anything about nomads. She didn't mention to him her experiences in the tram or the street. She wanted to be sure about them before causing Eson any alarm, and also to keep some knowledge locked away within her.

The storm clouds shot a crackle of energy through the air, sending people yelling and singing through the streets. She and Eson looked from the glass garden down into the streets where the world of people moved in elation within the greater, calm rain of the natural world. A very old man strode by below, singing a rejoicing song with a loud and somehow urgent voice.

"It must remind him of how it used to be here, when it rained much more reliably," said Eson, and then: "The dust storm made its impression on the city. It won't be forgotten easily." He looked as though the storm still affected him, even weeks later. He turned to her with a serious face that softened when she asked him where he had gone that day.

"Only to the trading houses on the commerce summit. There were just a lot of representatives sitting along tables in the hall. It was a prolonged and dull experience. ...You're enjoying the city again, aren't you?"

"I am! I'll tell you about what I saw today."

They spoke for a long time while the rain fell on the glass walls. It grew dark, and they saw a white branch of lightning in the plains just visible beyond the city. The storm brewed a strange sort of passion, and when the electric power switched off for a while in the deep of the storm, they only lit candles and further enjoyed the extreme uniqueness of the rainy night.

He said quietly, before falling asleep, "We never have power outages like this with the springs next to us in my mountain home."

Kyra wondered, before sleeping herself, how the mountains, the springs and the power they held could be brought closer to the Glass City and away from the domain of the steam capital. She dreamed that night of crackling electricity, of places that called themselves trading houses but were filled with hanging gardens of moss. She knew they were energy conductors, making electricity from the moss, but couldn't fit together anything else in the dream.

Eson was gone as usual when she awoke, and looking at the sparse clouds that strayed across the skylight, she decided it was an auspicious day for her to visit the tea shop. A thought surfaced as well about the Heiress: she had disappeared in a way that seemed complete, yet not altogether comforting. Her former employer had made definite threats about what would happen should Kyra run from her agreed duties, and she knew firsthand how tenacious the Heiress could be in settling old accounts.

The day was hard and bright after the storm, and she drank many cups of the Cascaradian tea Eson had brought home a few days before. She leafed through some of his books and read an entry about the celestial calendar of the western islands, and about the hostile takeover the islands had endured centuries earlier. She read also of other myths that had come over from the continent in the east, increasing her knowledge of the pantheon in which Eson had given her a role. Becoming restless, she ventured out into the city and once more found she could listen to impossible strains of conversation around her. She drifted through the bazaar and its shops, through galleries and small museums.

The tea shop was even smaller and more marginal-looking than she had remembered. The lighting was too dim to be intentional, and the countertop behind which Jado sat was cluttered. He was leaning in apparent frustration over a small device, and looking up, he put it aside with evident relief.

"You've finally come back," he said, as if speaking to someone who had been away for years. He looked pleased but mystified, and it was a few moments before he appeared to readjust to her presence.

"I'd been meaning to return, but hadn't found the time until now. You know how life carries you along with it." She sat on a chair near the counter. "I saw the festival yesterday in the courtyard with the round pattern of glass."

"You were in the Niyali neighborhood?" He sounded pleased and surprised, proud that his community would be of interest to an outsider. "We have festivals in that courtyard because the glass pattern looks like the ones we had on our temples in the islands. I would have been there, too, but we couldn't afford to shut down the shop for the day."

She looked around at the shop, empty but for her and him, and nodded understanding. "The music was intoxicating! And I ate some kind of food that was wrapped up in a packet, like sweet potato in bread."

"That was one of the favorite foods people used to eat on the islands, before we came here. It grew wild over there, but we grow it in enclosed gardens and eat it a few times a year."

They spent some minutes poring through jars, concocting a custom blend of tea, which soon sat steeping on the counter amid small pieces of metal. She felt calm with him, as though he expected little of her other than relaxed company.

"Where are you from?" he asked her.

"Recently? I've just come from the north." She gave a fast, wicked grin as she said it, knowing the words would have the power to surprise. She knew also that the answer was evasive as he'd asked where she was from, not where she'd just been, but she had always avoided telling people about her past, and would only do so if pressed.

"The north! Just into the plains, or beyond the border?"

"Into the mountains beyond the plains. I crossed the border, then crossed back again a few weeks later." It had a foreign ring to it, even to her.

"How did you manage that?"

"A temporary work permit," she said easily.

He nodded. "But what did you see there? I've heard rumors... It sounds so dangerous there."

"It's different from here. I think life is much harder for many people. But for others, life is easy. There's steam power, and hot springs welling up in the mountains."

"Did you stay in the mountains, or did you go to the capital?" The mere word *capital* was typically edged with dread in conversations about the north.

"I saw the capital, but I didn't go there. It was unbelievable, the steam and smoke and rough city outside a clear dome that had high technology, clean paths and clear air. I stayed in the mountains. There was a servant who looked like a holographic image, but who spoke to me once with the lucidity of a living person. There were ancient forces contained within the walls of the houses."

"Did they have other... strange technologies?"

She nodded. "I found a statue of a bird that could record everything its eyes saw, storing it in black orbs. I... " She tapered off, having been about to say that she had brought the bird back with her. She had already said too much about the north.

They sat without speaking again for a few minutes. "What about the things you're making here?" she asked him, to change the topic of conversation.

He told her about the small listening device he was fashioning, and she joked that she would be able to find a use for such an object if he ever perfected it.

"Wouldn't we all," was his answer. It was his turn to change the subject, and he did so, reiterating his question about her origins. "Where were you before you went to the north? Before you came here for the first time, I mean? Where did you grow up?"

She gave in, though tersely. "I grew up in an aeroponic garden cave." She paused and waited for the usual questions.

But Jado only nodded, clearly having heard of such places, and asked, "What was that like?"

She took a deep breath and, encouraged by his sympathetic question, spoke further. "The cave's in a broad sinkhole in the ground in the forest, and houses are secured on scaffolding on its walls. The sun shining through layers of garden and the mineral air from inside the cave cause the plants to grow. It wasn't really underground, but it was below the planet's surface. I left early. It was beautiful, but I wanted more of the world." *And you certainly got it*, she thought with some irony. "I wandered between different towns and cities, working, returning to the cave off and on. Eventually I came here." She shrugged, as if to say that was all, and looked to him. "Did you spend your whole life here?"

"Yes, all of it," he answered, then added, "But I'll be leaving soon. I'm going to the tidal shelf."

"Really? Why are you going there? It's difficult to live on the coast. Their money is worth more than ours, by far." She said it gently, thinking less of Jado than of Eson and of herself. She had recently been devoting much thought to the coast as she'd heard portions of Eson's plans.

He thought for a moment, and then said, carefully, "A friend of mine has offered me a job there."

She became thoughtful, and didn't ask him any more questions. They drank their tea without saying much more, only talking lightly of inconsequential things.

"Will you stop in again before I leave for the coast? I won't be going for a while."

"I will. I enjoy talking with you here."

He answered only with a nod.

Then she was once more outside, in the bright light of the afternoon. The past that had ebbed closer than was comfortable now receded again, and she absorbed the anonymity of the city.

It was only later, as she glanced again at the names in the stack of deeds resting in the desk in the suite, that she connected Jado with Eson's network. Could this be the same person, or was it someone who only shared a name? She couldn't go back and ask questions for some days now, as it would be odd for her to return to the tea shop very soon.

She would simply concentrate on other avenues in the meantime. He'd said he wouldn't be leaving for some time... but it was odd he had been offered a job on the coast when Eson was also speaking of going there. And hadn't he been more interested in her experience in the north than most people would have been?

But then, Eson wasn't in the habit of offering people jobs as far as she knew.

Eson returned in the late afternoon, after she had put the contracts away. He had been to the markets below the city, he told her, near the irrigation channels that fed through the plains. Out of a paper packet he brought a large, flat red fish that brought to mind prehistoric oceans and branching charts with Latinate descriptions of ancient fauna. "Is it edible?" she asked doubtfully.

"Not only is it edible, it's an extraordinary find! I had to bargain fiercely for the honor of bringing it home."

They cooked it with delicate greens and spices she'd bought at the local bazaar. "I bargained fiercely for these, too," she joked.

Once cooked, the fish stared up at them from its pond of greens, set on a star-shaped platter atop the jagged thorn-patterned tabletop between two spindly candles. Its flavor was both delicate and full of the richness of the distant lake its kind had dwelt in for eons. They washed it down with strong northern wine.

As it was on many days, their time together was carefree. There was talk of seeing a concert in the amphitheatre beside the monument. Their doubts were very far away from both of them, and the evening slipped away into the vault of idealized memories of which such evenings become part.

She decided she'd wait for an evening when Eson went out without her, and then she would go to the nightclub. In the course of her time in the Glass City she might begin visiting it often, especially after he left for the coast. What she was to discover there, and in places she learned of from people there, would remind her again of how the time in the mountains had made her different. She would remember herself earlier, how she had felt traitorous in investigating Eson's study. She would feel no such guilt now in the neutral landscape of the city that was as much hers as it was Eson's, even in the place that he had asked her not to visit. But underlying her determination to visit the club was an undercurrent of near superstitious disquiet, as if by moving out of the territory he approved she was subjecting herself to a risk she had been warned against. His words were not a moral command, but a floating, nearly supernatural edict. It was a subtler kind of control that filled in the spaces between the more direct forms she had been able to reject.

Her visits to the club, the tea shop and other places in the Glass City gave her life beyond what she knew as part of his world, and what she had seen during her time in the outlying aeroponics regions. She had the desire to create something she could think of as *home*. She wanted to own a landscape, the way Eson owned his springs and his homes, in a different way that was all her own. "You're inventing the world around you by mapping it in those orbs," had been Eson's observation, and it fit well with her way of looking at her situation.

He had told her gradually of his plans to relocate for a time to Waters Rising on the tidal shelf of the western coast. She was not receptive to these plans, and said so without any verbal cushioning. "It will only be for a short time, while I'm setting up some liaisons there," he promised her.

They lay awake one night, and he spoke of it again. "With a base of actions in Waters Rising, we can tap into the trade networks that branch out across the sea. We're in a closed circuit here, locked in by mountain and desert. It's beautiful, but isn't it sometimes stagnant here, too? I want us to grow beyond ourselves. We can't do that moored in one place. You're a wanderer. Have you really found the place that will satisfy your curiosity for years to come? You wanted to travel."

She chose not to engage in answering for the moment; instead she asked him if he would be taking anyone with him when he left.

"A friend of mine might be accompanying me," he said. And after another moment: "I have to keep finding new territory, because the people who are seeking me here in the Glass City restrict my movements. While I'm not in such danger as we find in the north, we're still vulnerable to the people who are wishing me ill. We have to be wary of attracting their attention. In the west, I would not face such encumbrances on my actions."

"I don't feel any stagnation here. It's only here I can live my life fully." She closed the conversation by turning away from him and closing her eyes to sleep.

"As your freedoms grow in some ways, they're curtailed in others," he said, still, stamping his voice's imprint into the silence.

"There are different kinds of freedom." But she said it softly, only to herself.

I had taken special passages down through the city the day I scored the Xanthus fish. I'd entered trading houses and markets that were a far cry from those official places of commerce in the loftier boroughs of the city. There are places for the doing of high things, and other places for the doing of low.

Leaving my suite in the early hours of the day, when my Kyra still lay sleeping, I took a unique route fashioned by personal necessity. The energy trails are safest if I follow a certain corridor north before looping upward along a winding stair. I am actually further from my destination, but am undetectable. Here there is a door under an archway, and it leads downward into a street that is otherwise hard to access but is a pure conduit down to the Mako tram station, a secure line into a sketchy area of town that is largely safe for me.

Getting off the tram at Silk Street, I passed by the bright banners that hang over the buildings, then through a rough garden onto Bridger's Way. I walked through a glass-roofed corridor that leads along a clear irrigation channel and then wove through the market at its opposite end.

Here on the lower slope are the hotels for transient workers, the old markets, and the gaming and trading halls that truly support much of this prim city's economy. There are stacks of houses, and many people live out respectable lives here, as in any part of the city, but there are undercurrents of rebellion, too, in cafés and pubs where dissenters from other nations, not excluding the Steam Territories, are known to meet. There are subcultural outposts of those who live for the thrill of the game or the sound of the electric music dens. There are psychics and oracles for those who wish to believe, and geomancers and astronomers for those of a more scientific bent. The buildings are a clash of old and new that is welcoming to the jaded eye.

I haunted one of the cleaner gaming houses on that day, trusting it with small fortunes and coming away with larger. It was a glassy, smoky place, ephemeral and with constant through-traffic of people who are never seen elsewhere.

I first won the lion's share at the glass chain game, which is a kind of tug-of-war, and a favorite of mine. In this game a tangled knot of glass rings, all set to break at the same point, is suspended above a table surrounded by the gamers. At a signal, we all pull toward our own spot at the table, and the winner is the one who comes away with the most rings. I've perfected this art, and when I moved on to the numbers-in-sand table I noted with satisfaction that all those who been part of my first game dispersed far from me for my second.

Numbers-in-sand is a slower, subtler game, requiring a focus of energy not easy for some. A table covered in a thin layer of sand is swept smooth, and each player draws some numbers in a sand block in front of them. Glass closes over the numbers that the players write, to prevent cheating. On the larger table, numbers gradually rise up out of the sand like mirages in the desert. Again I had the pleasure of seeing my luck demonstrated as my numbers arose.

I did so well at the trading house that I was able to treat myself to the Xanthus fish. I had to outbid some eagle-browed connoisseur who kept upping the ante. But I prevailed, and he left with only the lesser green angler-fish, with its grainy texture, for his evening meal.

But gaming was not my most urgent reason for coming down to the lower slope. After my gaming foray, I had a meeting to attend in one of the sleeker bars here, which have been renovated and sit next to the irrigation channels. In a city of warm colors, this place is entirely blue, and painted in designs from the rune books of the plains. The lighting is odd, and puts one in a certain mood not achieved elsewhere in the city. One block of windows looks out onto the channels, tinting them and the plains beyond with blue.

I arrived several minutes early and waited, watching the wheel-shaped machines churn by in the watery fields.

My contact arrived, a woman with a fluid, coastal gait and cool, casual clothes exuding tidal style. I had met her only once before, and we kept a distance that was appropriate for an arm's length exchange. She represented a faction I was to be dealing through on the western coast.

We caught up briefly before she apprised me of the situation in Waters Rising.

"There are people stopped over on the coast who want to make transactions with you now. They need your steam power and more tidal power besides," she said. "I understand you're a wealthy baronet in the northern territory? Your title means less to those on the coastal shelf, and you will find people there less obliged to wait for you than in these more impoverished places."

The western arrogance put me out a bit, but I knew she was speaking with a degree of honesty. I listened coolly. After my recent betrayals in the north, I found the honesty refreshing.

"It will be to your advantage to take up a position there soon. They're tired of meeting only a hologram. A suitable house has been secured for your use, temporarily. Can I tell them you will be arriving soon?" Her intonation drew lower at the end of the sentence: not a question, but an answer.

I looked off thoughtfully over the channel before answering.

"Tell them whatever they need to hear."

I gathered from her silence that the answer was not entirely satisfactory. Nonetheless, my determined nature made its way through to her, and we drew up an agreement written on my paper. She signed it not with her name but with a seal in the shape of a turtle, which was doubtlessly safeguarded. Still, I felt it was a kind of victory, a precursor to my actions on the coast.

I was in high spirits when I made my way back up through the city. I would be making my journey sooner than I'd expected and the thought made me feel alive.

Kyra was in a good mood that day, too, and I hoped there would be time for us to go to a concert in the amphitheater before I had to leave.

She knows I will only be gone for a while, though I haven't told her I must leave so soon. I think there may be some tension when I tell her, but it can't be helped. I am doing this for the good of both of us.

Communication from the north is slow lately. I can sense that the springs are protecting me as they have always done. It matters little what happens there, as long as the power of the springs still flows through my actions. Nonetheless, some news from that quarter would be reassuring to me.

In a way, I'll look forward to traveling with an assistant rather than a lover for a while. Jado's emotions will not be my responsibility the way Kyra's are. Sometimes one must be tough with others, and intimacy makes this difficult. But I will miss her. If she comes to visit me on the coast, she will see that it is like in those exotic places she has long wanted to go. Honestly, I think the journey into the north shocked her more than she admits, and now she wishes to forge stability in this easy city. It is a laudable wish, but I fear she will come to see that this place is not so simple as it appears.

Yet, she will keep a watch on this city while I am away, and will build her powers, contributing them to my own as they are bound to my purposes. The energy trail between the mountains and me will remain strong in part because Kyra will be here as a link. I suspect the searching she does here will have as much benefit for me as it does for her.

As for Jado, he will adapt to the coast with ease, as I can tell he is a resilient person. If it is difficult for him there, he will know that it is only with difficulty that growth comes, and that the road upward is the only one worth taking.

book three

harborfront at waters rising

Under the sealed darkness of night Jado crept across the smooth, cool tiles of a house's roof, a thin rope keeping him anchored to the solidity of a nearby tree. Reaching the peak, he displaced a tile and quickly positioned a tiny, almost invisible object beneath it. He put the tile back with rapid care and lowered himself backward down the dark side of the roof. A glowing light from the street illuminated the front half of the roof but he had come in from the back, allowing him to stay in shadow. He placed his feet carefully, not moving any loose tiles, and was soon close to the tree. The sloping bed of tiles receded before him as he backed his way onto a solid, bowlike branch.

The tree was of the smooth, towering variety, the bark approaching the quality of stone and the branches growing at sharp angles, elephantine parabolas. He had needed spurs on the soles of his shoes to climb up the tree and had taken them off when he moved onto the roof, so as not to scratch any of the fine, delicate tiles. He lowered himself down the branch, then partway up another so he could climb onto the wall that signified the completion of his task. He carefully untied the rope that had been his lifeline while on the roof.

For a few brief seconds he was below the level of the wall, and it was within those seconds he felt most as though he were trespassing. With the wall of the house to one side and the garden wall closing him in from the other, he was no longer occupying the free air of the night, but was enclosed within somebody else's property. He looked down and saw a yard he was not intended to see, plants and yard chairs that were not his. He did not feel as though he owned the garden as he had looking up in the courtyard of his youth.

He took a deep breath and pulled himself upward, bracing his arms on the smooth bark, until he was able to swing a foot onto the wall and pull himself over it. He felt as though he were emerging from a pool of wrongdoing, but the feeling faded as he put the wall between himself and the enclosed yard. He disappeared over the other side of the wall, this time lowering himself into the uncontrolled realm of the night streets where he became an anonymous shape, one who could easily be the random victim of other shapes in the dark.

This was one of many errands he had run since leaving the Glass City and becoming an active player in a network that expanded far beyond the small circle of people with whom Eson had put him in contact. His purposes here were many, and if he sometimes took part in things he found unsettling, it was a step toward an end that outweighed any temporary misgivings he had… though the misgivings had increased with the passing days, if he admitted it to himself.

The world around him had grown vertical, stormy, and wild in this new place, where everything was situated on steep hillsides, the wind was steaming and abrupt, and the trees profuse and varied. He did not consider it home. He had come here on a powerful whim that told him to abandon his static, comfortable world and seize the opportunity for something new and risky.

His hometown seemed to him civilized, the place where his culture lived. And while the Glass City was artificial in many ways, it was yet organic in its handcrafted, ancient construction, dry-aired, and warm-colored. Plants were largely confined to glass enclosures on the sides of buildings. All things were on a small scale, precious and ornate, usually antique. It had been the limits of his experience and had taken on the still, close aura of a place where he felt confined. Though it had contained all the meaning he had ever known, the Glass City now looked small in relation to the broader world.

This new place was besieged by plants and by rough, oceanic air, warm and constantly in motion. All buildings and gardens seemed recently to have sprung up, to be made of temporary fibers. He knew this was because of the city's placement on the continent, because of ocean currents and mountain ranges, but could not reconcile himself to the alien climate. The places he saw drifted by as nameless pieces of scenery, their meanings continually eluding him. Yet he did not return home, and likely could not have if he had chosen to do so.

He hadn't felt he was betraying his community in leaving. Niyali had traveled outward in the past, and now he did so as well. His family wondered that a job opportunity could come up so suddenly, as he had told them was the case, but he was an adult and nobody could tell him not to go where he pleased. And while he wouldn't ordinarily describe his current way of life as a job he could think of no other way to explain the situation while retaining its sense of legitimacy.

He had a mixed view of Eson now that he had spent more time in his presence. He had struck a deal with him quickly, after only a couple of meetings, and had gained the sense that he was capable of achieving something massive while following his lead. That sense had waned over the course of the week as he learned more of what Eson's real purposes were. He felt that he was, in a subtle way, being led in circles. Yet still, there was the sense that he was part of something his old life could never have offered. The mediocrity of the workshop and the shelter of his neighborhood and old friends were set up in contrast to the risks and high energy he was experiencing in Waters Rising. He missed the tea shop and its visitors, but felt there was now a balance in his relation to them. He no longer waited, stationary, for visitors to come to him. Instead he was in motion, an actor in his own drama.

He had waited some time before contacting Sarah. Though he considered her a much closer ally than the people surrounding him daily, he feared if he told her where he was and with whom, she would feel betrayed and refuse his explanations. She might even want to immediately follow him here and confront him. He had enough trouble understanding for himself why he had confidently closed up his shop and cajoled his cousin into looking after it in order to join Eson the enchanter, the very one Sarah had spoken of as a malevolent oppressor.

Night in this part of the city was tense and desolate. The wind whispered of hidden threats; corners could harbor surprises for the midnight walker. He listened closely and kept to shadows, cutting across gardened squares whenever he could. He kept an even pace, an even breath, measuring the shortening distance between himself and the relative safety of the house he would rest in that night.

A shudder of wind animated the trees. Innumerable walled gardens paced off the dark distances. His night vision set the world before him in murky shades of gray. He was walking uphill now, and would soon reach the house. This night would have a tranquil conclusion. He relaxed enough to enjoy the night walk, let his guard down a little for the last winding streets. The streets grew more eccentric as he climbed, the houses more idiosyncratic, mainly hidden from view, though upper stories and dark gardens could be seen above walls much like the one he had successfully climbed. It would all be his to climb, to explore and enjoy, were time frozen in the perfection of darkest night.

Quite suddenly, his shadow stretched before him in sharp relief. He turned to see vehicle headlights as a near-silent steam car with blackened windows approached and stopped before him. He had little time to think as a window slid down and two shapes in the dark interior looked out at him.

He stood completely still, trying to determine the expressions on the obscured faces, his heart thudding in his chest.

One of the shapes leaned away. "Not the one," a voice said, and the opaque black of the window rose again.

The steam car made a low hum in the night air as it sped away. He leaned against a wall to catch his breath and try to slow his drumming heartbeat. Aside from the possibility the residents had detected him on their roof, there were gangs in Waters Rising and much drug trade around the coastal ports. He could have easily been mistaken for a member of a gang or drug ring.

Nothing of the sort had ever happened to him in the Glass City. Casting a glance around, he began walking again, more quickly this time, and covered the last blocks at a near jog.

He reached the dark, smooth gate to his destination, pushed a button beside the gate, and was silently allowed access. Inside the wall the path wound upward, covered in light gravel, as if a path of moonlight or an asteroid belt were his trail.

The house above him took the form of three interlocking squares set into the hillslope and edged by bamboo. The second level was set into the slope beside and only halfway above the first level, several steps further back. The third level rested in the hillside above the first, but was further behind it. The result was a careful symmetry, a sense of progressive seclusion in the upper

the coast house

levels and of a sublime entity resting on the slope.

The paneled windows were closed to the night air and the three smooth faces of the house reigned over the garden like an immortal and dignified family. Light glowed inside the first and third levels. He stood on the path for a few moments, sheltered now from the street and the threat of dark steam cars, enjoying the still of the night, its simplicity beyond the maelstrom of human life. He felt reluctant to enter the storm, to let the maelstrum engulf him again.

He did so anyway, stepping onto the wooden porch before the door, then opening the smooth, etched-stone door. He removed his shoes once inside the doorway, standing in a lowered, screened area that served as a foyer. Stepping up onto the straw mat flooring in the main part of the room, he was now visible to the people in the room and they to him.

Eson and his guests were seated in the lowered area in the middle of the room, lounging within a square of embedded cushions surrounding a low table arrayed with late-night snacks, drinks and a gambling kit. The light was very dim, diffusing upward from floor lamps set near the gathering. The room was otherwise barely furnished, high-walled and lightly earth-toned, with a walled enclosure at one end serving as a kitchen. An entire wall on the right was given over to latticed paneling, which could be opened to the garden in warm weather. The far wall housed potted plants, and was lengthened by wall panels that spanned floor to ceiling, opening to the third floor above.

A square staircase between the floors formed an axis at the center of the house, was open to all the floors, and allowed light to spill between the floors in daylight. The wall visible behind the staircase had flame-like patterns etched onto it, and the high walls in the main room bore patterns of delicate trees, mountains, and waterfalls.

Eson's guests were two in number, and dressed in suits of an iridescent color that clashed alarmingly with the muted shades of the room around them. They sat opposite one another at the low table, providing inebriated, chortling growls as responses while Eson kept up a running commentary for their entertainment. They had slightly devious, handsome faces, and could have passed for sharpshooters were their outfits not so glaringly outdated, or their eyes not dulled by numerous drinks. They were evidently not important people, as Eson was displaying to them none of the refinement he reserved for his higher echelons of acquaintance.

Eson's tone took on a teasing edge as Jado approached the table and took up a position both defensive and reposed at the near end of the table. "You're back already? How quickly you must have flown through the night air." He was in his half-drunk entertainer's mode, and spoke in the gloating tone he reserved for use in the presence of guests, when he wanted to set most of them at ease by singling out one guest and making leisurely fun of him in front of the others.

Jado had never been the target of this before, and felt a return of his sense of irritation at Eson, a reverberation of what he had felt when he knew Eson only as an abstract encumbrance on Sarah's life. He studiously avoided eye contact and refused to show any reaction, instead looking at the oddments arrayed on the table before them, which the two guests were arranging in a much busier and more furtive fashion than was necessary. They were setting up some kind of game, and cast glances back and forth to each other, never at Eson or Jado, though their mouths broke into crooked grins at Eson's words.

"Interactions are all energy exchanges," Eson said unexpectedly, looking directly at Jado. "Whether you're interacting with a place or a person, there's a charge that goes beyond matter. Some people are tied together by these charges, like magnets. They can't escape each other, no matter what other bonds they may pretend they have forged."

Where is he going with this? Jado thought.

"Didn't you feel an almost electric charge around your friend Sarah, before you abandoned her to follow me? I could sense a deeply charged energy field surrounding every letter she sent to me."

Jado raised an eyebrow.

"You knew she was writing to me? Of course. You and she are always in lockstep, aren't you?" There was an accusatory tone to his last words, as though challenging and calling into question his loyalty. Eson let the words fall completely and pointedly before changing his tone and including again the other two in his

152

conversation.

"Another round, no?" He gestured at the gaming pieces that divided the four from each other. "Maybe Carstell can win back some of his money." Rueful laughter cut the air, changing the mood as sharply as if Eson had commanded it.

Still calm, Jado threw a spanner into Eson's careful redirection of the conversation, when answering was clearly no longer allowed. "All this talk of energy, and yet you still do nothing to help me with my plans for a solar generator."

Eson looked up, eyes blazing, before launching his defense. "Not help! Just tell me one thing I've done in order to 'not help' in the past while. I took you in, little brother. You're nothing outside my world. Gerson, deal out the briquettes." But the host was shaken and the words bundled out in an unruly mess.

Jado too felt ill at ease, and insulted, saying nothing now in response. He didn't easily confront others, and always felt drained by anything approaching anger or argument. He settled back away from the table, into the low cushions. The square formation of bodies was now an unbalanced diamond, one of its points refusing to cohere, stretching outward into isolation.

Gerson dealt out five sets of the intert black briquettes in a plain but somehow dishonest manner. Eson watched with a carefully detached laziness, taking the opportunity to regain his composure. Carstell, designated the unlucky one for the evening, watched impatiently, his eyes following Gerson's hand around the table as though checking for some sleight of hand. Jado kept back as well, regaining his own sense of calm.

Each player had a set of marking tags with a seal showing one of the four directions. The player at the south end of the table marked his pieces with the symbol for south, and so on around the table. Jado was seated at the western side, and marked his pieces as the three-dimensional game field hovered fluidly above the table with its gray, shifting squares. They would allow the briquettes to move in certain directions, then switch and change courses. It gave the impression of a translucent, geometric river of air, with a gauntlet of suspended gray stones altering its currents. Once set into this field, the briquettes would wander randomly on their paths, ever nearer collisions with others.

It was when these collisions occurred that bets were won and lost. As two pieces collided they would ignite, give off sparks, and war with each other until one piece won out over the other, disintegrating it completely. Each piece held an unknown degree of strength and endurance. If two pieces of equal worth collided, they could destroy each other, or one could win out by virtue of having hit the collision at a favorable angle. Points were tallied up after all the pieces collided, and winnings redistributed accordingly.

Jado leaned back into the center, and rather aimlessly placed a bet smaller than even the usual cautious wager he made when betting. Eson, he noticed with irritation, placed exactly the same bet. The other two players bet lavishly and without qualm, laughing in deep and exaggerated tones.

Gerson called out the word, and within seconds, all the pieces were roaming the field, their fates unknowable.

Two of Carstell's pieces collided with each other at the outset, but the surviving one became stronger as a result, so it was not a bad sign, though considered bad luck in traditional games. Jado watched absently, not in the mood to play, but obligated to sit in one round. The early part of the game moved quickly, pieces igniting and sparking, narrow misses, barks of surprise as pieces were destroyed, until only two pieces remained. Though mindless bits of chemical compound, these last briquettes seemed to circle each other and calculate their own trajectories. They avoided, they chased, they ambushed. This part of the game could drag on for several minutes.

Such was the case in this game, as both Eson and Jado's

coast house interior

pieces were eliminated, leaving only the other players to contend. Impatient for an outcome, Gerson and Carstell moved their last pieces so they were on a collision course and within seconds, Gerson was laughing his victory, Carstell shaking his head incredulously and handing over his cash. Eson and Jado owed each other nothing and sat back, not looking at each other and speaking only to the others.

As the two prepared to leave, Eson helping them pack up their betting kit, Gerson treated his friend to a resounding slap on the back and promised to buy him a drink on the way home. There was a show of teeth and more deep laughter as the two headed for their shoes by the front door.

When they had left, Eson at last turned to Jado, and said in a perfunctory way, "Help me move these couches back." He began to pick up the cushions and Jado did the same, until only the table was left in the lowered area. This they cleared of the evening's debris. Eson walked to the back of the room and brought out pieces of sturdy, reinforced matting, which he placed on the floor.

"Betting is a profane activity, and must take place in a lowered area," Eson said by way of explanation as he placed an embroidered mat over the floor and straightened the couches in their usual positions. Jado said nothing. His host followed some arcane religious tradition which declared many things to be wrongful actions, yet allowed one to do them anyway as long as they were carried out according to protocol.

"Don't you agree?" asked Eson in a voice that was pointedly absent and dismissive. He disappeared into the kitchen enclosure.

"Good night," Jado answered in as neutral a tone as he could manage, and moved toward the staircase, relieved to be finally approaching his own bed. On the second floor sliding walls had been set in place around a section on the front side of the house, to serve as his bedroom. He felt relegated to a childlike position in this room, yet still enjoyed it as a sanctuary. He slid the thin, lightweight doors shut, and was again alone with the night. He switched on a lamp so dim it served only to define the edges of the room in a soft, tan color, and sifted through a small tin he kept next to his bedroll, resting low on the soft reed mat floor. He slid open the low window panel next to it. It was the deep of night now, and only a sea of lights was visible in the city below him. These lights ended abruptly at the shoreline far below, and in the remaining space, as though a wall were suspended from a point high above, lay the dark surfaces of the ocean and the night sky, themselves riddled with lights. Wandering, vagrant lights signified boats, while static constellations marked out islands in the sea and stars in the sky.

In daylight, the islands were set in the turquoise wall of the sea, land and ocean angling into each other as though meeting at the bottom of a chasm. The horizon was unnaturally high, as were the tiny, rocky islands: pillars of green rock colonized by balancing, jutting houses, architectural gymnasts stoically maintaining their poses. They looked urban, the city having burrowed beneath the ocean and cast up pockets of human design. Paths zigzagged toward a temple at the top of a hill. There were wind generators turning like the slow pattern of the tides.

All this was his to survey from the high vantage point of his room. He had viewed it in daylight, and in its luminous nocturnal form. He contemplated the wind generators now, their endlessly turning points of light over the water, and thought of tidal power, bridges of tidal generators that could use the wild oceans to keep the sea of lights ablaze in the cities of the future. They were using generators on the tidal flat in front of this city, he knew, as this fact was at the crux of his involvement with Eson. He imagined the Niyali home islands as someday being a paradise of wind-driven, free power. Turning his mind toward utopian futures, he slept.

He dreamt of the cousin who had agreed, if begrudgingly, to look after his tea shop. The cousin was now asking Jado to watch over his own house, as he was leaving for a trip and was trying to pack. He asked Jado to bring him things from around the house that he needed, but Jado could only bring him wrong, useless things, delay his departure, and wander futilely about the house. The house became a vast shopping center, and Jado found himself in a music store listening to a recording that evoked a sense of belonging to a pure primordial pattern. On buying the music, he found that it had changed and become subtly flat to his ear. His mind struggled to remember the lost music and its perfection, but his thoughts ran like a cart along a rail track, always into the future, always in one direction.

The next day began very late for all in the house.

Eson arose even later than Jado and was once again the civilized host, smoothing over the night before by concocting an opulent breakfast, a tacit acknowledgment that he had perhaps overstepped a line in his treatment of Jado.

"You like tea? I call this 'The Tea of the Gods'," he said, pouring an aromatic brew into mugs beside plates heaped with fruits, pancakes and the honey given to them by the retired neighbor who kept a special breed of bees in her yard next door. She had zealously regaled them with the merits of the bees on a welcoming visit soon after they had moved in. "The bees were developed in our research program over at the university," she'd explained. "The genes of a rare herbal element known to prevent disease have been used to enhance them. That accounts for the honey's strange color." The two young men had been astounded at the healing properties said to be present in the honey, and had nodded, tongue-tied throughout the visit.

"You learn something new every day!" Eson had said after she left, as he and Jado stood investigating the murky jar on the table. It had taken some getting used to, but they now garnished a surprising variety of their foods with the fruit of the ever-diminishing jar. This morning was no exception. They spooned it into The Tea of the Gods and stayed at the table for a long time after breakfast, feeling health percolate through them, counteracting the effects of the late night.

Jado was at last thanked properly for his work of the night before. "I simply can't pull off those rooftop maneuvers anymore. I'm no longer twenty!" Eson said, with a slightly nostalgic tone.

He looked at Eson, who was sitting with an elbow propped on the table and a look of reflection on his unworn face. He felt young in his presence, but sensed also that the difference in their ages was not as great as Eson made it out to be. *He can't be much more than thirty,* he thought, but kept the conjecture to himself, enjoying the peace of the morning.

The letter traveled thinly and innocently, no one knowing it had been sent, no one expecting its arrival. It was a simple white envelope with proud, garish stamps from one of the wealthy nations of the western coast.

Sarah,

You may know by now that I've gone to the coast. I traveled here with Eson, and have been drawn into some things that I don't feel comfortable discussing in letters. Please don't see this as a betrayal. There is a young woman he speaks of sometimes. It seems she has access to his apartment in the Glass City, and to his records. I think you should find her, if you haven't already. She knows of our location here, and may be able to give you direct information for finding us here, should you ever need it. I regret that I can't give you that information. I feel that if I did, he would somehow find out. It's difficult to explain, but a disconcerting force pervades his surroundings. I have stepped out of the house to write even this much. He plans to make a trip back to the Glass City to visit her, and then I will be free in this city. But it will never be my home. Someday we will meet again, and speak openly as we always have.

Be well,

Jado

The air of the nightclub was perfumed ambiguously and artificially through vents hidden in the walls. The indefinable scent of a social atmosphere brought visitors back into the memory of earlier sensations and enrobed the crowds that gathered there, as a breeze on the ocean swerves its way around islets and sandbars.

Kyra inhaled deeply as she passed through the insubstantial door that led to the club and immediately stood to one side, in a spot remote from the lanterns' illumination, wanting to watch for a time without being seen. In her small shoulder bag were a black orb and the beaded control device of the vision bird, which was stationed above the hidden door on the club's third story. She carried also a satchel with some blank parchments and a vial of ink. She didn't think there would be occasion to use them quite yet, but felt secure with them near her.

Her memory of Eson's offering of the parchments replayed

in her mind. He had left more than a week before, and she missed him, more some days than others. She was glad in a way that he had gone west, as he would be further away from the steam capital and the dangers it posed to him—but in another way, he was such a part of her life in the Glass City that she felt a loss of dimension without him there. In coming to the club, she built her world outward in another direction. She had come here before but had not yet sensed anyone there from the circle of people she was now seeking, the people named in Eson's deed.

They were here tonight, she could tell, except for Sarah and Jado, whom she now knew must have gone with Eson to the coast. She suspected Sarah would be the most difficult to track of the group, and hoped that Sarah herself would make the first move, perhaps even contact her. She must speak with her. Sarah almost certainly knew things about Eson's contracts and about the mystery surrounding them that Kyra did not, despite her close relationship to him.

There were things he would tell her about them, such as his reasons for striking a deal with someone, and things he kept hidden, like the way he managed to gain signatures from others. She freely looked over the contracts even while he was there, and had made note of the names captured on the pages. She had focused her new search on the ten debtors of a single contract because she knew they were all located in the Glass City, while other contracts referred to people and places further away.

She couldn't see them in the thick crowd, but as she contemplated the closed system of the nightclub she became aware of each of them. They were not grouped together but arrayed, as though in strategic positions, throughout the club's three levels. She passed her eyes through the nightclub and attuned her ears to hearing beneath the loud music that resonated outward from the musicians at the end of the room. They were a visiting group from the underworld of a distant metropolis, and their sound was incongruously modern in the dilapidated, wood-banister club. The crowd was a bit thrown off by the sound, and only a few were braving the open area of the central floor. Most others hung back around tables or bar counters, and the walls were more noticeable than they had been on other nights when she had visited. It would not be as easy to move with anonymity in the crowd this night.

She circulated toward the side of the room until she was under one of the upper terraces. She ordered a drink casually, and stood back to become part of the scenery of the club's lowest tier. Beside her was a crowd belonging to a celebrity impersonators cult, who exclaimed at one another and paraded their costumes in front of old film posters glorifying their idols. They made for a raucous distraction for any eyes that passed the way of a small young woman who carried more in her shoulder bag than most, but was otherwise unremarkable. This was one night when she did not want to receive any special treatment or attention. She made as if to be indistinguishable from the decaying, smoke-mottled wallpaper tearing off in strips from the dim walls. She noticed eyes upon her from the nearby bar, then, and experienced a momentary spike of panic—but it was not one of the debtor's circle, only a young man who had noticed her long dark hair. He looked away into the crowd, and she was once more alone.

She lowered her eyes and brought her concentration to the terrace above her. There were two debtors, though she couldn't tell which two, almost directly above her. Another was at a table on the opposite end of the terrace, and two more sat at a table on a lowered area that jutted out over the first level. A sixth was at a table on the third floor, and the last two were opposite her, beside one of the bars on the first floor. She moved so the celebrity crowd further blocked her from view. Though she knew the debtors couldn't recognize her by sight, except for the two that she had met at the club previously, she couldn't be certain that some of them didn't possess abilities of the sort she was developing. They had known to come here, after all, when she had been frequenting this place for the last few days. Their sudden appearance and deployment in the club was too definitive to be written off as a casual night out. Those who travel in a pack lose out somewhat in stealth and subtlety. She glanced out from beside an oversized paper lantern that also shielded her from view, feeling the lantern's glow on her face.

The warm light of the club lit the room in sepia tones. The murky wallpaper, covered in vintage posters, gave the impression of layered parchment. The frail wooden beams that held up the terraces and staircases were the only solid material in the club, and people were drawn into this landscape as insubstantially as the figures in the posters. Even the costumed people before her were like thin cutouts of people enjoying a night in a club. She intuited the debtors as points of space around her in a field of energy. The one on the top floor had gotten up and was moving toward the back door where she had her bird. The two debtors she could see looked disillusioned as they stared dully at the musicians on the platform. They didn't appear to be aware of her at all.

Staying behind the cover of the lantern, she covertly brought out the small orb she'd brought with her and directed the bird to watch as the person she sensed moving walked out through the back door of the club. She decided to postpone her observation of the group as a whole and see where the solitary mover went. She couldn't discreetly track the person while inside the club, so she moved toward the door.

She slipped carefully out the front door and stood in the shadow of the nightclub's façade. Knots of people and solitary walkers filtered past, few of them noticing her as she stared intently into the small black orb cradled in her hands. She stepped further back into an alcove that housed a garish poster for a dance performance that had long passed. Sconces held burnt-out lanterns in the carved paws of wooden lions on the alcove's walls, shabby relics of an earlier era of glory. They watched her silently, and she in turn watched the tiny image of a man descending the stairway at the back of the club. He was not the man of the pair she had been threatened by earlier, but looked a bit younger, more clean-edged, and slightly furtive as he dodged out of the light that shone over the landing. His movements were light but somehow aggressive as he glanced off the surfaces of the stairs, touching each foot down for only the barest moment. He moved as someone who feels a force of repulsion between himself and the world. Kyra recited the names of the debtors silently, but couldn't form an idea of which name fit the man she was watching. He gained the level of the street, and lowered his body somewhat as he moved down the narrow lane. The bird floated after him.

The man disappeared into a wall… which somehow had grown a door! She would never have seen this during her walks through the city. Fortunately, the bird was able to pass over the doorway's wall, and continued to trail him along a narrow walkway lined with trees that gripped the wall like sinuous waterfalls traveling the wrong way. He passed through an arch and up a staircase, which narrowed to a point that forced him turn sideways to pass through it. Above this, the staircase widened again and came out into a small, walled court. The bird passed through all this, but when it came out into the courtyard the image in the orb faded to darkness, and she glimpsed for only a second which direction the man turned.

She shook her head and commanded the bird to come to rest as soon as it could. When it did so the image returned, but the bird was in a different place, and the man was nowhere to be seen. She had lost him in one of the places that the bird refused, or was unable, to show her. Why was this? She made a note to herself of where the door had appeared in the wall. If she couldn't track the man she had seen leaving the club, she could at least explore the unseen place into which he had disappeared, and gain a sense of whether it was related to the doings of the circle.

If Jado were still in the city, she would have found a way to ask him about the situation. But he was gone, presumably with Eson, and she had no way of contacting him. She couldn't very well ask to speak to him on the phone when she spoke to Eson. Besides, the idea felt to her dishonest. She didn't want to pry directly into Eson's dealings, only to find out what was happening around her in the city as it related to her powers and her own security. In a way, she was keeping an eye on situations here while Eson was away. She thought of these things while standing in the lion alcove, and looking at a nearby clock, decided there was time for her to go back into the nightclub and salvage something of the evening. She would follow the path the man had taken, but would do so in the light of day.

Reentering the club, she made the trek upward to the second level. The energy trails within the space were cleared now and she could sense that all of the debtors had left. Had they gone suddenly? Had they taken the same path as the first one to leave? And where had they gone? She clenched her fists as she realized she would have to wait until another night to find out. Tracing them anywhere else in the city would be a random and fruitless effort.

She ordered one of the desert oasis drinks that she'd had with Eson. It had a muddy under-flavor that stayed with her, and its color was aqueous but mineral-soaked. With the debtors gone, she stepped out from the sidelines and stood near the edge of the terrace, looking down into the crowd below, which had thickened slightly in the past minutes. She watched a diva from the celebrity impersonators cult flirting extravagantly with an athletic type in a west-coast uniform. The dust storm hadn't deterred all of the city's visitors; they'd returned in droves to take in the idiosyncrasies of the City of Glass. Where else could one come face-to-face with the film star Elis, who had disappeared over the southern sea decades ago? The athletes were in the club as a team, and were taking to the floor as to the playing field, joined by others who finally gave in to the forces of the night and forgot who they were.

"Party's getting rough, no?"

She turned around from the railing. One of the nightclub's intrepid bevy of servers was speaking to her. She smiled noncommittally and looked into the face of the server, which was framed grandly by a red mane. Something welled up in Kyra's mind instantaneously, a recollection of shared food, a crowded bazaar, a book etched with hand-drawn characters.

With curious eyes, the server joked, "You didn't recognize me?" And in that instant, Kyra did. Her face lit up, and she clasped her friend's hand before moving with her and the drink to a narrow table in a quieter section nearby. She hadn't noticed how alone she'd been since Eson left, and seeing Neriv again brought her back to life in a small, subtle way.

"How did you end up back here in the city?" she asked Neriv anxiously, concerned that Neriv's plan to take a job in the north hadn't been successful. For the first time, she wondered exactly where Neriv had been speaking of when she mentioned going north.

"I'll tell you what happened," Neriv said, with a certain weight behind her words that Kyra hadn't remembered hearing when they had spoken many weeks ago. "Do you have time? I have a break coming, and we can talk at a table on the third floor. I haven't had a moment's peace this evening with the group that just left, getting after me to pass letters among their tables. They were bizarre and insistent, pushing money at me with the letters, addressed to these tables as if they were proper addresses and I were a courier! Unbelievable! I'll return soon." Neriv stood up and hurried away to finish her shift, leaving Kyra to finish her drink under the leafy shadow of an artificial tree.

She checked in with the vision bird, which she had directed homeward. It was flying close to Eson's building, where it would sit upon the roof of the glass garden. Kyra caught sight of a figure gliding, unidentifiable in the night, to the box that kept Eson's letters, and dropping something in before dashing away. The person disappeared too quickly for Kyra to redirect the bird after it. She felt a twinge of shock. Evidently, she and Eson were still under the surveillance of a third party.

She put the orb away, making a note to check the letterbox on her way in that night, and turned her attention back to the interior wilderness of the club, doubly relieved to have found an ally in the city again. Security rose around her like a tide. The people who had made themselves a nuisance to Neriv—were they the circle she had been monitoring?

Neriv returned and they ascended to the third level, above the noise of the music, taking a table where they could still see over the edge into the abyss of lanterns below.

Neriv told Kyra her story. "I was supposed to take a job at an experimental new research station in the plains north of here, an area I didn't know anything about. I imagined there would be some settlement there, though I had no idea what else to expect.

"I took a train as far as I could up into the remote areas of the plains, where the rocky foothills begin. There were a lot of small towns, and when the train reached the last stop, we were really at a dead end. I couldn't imagine how anything advanced or innovative was supposed to exist anywhere around there. I hitched a lift by steam-truck to the next town I was supposed to come to, and people there only shook their heads at my questions. I'd come to a place where few people speak our language, as they have never left their towns. It was toward nightfall. The irrigation channels don't reach out that far, and the fields stretch out in all directions, with endless grass.

"I came to a café where someone spoke the dialect we're used to. I asked if they'd heard of the research station and they gave me this odd look, saying it had been there recently, but had been dismantled, suddenly, only a few days earlier.

"I wondered how something like that could be dismantled, like a carnival tent! The café served rich food, though, that was good after the long journey. There was a hostel next door, the beds new-made of pine from the mountains. There were only two other travelers in the room. I met them the next morning at the same café. It turns out they were in the same boat as me, so we went walking, with some food in our packs, to the place we were supposed to be. Just as the café owner had said, the station was gone, only some closed-up buildings left by the banks of a river. We looked at each other and couldn't believe it! We'd traveled a long way, each one of us..."

Neriv trailed off, still mystified by the experience.

"So you came back here?" Kyra asked.

"Soon after. One of the others had a tent, so we stayed there a couple of nights, in the fresh air of the river valley." She smiled to herself, as if looking out over the river in her mind's eye.

Kyra sighed enviously at the thought of the beautiful, if empty and wild, place. "I used to love camping in the forests near my home," she said, sharing in Neriv's nostalgia. "What kind of research station was it supposed to be?"

"I didn't quite understand the specifics of it myself, but we were to help with the horticultural work for some river algae they thought could be used to produce electric power. Unbelievable, that someone could just pack up and abandon a project like that. Who runs these energy companies, anyway?" She shook her head and cynically pushed her chair back a bit from the table, crossing her arms.

Kyra was jarred by her mention that the research station had been involved in electric power, and was situated in the mountains. It hit a bit too close to home.

Neriv leaned back in her chair and surveyed the club as she spoke. "So we stayed there for a couple of days, and went hiking some in the hills. As we were returning one day, we saw some people on the riverbank near our camp who looked like they were gathering clay from the banks. They didn't look like anyone we'd seen in the nearby town, didn't even look like they belonged in the area. They were cutting blocks of clay and loading them into a strange kind of travois, then carrying it away into the hills opposite. We waved to them, and they waved back, but by the time we'd reached the river they were gone. They left only the dents where their blades had gathered the clay.

"We didn't know what to make of it, so we just fell to telling tales of things we'd seen that we didn't know the who and what of. I really liked both of them, but soon they had to leave, and I did as well. We couldn't live in the valley forever telling stories.

"By the time I got back here, I was low on money, and had to get a job as quickly as I could, while staying with some friends. And so you're here, waiting for me to find you again. I thought I'd lost you, but we're meant to be friends after all!"

It was late when she at last left the club, and arm-in-arm with Neriv and two or three others caught a tram going upward. They got off several stops before her, and she stayed on until the tram reached Eson's upper-strata neighborhood. The late-night faces of those going home or on to house parties were varied, from the sullen and tired to the cackling and manic. The tram lurched to a halt and everyone swayed as it stopped just long enough for her to slip out. There was no one in the quiet street as she came back to the building, and the creak of the letterbox carved loudly into the still air.

She exhaled deeply as she entered the dark suite, conscious of how empty it was without Eson. She slid toward the bed without opening the letter. It would become an element of the next morning, she decided, as the evening had already filled her mind's reservoirs with myriad questions. It was only now as she attempted sleep that her head spun again with myths, power sources and binding pacts. Even the Heiress loomed over her again for a brief moment before her cyclic mind turned onward. Her awareness was different without Eson nearby, as he had been a solid structure, making her reflect on things she would have otherwise never considered.

She'd told Neriv much more than she'd intended about her trip to the north and about Eson, letting rush out the emotions and vivid realizations she had kept locked in. It wasn't that she didn't share her feelings with Eson, only that she angled them a certain way, and with Neriv could relive them more fully. They'd met and recapped their lives with the camaraderie of those whose roads cross again on an unsteady landscape. As she drifted to sleep, she meditated on the life of the other woman, and gained distance from her own life momentarily. Then she imagined Eson had taken a breath beside her and turned toward his side of the bed, finding only emptiness, and felt alone with a finality that is only possible at the moment before sleep.

In the light of morning, which flooded the suite from the glass garden, she opened the small letter. It was but a small sheet, written in a script so neat as to be almost machine-made, the same script that had appeared in the letters that Eson kept. This letter was not addressed to Eson, though, but to Kyra herself, her name emblazoned on the envelope in a wild flurry at odds with the composed order of the letter.

She made coffee with the small apparatus Eson used most mornings, and paused to think of him and his odd relation with Sarah. Then, when she had cleared her mind enough to take in the letter, she sat comfortably in the sunny glass room to read.

> *Kyra,*
>
> *The time has come for you and I to meet. Do you know the Keviya Gallery that is below the monument, at its eastern edge? I'll be there the day after tomorrow in the Jaguar Room (anyone can tell you where that is), by a painting of the creator deity, Sarhul. I'll be there at the Hour of Lions, and for only a short time after that.*
>
> *By the way, please don't go back to the nightclub before you have met with me. I'll tell you about that when we meet.*
>
> *Sarah*

That someone she had never met was casually arranging an appointment with her was normal to her only because it was Sarah. Kyra felt she knew her in an odd way, such that it felt logical for Sarah to have the authority to summon her. The letter was much more casual than the ones Sarah had sent to Eson, which didn't bother her, as it cut through a layer of artifice she had sensed in Sarah's other letters. After a few moments' reflection, she felt elated that she would finally be meeting Sarah, the one who had played such an important hand in their lives!

But to stay away from the nightclub that evening… It would be difficult, knowing that the debtors were likely there, and Neriv as well. It was stranger still that Sarah agreed with Eson on this matter, but Kyra was no more likely to obey two people than one. She would decide later, maybe going to the club, maybe not. She'd made vague plans with Neriv to meet there.

For the meantime, she was eager to retrace the steps of the man she'd seen leaving the club. She was struck again by the anger infused in his long-limbed movements. She didn't regret her decision not to track him on foot in the night, when the character of the streets took a turn for the menacing, and with that she re-thought her stance on the nightclub, and planned that she would go only for a short time, in early evening.

Before she went out into the streets, though, she would call Eson. It had been a few days since they'd spoken, and she craved the connection. She was also curious about his life in Waters Rising. The place sounded lush and marine, and though she was strongly resolved to keep living in the Glass City, she felt a pull toward visiting the exotic tidal city as well.

She and Eson communicated through the static ether, their voices meeting in a vacuum between cities.

"Kyra! It's so good to hear you."

"You too! I've missed you."

"Yes, I as well. Though we're busy here, there is infinite time for me to feel lonely. ...And is the city keeping you entertained?" he asked with the slightly indulgent tone he used when contrasting his life with hers, the industrious asking after the leisurely.

"I'm going to the gallery under the monument tomorrow. I met up with some friends last night for a drink. Do you know the gallery well?"

"I used to spend a lot of time there. There's a room with jaguars poised above every doorway. You can't see them until you're underneath them. You're looking at the jaguars over the doorway opposite, and then see that there are two more right over you! There's a painting of the goddess in that room as well. The entire room hinges on a sense of wildness, and Sarhul presides over the paintings and beasts, a rebel queen. I like the thought of you there."

Where all wild creatures are caged in a room... she thought for a moment back to Neriv's story of the wild river valley, and felt tame in comparison to her. She laughed and asked Eson about his own adventures on the coast. "How is it in Waters Rising?"

"It's swimming ahead well. I've got some traders from overseas who've signed on for electric power."

"Steam power? How will you get it to them?"

"Oh, there's a line under the mountains already, but those springs can only produce so much. We're going to augment the supply with tidal power."

"Tidal power! They have generators on the coast already? Will you buy one?"

"That's still in the works. We can get the power to them, but it's contingent on my personal influence to get everything and everyone lined up properly. We have to do a bit of technology development work before it comes together. I know it sounds vague, but the border between science and metaphysics usually is."

She noticed he was speaking of himself as part of a group, using the term *we*. "Did somebody from here end up going with you?"

"Yes, the friend I told you about came with me. His name's Jado." He said it as though cautiously staving off an accusation. Had he thought she was probing him for information about a possible woman? She hadn't wanted to imply that at all. Now that Eson had confirmed it was Jado working with him on the coast, though, she was satisfied to be putting pieces firmly together at last. Jado's presence also explained somewhat the 'technology development work' Eson spoke of.

"Actually, I know Jado, I think. Does he run a tea shop near the monument?"

"Yeah, I think he was running the place. That tea shop I told you about, with the maps. You've been there?"

"A couple of times. I went there during the dust storm, just before we met."

"Aha, that explains how you were able to keep so cool and calm in the dust! Did you see the machines he was making?"

"I was amazed. Do you think he can make something like the vision bird?"

173

"That technology can never be duplicated. It needs elements from the old world. But he's continually surprising me with his abilities. I'll show you some of his work when you visit. Will you come soon?"

She thought for a moment. "Yes, I'd like to. Give me a few more days here. I'd like to spend some time with friends before going to a new city, to get my moorings settled here, you know."

"I understand. One's magnetic fields should be strong before you enter a different domain. Were you upset when I left?"

"No. I was happy for you. I want you to be working on exciting things. And at least I knew you were leaving in advance this time." She hadn't meant it to sound reproachful, but the words could not be innocent, in view of the time he had left her in the mountains without telling her he would go.

There was a brief silence, bordering on awkwardness, before Eson answered.

"You are very patient." He said it quietly, as though they were very close, in his cool bed below the starry skylight.

"You're being patient, too. I didn't mean to bring up what happened in the mountains. I know it was a difficult time for you. And I'll visit you soon."

"I'd love that. Can I call you the day after next?"

"Okay. Then we can figure out train schedules."

"Enjoy the gallery, love," he said, and she felt aware of her many omissions in the conversation. She would tell him about Sarah, but afterward, in case he worried for her.

She quietly said goodbye and replaced the phone.

Before visiting Waters Rising she wanted to explore the places in the Glass City the vision bird wouldn't show her. She hadn't been overly curious about the bird's systematic blackouts until she had seen the man disappearing after leaving the nightclub.

There were so many places in the city to observe that missing out on a few hadn't seemed important to her, but now they took on significance.

Soon after speaking with Eson, she was at the place in the narrow road where the young man had caused a door to appear. When the street was empty, she pushed on the wall lightly, and an area outlined subtly in glass pieces sank inward. She cautiously entered the space behind it, and walked with trepidation along the garden walkway. She was certain she wasn't on anybody's property, but traversing the hidden path made her feel as though she were invading an area of the city not open to those like her, who were guests.

The trees were less serpentine by day, and the dusty earth beneath them lent the walkway an air of desertion. There weren't many places in the city where bare earth interrupted the solidity of the built stonework. She passed through the arch and up the stairs, pausing to watch through the narrow space in the stairs before moving through it. She could see a sliver of courtyard beyond, bright under the midday sun: the courtyard the bird had kept from her. She walked up into it and surveyed its tiled ground, ringed by high-windowed houses. Narrow streets and walkways branched off in several places, but few people passed through. The rosy walls trapped light and warmth within them.

None of these things were remarkable to her, as she had now spent some time in a city full of such places, but there was something unique about this courtyard. Anchored to a wall opposite was a fountain, boxed in with greenish stone. It was not working, and looked as though no water had flowed from it in many years. The basin was dusty and cracked, the stones worn. But the strangest feature of all was the pattern of live roses growing defiantly from spaces between the stones of the basin.

As if from nothing... She marveled at the tenacity of the plants. Did some vapors leech from below the ground to keep the roses alive? This had been the case in the aeroponics cave, where airborne minerals fortified the growing plants, but she'd heard of nothing like this in the Glass City.

Looking upward from the thin roses she noticed a shallow alcove in the wall, an echo of the alcove above Eson's spring in the mountains. There was a small object placed in it, but she couldn't make out what it was from where she was standing. Looking to see that no one was walking past, she stepped into the dry basin, and it made a crackling, yielding sound beneath her feet. She stepped carefully through the roses and reached the alcove, which was lined with the same greenish stones as the fountain. The object within was a small wooden box, plain and unpainted. Within it was a small, folded piece of rough paper with only the initials *L.B.* written on it in dark ink.

Realizing she'd stumbled on somebody's prayer offering, she swiftly closed the box and placed it back on the shelf, retracing her steps through the basin and stepping out onto the floor of the courtyard. She made a sign of respect and moved away from the fountain. The initials coalesced with one of the names she remembered from Eson's deed, Loken Birch. It was possible that the young man from the club, if he were Loken Birch, had placed the box in the alcove late that night.

She glanced down the walkways branching off from the courtyard, but there was no way to know which road he had taken. She started off down one narrow lane, which eventually led out through a gate into the ordinary streets. The light changed as she walked, as if asking her to step back from her actions and think about what she was doing in a new light.

Back at the suite, she arrayed the black orbs over the floor and scanned them, looking for the places the bird's sight had blanked out. She activated several at once, watching for fade-outs.

They were like inert planets that had been harvested for a celestial game of marbles, and on each surface was a contained, detailed voyage over the city.

She found there were ten or so places, all within the central area of the Glass City, where the bird had blanked out inexplicably and then reappeared a short distance away. She brought these orbs out in front of the others, and reordered the rest in the corner they usually occupied.

She marked the places as best she could on a map of the city, and in doing so noticed that Eson had lightly traced his own pathways over the city with temporary, uncertain-looking ink, and had written some illegible notes on the edge of the paper. She realized they were the pathways he was safe traversing, and imagined him, innocent and vulnerable, moving quickly through the streets. In picturing that innocence, she felt a dark shift of guilt at her deceptions. She remembered him on the train, sleeping fox-like while the mountain landscape passed by, and was mystified again that he could be the same person who indentured people to him by way of the deeds.

She noticed his pathways universally evaded the places that she had just marked on the map. She vaguely wondered why, and though a spark of caution raised an eyebrow inside her head she set out with the map, drawn along in a trance of curiosity. Before leaving the suite, she looked back over the deed that secured the group to Eson, and copied all of their names carefully onto a small piece of paper.

Making her way through the mysterious inner pathways of the city, she found fountains much like the first at every spot the orbs had blanked out. She finished her search near the monument and walked up the hill to survey the city from above in the early evening light, standing within a protective, smooth arch of the monument and looking out over the city, imagining the fountains scattered in a network below. She was no closer to understanding what the fountains meant to the people of the city or to the debtors, or why the otherwise amenable vision bird had hid them from her. She looked with hope to her rendezvous with Sarah.

The hour was approaching when she had agreed to meet Neriv at the nightclub for an early drink, before her friend's work shift started. She rested in the spot where she had sat with Eson when they had first met. She had begun deceiving him from that moment, she told herself harshly, and now felt that she was keeping too much from him, far too much. She remembered the imprint that his voice and his calm, steady gaze had had on her on that first day, how she had changed her direction completely upon meeting him. While he had sometimes been careless with her, she owed him an honesty that she was not fulfilling. She had a momentary flash of anger at his decision to leave for Waters Rising. He'd included her in this plan, assuming she would agree, until she said directly that she planned to stay in the Glass City. But she felt too that anger was unfair, and that she herself was not always easy to be with.

The mysterious story Neriv had told her about the journey and her stay in the wilderness made her remember how she had wandered before coming to the Glass City. Looking west from the monument, she suddenly did want to go to Waters Rising. But first she would try to observe more of the happenings at the club, and would meet with Sarah.

The monument was riddled with relaxed evening walkers and she felt a momentary calm, both because her life and Eson's seemed to be changing for the better, and in the thought that she could always return to her wandering lifestyle if she chose. She was part of Eson's world by choice, not because of his power, but because she cared for him. She vowed to tell him the next time they spoke about all that was happening in his absence. And wasn't her small deception in aid of finding out really about the ethics of his actions? The servant's words still caught up with her at times.

The history of the city arched over her in the monument's stone surfaces, a comforting assurance that everything in their small lives would someday be overlooked as but a detail in the macrocosm of history. What was individual action or inaction, unless its outcome helped or harmed large numbers of others? Someone powerful like Eson could shift lives, and perhaps she could, too, with her developing abilities. He had all these people in his shadow by way of the deeds. She knew also that she was bound by a deed, and so felt that a thin, strong thread connected the debtors to her. She needed to find out what they were after, and to know the meaning of Eson's deeds from their side. She resolved to do this without betraying Eson. *No matter what I find out about him*, she told herself.

She thought of the meager, striving roses she had found in each of the fountains. They seemed to embody a kind of truth, like ascetics that are fueled by the planet itself and need very little from the material world. If she could understand the meaning in the fountains and become like their roses, she would be led toward truth, and could hope to overcome her own deceptive nature.

She would have a quick word with Neriv, and then she would leave the club. The debtors were there again, and she could intuit their group connection as a quick wave that traveled between them. The wave lost intensity as the group fanned out over the nightclub's first floor.

"Oh, they're here again!" hissed Neriv. She and Kyra were sitting once again at their table on the third floor, watching the crowd slowly filter in. It was early evening, and light still came in the windows. A waiter was only now lighting the lanterns, floating with a levitation platform beneath his feet. Kyra followed Neriv's eyes down to a knot of people dispersing on the first floor, among them the man she thought of as Loken Birch, and the man and woman who had blocked her way in this club many weeks earlier. She felt an instinctive wariness on seeing them. She could see the group briefly, then relied only on her intuition as they disappeared under the terraces of the club. Some of the group were making their way toward the staircases. She cast a glance at the small door behind her, ready to leave quickly if the debtors confronted her.

"What kinds of letters were they asking you to pass?" she asked Neriv.

"The unfolded letters were pretty insignificant, like 'Meet us outside at the Dog's Hour', and that kind of thing. A couple of the letters were folded up, so I didn't read those. I have to start work in a couple of minutes. Are you staying around here?"

"I'll stay here for a little while, but I'd like to leave soon. There's a show I want to catch at the theater in my neighborhood."

"Yeah, which show?"

"It's called 'The Storm Land'. It's by a northern director named Leda Riso."

"Classic! It really amazes me what goes on up there in the north. People have been arrested just for making films."

She nodded. It had amazed her, too, when Eson's friend had told her of the secrecy and the danger of the underground media work in the north.

Neriv waved and moved off to start her shift. Kyra took stock of the situation, having lost track of the group. She attuned her senses and realized that two members of the circle were visible on the second floor terrace, and that Neriv had just passed by, pointedly ignoring them: Loken Birch and a young woman whose clean, slightly bland version of the urban punk style matched his. They wore their hair choppy and dressed in sleek designer clothes. He looked calmer than he had the previous night, and his companion at first appeared quite emotionless—but her eyes widened as she looked up to where Kyra was sitting. She motioned to Loken and he looked up at Kyra as well. There was little anger in their expressions and the aggression Kyra had noted in Loken's movements seemed almost completely transformed. Maybe she had been projecting her fear onto him in her first perception of him in motion.

She had been glancing at them through lowered eyes, but under their steady, open gaze, she raised her eyes and met theirs. There was an overtone of infatuation in the look she shared with them, traversing the open, lantern-lit space of the nightclub. The two had a striking and intriguingly rebellious look, and it was because of this that she let her guard down and allowed a visual connection to be made. They knew and she knew they were bound to Eson by threads of ink and parchment. She thought also of Jado, and of how she had trusted him instantly, not even knowing he was a member of the circle. Perhaps she'd met the toughest elements of the circle that other night in the club, and had nothing to fear from the other members. She held onto her caution, though, and prepared to exit the club at a moment's notice.

They were walking toward the staircase that would bring them to the uppermost floor. She saw them give a signal across the terrace to some others she couldn't see, but could sense. They were scattered in knots below her, but were now gradually coalescing upward. It would be some minutes before they all reached her, if that was what they were intending. She sensed one group below her stopping and milling around by the bar, while at the same moment Loken and his companion appeared at the top of the stairs opposite her.

She breathed in and prepared to meet them, reminding herself of the power she now had, feeling the charismatic grace that surrounded Eson growing outward from her. She pulled strength up from an ethereal void within her, relaxing into it.

Loken and the woman arrived at her table. With a feigned casualness, he asked, "May we sit down?"

She could see a spark of anger in his eye, not quite veiled by his genteel manner. Despite her apprehension, she made an expansive gesture toward the available seats.

The two sat.

"We have wanted to meet you. We've come here every night hoping you would come to us." Loken indicated himself and then the woman. "I'm Loken, and this is my cousin Illusi."

When they spoke, it was as people who have suffered an innocent pain and are demanding to know why they have been subjected to it. They didn't reproach her, but tried instead to solicit her, tried subtly to pull her aside from Eson. It was clear they saw her in quite a different light than Eson, and that they believed she could be a beacon of hope for them.

Their guileless optimism made her want to cry out with the absurdity of her position in their lives. She realized she had committed the dangerous act of forming a connection with them, and so had placed herself on the narrow bridge of disputed land between Eson and the people with whom he bolstered himself. Was she of them, or was she of Eson? The ground on which she stood was muddied and volatile. She felt an echo of understanding now at both Sarah's and Eson's warnings—but the counter-warning the servant in the mountains had given her still echoed down from steam-clouded heights.

She would hear their side of the situation, and then know better her own role. "What do you know about me?" she asked them, with patience.

"We know that you are very close to the one who holds us all under his power. We know that he has a deed with our names on it, and that the life is sapped from us daily so that we fear and resent him. We know you have access to this deed, and that you have reasons both for helping us, and for helping him. We hope your conscience will tell you that you must listen to us, that you aren't much different from us. Beyond that, we know little about you, and would not impose on your life where it doesn't overlap with ours." He maintained his diplomatic poise, but tension was creeping in to the edges of his speech as he added another comment. "We also know that you impersonated Sarah, and we have no idea why you did this."

She brushed aside the last remark and answered only to his other statements. "The deed you speak of is beyond my power, because I'm also bound by a deed, and by other bonds besides." She paused, then, as three more people were now approaching the table.

They came to stand behind the other two in a solid formation, one of the two women leaning her weight on a chair between the other two. The man, who looked tougher, younger, and poorer than Loken, was introduced as Hesek, the woman sitting beside him was his sister, Charis, and the young woman beside them was Alon. Framed together, the three looked respectively like embodiments of terseness, curiosity, and impatience. They were all attired in black fabrics with slashes of bright hard colors, and together they resembled a cubist group portrait with an overlay of graffiti. Alon and Hesek came prepared with cynical looks, while Charis appeared to reconcile with her. Loken and Illusi exchanged a glance, as if tacitly agreeing to neither believe nor disbelieve her claims, and the group before her took on a collective wired presence, a hard-edged sheen of urban vitality.

"Tell me what it is that you think I can do for you." Kyra leaned forward. She met the eyes of at least three of the five, conscious that there were two other debtors still on the second floor below them, while the last was now advancing up the stairs. She'd walked into the center of their web, and now they were closing in on her. She had to appear solid. They were not the Heiress, after all, but were a pack, and unpredictable. She quelled her fears and waited, firmly, for a response.

The tall, leather-clad woman from Kyra's first evening with Eson was last to approach the table. She stood back, scanning the terrace and over the edge as if guarding the group against others who might be watching them. Then she spoke abruptly, an open challenge in her voice. It seemed to sway the others who stood behind Loken and Illusi, as if spreading a net over them.

"Mersad refuses to meet with you. He says you will be just like Eson. He and Stas remain below." She didn't offer her own name.

Kyra sat up straighter, taking on a voice not her own. "I've been to the north and I've seen how Eson suffers, likely more than anyone here does. The rules are different there, and it's difficult for us to understand them, living in a free country as we do. This deed, do you have any proof it exists?"

They were visibly moved, all except the tall woman with the ragged voice, who stood with her body turned partially away.

"Waren told us about it the night after he signed it," offered Charis, who looked as though she was trying to assemble the fractured situation in her mind.

"We believed Waren when things started going wrong for each of us," said Illusi, but offered no more.

Charis spoke again. "Just because the north is a hideous place, does it mean we should shoulder a piece of its suffering?" The others looked around with disjointed expressions, and the question went unanswered, rhetorical by default.

Kyra felt she wasn't warming them to her enough, so she pushed further. "How do you suffer from his contract? Do you really think this man is the one responsible for all that's wrong in your lives?" She asked it in an accommodating tone, conscious of romancing the crowd with an influence she developed as she spoke. It didn't feel natural coming from her own mouth, but she marveled inside at its effect. "What things have gone wrong?" she continued in a tone of great concern that was genuine, but much more demonstrative than she was accustomed to using.

A moment passed, and they began to spill their tales of hardship to her, small troubles at first, then with a greater release.

"I lost every bet I placed," said Hesek vaguely, as if to offer the first example. Charis kicked his foot gently. Hesek was young and lean, edged in black clothes. Charis, also lean and adorned with subtle tattoos, appeared a few years older, but they were clearly quite close, reacting intuitively to each other.

"I had all my money stolen and had to move back home," said Alon, without looking at Kyra. She was young and round-faced, though she might have been older than Kyra. She was decked out for a night in the deep catacombs of the underground scene, and her arm was lightly wound around Hesek's waist. Kyra could picture the two of them sliding with ease through the pulsing music and deep shadowy scenes of the club.

Illusi looked at Kyra with greater seriousness and said, "The business we started was doing really well until that time. Then the floor was swept out from under us, and we fell into debt, everything collapsing."

Charis added, "I began to feel ill whenever I was around anything electric, as if my inner power were being drained into the circuits and the power lines, being channeled toward him." The word *him* was emphasized, endowed with a godlike sense of portent.

The others vouched also for an enervation, as though the electric reactions of their inner cells were being drained like batteries. There was a moment in which the group was balanced on a hinge, evidently not sure whether to see Kyra as a hostile extension of Eson or as a possible ally for their salvation.

The intimidating woman, Mersad's companion, broke the moment and swayed the group back toward her with a bold threat.

"What if we were to make you help us?" she asked, and the others seemed to rise up, leaning in toward Kyra, demanding that she submit to the larger will of the collective. "We could take you with us right now, and then you would have no choice but to help us convince Eson to release us from the deed. You would know then how much he values you!"

Kyra stood her ground without faltering, glad that Mersad and the other, who was likely as dangerous as this woman, had stayed away. She was conscious of them both, large and unnerving presences below the floor of the terrace.

Loken and Illusi shed a layer of nicety and looked as though they could be pushed to act in desperation. Loken once again began to show his anger, with lashing eyes and a clenched hand. The two young people, Hesek and Alon, began to slouch and lour. Charis remained neutral between them but fastened a look of spiritual hunger on Kyra, reminding her eerily of the stranger who had shaken her arm in the street. She had stepped in over her head, as Eson, Sarah and even the Heiress and her agent had warned her not to do.

The circle of people now before her was taut as a bow with potential energy, a linked circuit of resistors who bore too high a burden of electrical current. Eson could have drained their collective force into his own stores with a well-placed word, but her own powers weren't so developed, and she felt sick at the implications of using people this way. In viewing the hungry debtors before her, she truly felt incapable of understanding Eson's moral justifications.

In her power and good fortune, was she too drawing life away from this group?

The thought filled her with distaste, and she tried consciously to send a wave of compassion over the group. An image of the desolate roses in their dry fountains appeared in her mind.

The circle softened slightly, relaxing at the edges. A voice broke into the silence, then, as the music from far below washed over them: Neriv had materialized next to Kyra, facing the group. "Is there a problem here?" she demanded. "I've already asked your two friends to leave, and I'll have to ask you not to intrude on the other patrons."

The debtors glanced around, hesitated, and finally began to grudgingly disperse.

Kyra clasped Neriv's arm in gratitude, and nodded to Charis, Illusi and Loken as they turned to leave. The others didn't look back.

"Do you need to call a shuttle-car to get home?" asked Neriv, very real and grounded after the bizarre energy of the group. "You probably shouldn't walk around in the streets near here."

Kyra nodded and thanked her dear friend, walking to the bar with her to call the shuttle-car. She realized that she indeed would have to curtail her movements, as Eson did his. It had happened without her being aware, but now she was locked into the quasi-vampiric world he also inhabited. She could never go back to her wandering days, she thought, and held onto Neriv as she made the call. Neriv was her link to a way of life that guided itself by freedom and honest desires.

Neriv took a break and waited with her for the rattling, steam-powered shuttle-car, which came to the lane underneath the back exit as Kyra had asked.

"I can't come back here anymore," she told Neriv as they walked down the narrow stairs. Neriv looked deeply at her and nodded.

Next to the car Neriv jotted her address on a piece of paper. "This is where I'm staying. Come by anytime you need to. You can stay there too, if you don't feel safe where you are now." She didn't let go of Kyra until she was safely in the shuttle car. The tinted glass door of the car slid in front of her, then, and was a darkened film between her and Neriv.

When the car dropped her in the quiet, safe street in front of the suite, Kyra found a note card in the letterbox identical to the one she had found the previous night. She sighed, guessing it would contain a recrimination from Sarah. She ran inside and locked the inside door of the suite, savoring the feeling of height and security that came with being able to look down over the city through the wall of glass.

The note was very short.

> *Kyra,*
>
> *I know that you have been at the club. Do you now see why I warned you? I'm sending you this because I want you to know that I will not be bringing any of them with me to our meeting tomorrow. In your state of mind right now, it would be easy for you to stay away, fearing I would be in connection with them, or bring some of them with me. That is not the case. The group is scattered, out of control. They can't be reasoned with as a whole. I assume you will meet me tomorrow. This is your chance to prove yourself worthy of having used my name as your own.*
>
> *Sarah*

While she knew that meeting Sarah could provide her with answers vital to her, she couldn't help feeling irritated by Sarah's presumptive and arrogant tone. The evening was young, though, and she drew a bath, musing on whether she should call Eson and tell him all that had transpired. He'd put things in perspective somehow—but she was at a loss as to how to explain her short-comings, her actions which now seemed nothing but impulsive and foolish.

She mixed a drink from some of Eson's elixirs, kept in dark bottles in the cupboard, following the instructions in a book of exotic and potent northern drinks. It was not like her to drink strongly, but this night seemed a special case. She lowered the lights and sank into the bath, taking brooding sips of the drink, confused and feeling no more secure in her situation than she had before meeting the debtors. She felt she hadn't helped them but had damaged her solidarity with Eson, and wrestled with how she would explain herself to him without casting doubt on her loyalty. Would he trust her, knowing she had met with the people in his deed?

She awoke to the dawn on the morning she was to meet Sarah with a very different feeling: a similarity to Eson, much greater than before. Her devotion grew, and she slid a dividing wall between herself and the people she had encountered at the nightclub. They were not to be trusted, though she still struggled with feeling a tie to them, an obligation to at least improve their situation if she had the ability to do so. She was haunted by images of them, and wrestled in her mind with how she could come to a resolution with the different personalities in the group.

Loken and Illusi were people she could speak with easily, though cautiously. The two youngest, Alon and Hesek, were unpredictable and capricious in their personalities, she felt, and could be swayed to her if she were lucky.

Charis was a mystery, though likely she would align with Kyra if she thought it suited her purposes. The other three were another matter. She wanted to stay away from them entirely if she could. Whatever was to take place, she couldn't count on them or trust their intentions.

She looked quickly over Eson's deed, guarding it with her body and putting it back in its case after only a moment. Looking over the names, she determined that the tall, ragged-voiced woman was named Carda Medean... and now she knew the identities of the entire circle of debtors, and could put a seal of completeness over them.

She was aware of her changed state of being that morning, and though she had known great fear, she was more like an immortal now, having drawn power from the group. She realized this must be how Eson fostered his power, though at a distance from the circle, using his contracts. Were they a kind of vampire, the people in his lineage? Was she becoming this kind of being? She felt an obsession now for Eson's presence, for his understanding of this way of being that was so powerful yet so constrained. A dark net suspended itself above her and the city, tangible to her for the first time. The suite became like a vault where they had been entombed together. Had he intended that she would become like him, in binding her to himself? The vision bird looked at her with its unblinking eye, as she in turn looked over the city morning. She silently asked the bird what it knew, but the bird only gave her its constant, serene gaze.

She used the lines Eson had traced on his map to chart her own journey to the gallery, and set out very early, not wanting to miss her liaison with Sarah. After the previous night, travel within the city would be a much more cautious and calculated affair.

Her path was not as indirect as she'd feared it would have to be, and she arrived at the foot of the gallery's stairs, under the benign presence of the monument, as the gallery doors were swinging open for the day.

The gallery itself was a warm stone cave made of the same rock as the monument above it. She entered an open, spacious hall and observed the vestiges of the massive glass-making machine that lay enshrined there. It had been the hallmark of the city's growth, and while now obsolete, it contained the majesty of the city's past and was a tribute to it.

This was a gallery, though, not only a museum, and the ancient machine was now being worked into conceptual art pieces that changed with the seasons. When she entered, the machine was covered with a large silken canopy, the crenellations of the machine visible beneath it. Inscribed on the canopy were the many names of the people who had been enslaved in the glass foundries until the last century. Over an audio system were the ghostly strains of an ancient, broadcasted publicity report on the city's prosperity and comfort. The machine lurked under its shroud as though it were in penitence for the crime of its makers, but the beauty of its design glowed through, underscoring the perversity of its history.

She stood taking this in, and a gallery assistant nearby spoke to her candidly. "There is nothing in this city that is purely beautiful, or purely terrible."

"What about the meteor tower?" she replied, glancing aside at him. He was tall, much taller than Eson, and fairly young. "Wasn't that built as an alliance between the desert and the city?"

"There's an alliance now. Luckily, we have peace. Do you live in the city, or are you a visitor?"

"I'm here for now, but I'll be going to the western tidal lands soon."

"Now there's a different place entirely from our city." The guide gave her a friendly look before moving away to patrol the gallery.

The normal, easy interaction set her comfortably back in the ordinary world, and she became simply a person enjoying a morning out at a gallery. There were few people there so early.

She moved upward on a stairwell that led to other, smaller galleries and entered a darkened, subdued hall with very modern paintings in sharp primary colors and black. There was a long painting with human figures caught at a moment of intense action, which echoed for a moment her memory of the debtors, their intensity and hard-edged aesthetic.

Next was a recreation of a historical gambling den of a now illegal variety. There were padded enclosures for the bettors, who would face a barrage of physical sensations and experiences in order to win prizes of the rarest order. The walls were covered in deep, musky fabrics, and audio speakers played out firsthand account of the games, complete with the screams of the shocked competitors and audiences. She passed through it quickly, shivering with the thought of what people had endured for money and fame. These were temporary exhibits, all geared toward unmasking the violence and oppression that went into the making of the modern, genteel city.

She passed into galleries that were more tame but no less ornate, with interactive machine installations and schematic drawings displayed in the manner of religious artifacts. Some adolescent visitors were making this room into their amusement park, and their rebellious, hyperactive and satiric laughter echoed around the rooms. She moved on into the old-world historical and zoological collections. The guide from the main gallery breezed up to her again, and with a conspiratorial smile gave her an ornamental key on a chain. "Turn this key in the wall next to the carved door in the Jaguar Room," he said.

She thanked him and waited until he had gone before making her way into the room.

Just as Eson had predicted, she fixated her eyes on the jaguars she could see at the opposite end of the room, and as she entered, became aware of two large, stony shadows looming above her. The jaguars, polished to a lustrous sheen and made of rock even darker than that of the black orbs, had their claws stretched over her in a pounce they'd held for decades. She instinctively ducked.

The rest of the room spilled over with paintings, sculptures, and furniture, all with a theme of wildness and animal ferocity. She wandered, transfixed by the grand and monstrous specimens of bestiary, and came to a series of paintings on the wall that she knew must be her meeting point with Sarah.

Sculptures hid her from view of the two entryways, as the room was quite large. She observed the dark, rich colors of the paintings before her, realizing suddenly that they related to Eson's distant ancestors in the old world. There was a triptych showing a vast hunting party, scouring the rugged hills for beasts. A youth riding among the tangled briars of the hillside looked to her like a miniature rendition of Eson.

There was a heavy, gothic pall over these old-world landscapes, which were alive with feuds and frightening beasts. There were some gentler scenes showing vineyards, sunlight and villages, and though all the paintings had a grim beauty, they did not describe a modern or secure way of life. In many of the paintings a forboding, lupine threat loomed behind very dark trees. She remembered how Eson had spoken of remodeling his mountain house, and understood it must have been the archaic oppression of the old world he had sought to cover.

The most enchanting of the images was that of the creator, Sarhul, depicted in a classic stance beside a dark, clear divining pool. She settled onto a bench before this painting and observed it while she waited for Sarah. Howling beasts threatened inward at the edges of the picture, but all were cowed by the presence of the creator. Suddenly conscious of the animal shapes that filled the room behind her, she leaned toward the painting, as if to shield herself within Sarhul's aura. An audio reel had just begun releasing the eldritch sounds of howling beasts into the room. She turned to let the painting of the creator guard her back, and noted the great skeleton behind her of what was said to be a werewolf creature, the last of which had been seen in the old-world hills some centuries earlier. The air felt chilled, and she pulled her coat tighter around her... and something fell out of her coat pocket. She bent to pick it up, and saw that it was the tiny envelope Eson had bestowed on her at their first meeting. He'd asked her to keep it close to her body, and she had done so, at least whenever she was wearing her own coat. She'd forgotten about the envelope and his request. She would look over it again later, but for now put it safely away in her inner pocket.

She felt a presence moving behind her, then, and with an instinct of curiosity rather than fear, turned to face a vivid incarnation of Sarhul standing still and looking down toward her. She looked back at the painting in confusion, and the living version of Sarhul raised both an eyebrow and a corner of her mouth into a wry smile.

Kyra stood, and was several inches shorter than the woman before her.

"Uncanny resemblance, isn't it?" said the woman, and Kyra slid toward the truth of the matter: the woman standing before her was Sarah. They sat down on the bench, a few inches of space separating them, a magnetic barrier protecting each from the other's influence. Kyra felt a dissonance between them, a sense that the veil of energy she'd acquired from Eson was at odds with the field surrounding Sarah, and felt, too, a mixture of awe and shame at being in Sarah's presence, knowing that Sarah knew of her impersonation, feeling the ridiculousness of her act of subterfuge.

She could think of no appropriate way of smoothing the rift between them, and casual introductions seemed irrelevant, given the nature of their relationship. She said only, "You look much more like her than I do." She felt an odd, talismanic protection from Sarah as well, as if the beasts in the room would leave her in peace while Sarah remained with her.

"There *is* something about these old-world beasts that's terrifying, isn't there? The people who hunted them and lived in concert with them were equally terrifying," Sarah said, still facing the painting. "While others were afraid of the beasts, Sarhul's followers were kept safe by their creator. Naturally they were blamed for the beasts' predations. Eson's family was among those people. There is a legacy of immunity and impermeability that survives to this day." She turned her eyes toward her. "You're drinking from that ancestral spring, you know, in your current state of collusion with him. I can understand how it must be alluring to you. …At any rate, how did you enjoy your evening out last night?" The words were tinged with irony, but not with real venom.

Kyra shook her head and spoke as though confiding to her. "I think I made a mistake. I can't make things any better for them."

"You can, and you will. They won't let you ignore them now that you've set hooks into them and they into you. They'll pull at you just as strongly as Eson can. Look over there." She pointed to a corner of the room where the animal forms had a mechanistic, sleek look, as if fallen from the same technological heights as the vision bird. "Those are non-functioning remnants of the old technologies. You have a bird that is of this type, and it is in working order?"

Kyra nodded, looking over at the animals. Fixed to the wall was a beautifully constructed metallic hunting hound, its dark eyes fastened inertly on a point before its once functioning metal eyes. There were also a horse, a deer, a lizard, several small birds and rodents, a cat, a larger wildcat, and other animals of ancient, extinct categorizations. She told Sarah what she knew of the animals. "They each have their own ability. The bird makes recordings of all it sees. I find it quite useful."

"Yes, I imagine you do," said Sarah, again with the ironic hint. "There are many disused technologies, and some of them could be brought back into use if they were known of and dealt with properly. These relics are museum pieces, and we would need ludicrously rare elements from across the sea to make them work again. But there are things in this city that can be made to work as they once did." She paused, and Kyra gauged there was a hint involved, something Sarah expected her to understand.

"The group you met last night are aware of one type of technology that could be of use to them. You've discovered this on your own already," Sarah pressed.

She was speaking of the fountains! Was it possible Sarah had been observing her movements as she charted the fountains' coordinates? The possibility made her nerves twinge with a sense of invasion. Her movements in the city had been less secure than she'd assumed.

"Do you mean the dry fountains?" She felt the barrier between them beginning to dull, as if melted slightly by Sarah's succoring manner. Was she really a manifestation of Sarhul? She couldn't be, because Sarhul would take a protective stance toward Eson, and Sarah seemed bent on confounding him.

She must not allow herself to become entranced by Sarah, as Sarhul subdued the beasts in the painting.

Sarah smiled with a radiant satisfaction. She had an odd, mythic beauty, and Kyra was thankful on a certain level that Sarah hadn't met Eson in person. She knew the enchanter was not immune from enchantment, and he already had her fascinating letters—

"Yes, the fountains, with their tenacious, resourceful flora. You wondered, didn't you, what was allowing the roses to grow?"

Kyra admitted she'd been intrigued by the roses, their aroma made dry as it mixed with the dust of the fountains. "We have plants fueled by hidden mineral emissions in the aeroponics regions," she offered, and felt like the dust of the backwoods speaking of her rural home to this urbane woman. She began to speak again of the fountains instead. "I also wondered why my vision bird hadn't shown them to me."

"Quite honestly, it was programmed hundreds of years ago, and religious decree forbade the construction of technologies that could infiltrate sacred sites. It's hard-wired to keep a respectful distance from places like the sacred pools and springs." Sarah stood abruptly. "Now, do you have the key that the gallery host provides? I asked for it in the front room, but it was already taken."

She fumbled for a moment and found the key, looking over the wall before her for the space the key might fit. Sarah motioned her to a corner of the room opposite the vision bird's kin.

The key fit into a groove in the wall next to a heavy, carved door that exhaled a woody scent, its surface depicting geometric sea creatures and huge canoes. It swung open a bit when the key was turned, and Sarah carefully opened it further, using a delicately carved copper handle on the door's edge. They passed through, Kyra feeling like a disciple invited into a sanctuary. She pulled the door softly closed behind her.

They were enclosed in a small inner room that bore little resemblance either to the room they'd just left or the door they had closed. The room was quiet, edged in a material that muffled sound. There were no windows or skylights, and the illumination was dim. In the middle of the room was a small-scale model of a fountain much like the ones placed throughout the city. Two of the walls were covered in schematics diagrams of the fountains.

A third wall was given over to a large painting of the ancient explorers who had founded the city, making their way up through the southern desert during a famine in the south. They stood under a stone outcropping on an exposed hill surrounded by dry plains, and a spring of water before them flowed down over the stones.

Sarah began to tell her about the history of the fountains. "The original settlers, driven into the wilderness from the famine in the south, decided to set up a small outpost here. The city grew up over the top of the springs, covering them with a network of pipes, roads, and stone buildings. The fountains were, until recent centuries, the conduits through which the springs had arisen into the city. They stopped providing water many years ago, and the city, now supplied by powerful water sources to the north, west and east, forgot about the meager wells that had allowed it to grow from its earliest roots. Layers of history left these fountains as the only relics of the ancient underground watercourse."

Kyra listened restlessly, beginning to pace before the schematic drawings. The fountains looked much too complex to be simply water fountains... were those turbines? "What are those complex mechanisms within the fountains?"

Sarah looked pleased. "Yes, there you've found what the crux of the matter! The fountains are really power conduits. They were used as a backup power supply to many of the city's districts in the early days of electricity."

Kyra shrugged. "So they were fountains as well as power sources, and now some people in the city still use them as places of prayer and offering. How come the water supply stopped? The springs in the mountains continue to flow and provide steam power. They weren't hot springs here, were they?"

"No, the springs here didn't produce steam as those in the mountains did. Hydropower could be taken from them, but no heat. Luckily we don't need heat here on the plains, with the desert air coming up from the south. I don't know why they stopped working. I don't know everything." Sarah gave her a suddenly reproachful look, reminiscent of the condescension Kyra had noticed in her letter.

She felt it unwise to ask any further questions for the moment. She said, instead, "The fountains mean a lot to the group in the deed. I know that much. Maybe they think they'll be free if they can harness a power source that would rival Eson's."

"Yes. But they know also that they have no power of their own to reactivate the fountains. So they're taking an interest in you, knowing you can tap into Eson's supply."

"I have no interest in doing that," she said, turning away toward the wall.

"I will tell you how to find them and bind them to you individually. It will be much easier to work with them separately than as a group. If you can tie your power to that of the circle, you can make yourself more powerful. With each of the circle working with you to activate the fountains, you could soon have access to your own power supply and feed off this civilization's hunger for electric power, just as Eson does."

Sarah was telling her only a certain version of the situation, of this she was now sure. It was not at all certain that in working with Sarah she'd be protecting Eson or his power. She did not trust Sarah, despite her forceful and plausible argument. Sarah was merely proving herself to be as skilled as Eson at making her views seem logical and right simply by presenting them as such.

"I'm sorry, I can't help you in this matter," she said, using formality of speech both as a defensive tactic and a means of closing the conversation.

"Charis wants to help you. So do Loken and Illusi. They really don't want any harm to come to you or Eson. It'd be best to work with them, I think, before the others convince them to go ahead without your help. You and Eson could both be in danger if they find a way to work around his deed without your guidance. You must take control of this situation before someone else does!"

How much of this was truth, and how much poisoned by

Sarah's own desire for revenge and control? She refused to answer to her claims, and only extended her hand to Sarah. "It was a pleasure meeting with you," she said flatly, and rather weakly.

Sarah grasped her hand with feral warmth, and in that moment Kyra was almost lost, much as she had been when Eson's arm had first encircled her shoulders. The grip lasted longer than was usual at the end of a casual meeting, and she disengaged her hand, turning quickly away from Sarah's strong, almost supernaturally handsome face. She slipped out through the wooden door and into the larger air of the open galleries, exiting the Jaguar Room in only a few quick strides.

She let out her breath as she took the long stairs down into the front lobby. The ghostly audio reel was still filling the air with a siren's song about the wonders of the Glass City, while the covered machine was still a silent testament to its muddied past. She usually had little patience for such abstract artistic statements, but the contradictions of the city seemed very alive to her today.

"I left the key with my companion," she said to the smiling guide as she passed his desk. He only nodded, not appearing to intuit anything out of the ordinary in her brusque manner, and she escaped into the breezy, hazy afternoon outside the gallery, standing for a moment before remembering that she must now keep out of view much more than she had.

She walked back along the route that had brought her to the gallery, and stopped in a small café in one of the peaceful side streets, letting the calm, everyday city activity wash over her. She ordered a cool, mint drink, which was served in a desert flask with a few artfully placed grapes lying on the plate next to it.

She took out the envelope she'd remembered earlier. The paper contained a beautiful swirl of calligraphic design that was so stylized as to be unreadable. It may have been a prayer offering or an amulet, a token of Eson's lineage. It was composed of the same parchment and ink as his deeds, and written with the same character. If she'd remembered it sooner, she might have been tempted to tear it up, as it was almost certainly the document binding her into the deed that had been meant for Sarah. But now, she saw it as the tangible link that held her to Eson. It was his beautiful penmanship, a small token of his desire to forge a connection with her.

She sipped the cool drink and placed the calligraphic emblem back in its envelope, slipping it back into her coat pocket.

It was time, she decided, to take her trip to Waters Rising. She would call Eson as soon as she reached the suite. She had gathered from Eson's carefree, elated tone in speaking about the coast that they could stay peacefully there, away from the people with whom Eson had dangerous bonds. She wanted only to visit Neriv before leaving the city now so fraught with hazard to her and to Eson. Neriv would be worried about her if she disappeared without contact, and Kyra felt the depth of their friendship buoying her upward to safety.

book four

aquarium wall at the high bank

It was warm under the eaves of the comfortable, tightly constructed west coast house. The tiny listening device fed off this
warmth, pulling energy into its efficient, minute battery coils.
It resembled a mouse, and its metal ears were energy receptors,
listening equipment and communication device all in one. It was
Jado's finest work to date, and was constructed with rare elements
Eson possessed, infused with a power only Eson could access.

The mouse fanned its ears in the absolute darkness of the
rooftop and navigated its way deeper into the house, chewing
through layers of good quality insulation, tasting no bitterness
with its synthetic mouth. As it gained access to the warm, secure
attic of the house, it began to pick up low vibrations below it. It
guided itself toward the voices, and dropped down into the space
between the inner walls of the house until it was level with one
of the inner rooms. This room was a series of resonating, sound-
conducting surfaces, and the mouse began to position itself for

optimum volume. The wall contained a wiry network of devices that ensured the complete comfort of the people inside the house, and the mouse burrowed its way into the nexus of these wires, feeding off their energy traces and currents. It could clearly hear the voices now, and began recording and broadcasting all that it heard back to its control device, which rested distantly in a borrowed house on the hillside. It heard things about tides, about generators, about passageways into the city.

Jado has been telling me much about the workings of electrical power devices, some of which catches in my mind, and some of which melts away soon after it is told. I know something of steam power and power production, of course, but the actual workings of photovoltaic cells and power inverters leaves me flummoxed. It's so much simpler to pull power out of the ether of the past and the planet—but such metaphysical power can only do so much. We must interface with the physical world if that is the world in which we are trying to advance. It is the combination of personal magnetism and concrete action that has allowed my family to succeed since the beginning days. I uphold this legacy, and do honor to the ancestral springs.

The most exciting aspect of the technology is for me the results purveyed so efficiently and seamlessly. I have learned what I need to know about the tidal power systems, and have a date in mind now for the accomplishment of our maneuver. There is an element of chance, but the basic elements are engineered in our favor.

There are ten battery collectors. Each one must be placed on one of the tidal turbines that line the shore. This is a simple matter, as I have a mechanical dog arriving, procured from old-world traders at much cost, that will be able to run the length of the tidal basin without tiring. The battery collectors will siphon an undetectable amount of current from the tidal generators. When the tide retreats, there will be full battery cells waiting. I have sold them all to sea traders who hover in ships in the outer bay, reliant on unconventional forms of power to make their way back across the sea. If Jado were better at networking with the sea traders, he could now be arranging to sell them solar generators when next they put in at this port... but we each have our own talents, and so collaboration becomes profitable for all of us.

The troubling hinge of the maneuver is that someone must activate the battery cells by way of a centrally placed control module, and this must be done almost immediately prior to the influx of the great tide. The tides here run on a very large, infrequent and sudden scale. They course inward across the tidal plain. The person who is to activate the batteries must do so swiftly and then escape into one of the hidden passages that run behind the city waterfront before the tide engulfs him.

I haven't told Jado of the details of this plan, as it may not suit his code of ethics well. But it will work, and I will give him enough money to buy a solar generator when he has finished aiding me. The sea traders have all signed contracts which ensure that the profit I make from selling them the power cells will continue to flow to me even after the traders have crossed the distant ocean. They will not be able to hound me as those in the Glass City do.

I've found a new level of freedom here, and now Kyra is with me, if only for a few days. I met her at the train station, and we walked, in a leisurely way, mindless of which streets we chose. It is happening to her, too. I could tell in her measured glance as she stepped off the train that the Glass City has thrown a net over her as it has done to me.

Jado was weighing the benefits of crystalline, thin-film, and string ribbon solar cells with part of his mind. The other part was engaged in homesickness for his family and friends in the Glass City. He had a new niece, and his family had been sending him letters asking him to come home. He had written back, saying he would return as soon as he could find time away from Eson's project.

Eson seemed to have a somewhat flat understanding of how important Jado's family and community were to him. Though Eson spoke of his ancestors and of legacy and honor, he rarely mentioned the real people who had shaped his life. "His family have all gone into the past," thought Jado, and felt a kind of sad pity for Eson that would have been unimaginable during their first meetings. Eson was a charismatic enchanter with every privilege, but his life now seemed, in Jado's eyes, to be disadvantaged.

Still, he envied Eson's romantic success, as Eson had gradually unfolded to him more than one story from his cache of baroquely detailed anecdotes. Jado had never had trouble attracting people to him, but his successes seemed meager when compared to the history at which Eson hinted. Jado knew of the Heiress and others before her, and now, of course, he knew of Eson's relationship with Kyra, the girl from the storm. After their breakfast, Eson had said he was going out for the day to meet with a woman named Kyra, who'd arrived the day before from the Glass City.

That he could lose her to another ordinary person he could accept, but to Eson, who was so unlike other people... He could not understand it, did not want to think about it, and tried, now that it had surfaced again, to put it from his mind. To think of solar cells and his family was safer.

Eson had asked, right after that, if he thought the batteries would be finished that day.

"It's unlikely," he'd managed to reply, and focused on the technical details of the question instead. "You have to add the rare earth elements in a particular sequence, and wait to see if each one has reacted properly with others. Sometimes you have to redo them, or fine-tune the conversion mechanisms... I think the magnetic fields here have an effect on the timing of everything." Eson had stood in the doorway of the room, looking outward and nodding distractedly, though politely. "I think Kyra came to my shop a couple of times," he had added, after a pause.

"Yes, she knew you when I mentioned your name. You can talk with her when we come back. I'll be here before evening, as I'm eager to find out if our mouse has reeled in anything more for us." Eson had left the room and prepared to leave the house, then called out to Jado, "Don't burn out over the machines today. We have a few days before the tide comes in, and anyway, we can't place the batteries until the running dog arrives. Please sign for it if it does." His voice had been even and consoling, and the rift that had threatened to form earlier was mended.

Though he still harbored doubts about Eson and about the ethics of their current project, Jado felt a sense that he was doing good work and developing his talents. He was helping Eson provide power to some marginalized seafarers, and was only taking a minute quantity of power from the surplus of tide-borne energy that served this rich coastal region. And he would have a solar generator.

As he worked on the batteries the house was filled with light around him, and the high, papery walls filtered calmness downward onto him. For a moment, he turned away from the battery he was creating and put on some of his favorite music to further soothe his mind.

There's a waterfall running over the side of a particular building in Waters Rising, trickling down an indigo wall nearly like water itself. I've come here to convince someone of their need for me, and my energies rush out temporarily as do tidal waters before a great wave hits. I feel light and quick as I pass through the building's high door into the dark, translucent interior. There is nothing I enjoy more than this, really. I've brought my contracts and ink, stowed in an immaculate and finely made case that has been my accomplice in many such ventures. There is often a thread of guilt in the moment of the inevitable agreement, but now, before the real negotiation begins, there is only the elated vault of possibility in my mind. The sea is very close at hand, and whether that will work to my advantage or to the other player's is still unknown.

The cool woman I'd met on the lower slope of the Glass City, my ally, appears in an upper doorway of the translucent room and waits for me to ascend the shallow stairs to the upper floor.

With a sidelong glance, she assesses me before offering her invitation. "The other negotiator is already waiting. He will see you for only a short time, as it seems the venue does not suit his comfort for a long meeting—yet I wouldn't rate him an easy mark for your purposes."

Even though she has signed my contract, she will convince herself she is an impartial mediator for our consultation, will not admit to herself that she is on my side. I respect this in the utmost, though it matters little to the outcome of our gathering. I grant her the sense of honor, and respond to her as though she is indeed an impartial mediator.

"Please assure him I will waste little of his time." I say it with care, not wanting to sound dismissive or overconfident.

"You may assure him yourself." We approach a light door that swings outward at her touch. She gestures for me to precede her into the room, where there is a comfortable sitting area. A solitary occupant sits there, his back to the high wall opposite the door. The sea, visible beyond a great pane of glass, seems somehow to radiate expansively from him. He has the composure of one who knows the sea, who is a visiting dignitary when walking upon land. His face is broad and strong, polished by the ocean wind, a face from beyond the western sea. His age would be greater than mine, but not by much, I'm sure.

"You're the tidal magnate, then." His voice is solid and unquestioning, with no room accorded to doubts.

"I am an entrepreneur of sorts, not nearly the tycoon some would have me be."

"Your reputation precedes you."

I doubt if all the layers of my reputation have met his notice, or he would not have granted me this consultation. Though impermeable in his manner, he is not hostile. He will not allow me to step in to take advantage of the situation.

I already enjoy the company of this sea trader, whether or not he affords me the same sentiment.

Our mediator has taken a seat on a long, low couch, and there is a seat left for me, an archaic and curved wooden piece that encloses me with cushioned comfort.

"My reputation is an entity unto itself, bearing little relation to my true character. If you might rest easily in my presence, I'd also be much set at ease." These formalities seem suited to the venue and persons present, and indeed I notice a softening of the sea trader's countenance. The coastal woman wears an unchanging expression, her position as mediator allowing her to enforce the proper conduct of either party while we are her visitors. She will collect a good fee for these meetings of mine.

The sea trader looks at me steadily. "So, then, what is it you can offer to me, as an entrepreneur or a magnate or such?" His question is not really a question but an invitation to let me state my case. I will begin as the supplicant, then, if it suits him.

"Not very much, I would assume, given my means here in this wealthy nation. I have only electric power, in a form you can transport with you across the sea. "For your... delicate cargo," I say, and pause for emphasis, "you have need of the most efficient and lightweight of power sources." From the case I take one of Jado's drawings of the battery collectors. "My gifted technician has devised a battery that's extaordinarily powerful and light."

He gives me an appraising look, then passes his wary eye over the drawing. "You're from the north, aren't you? I don't like what I've heard about your country."

I speak simply, feeling no need to defend the country that has long been my cage. "I don't like the north any more than you do. I don't consider it my country." I replace the drawing in my case. "You may consider me a free agent, as you yourself no doubt are. When do you need these batteries?"

"I arrived early on a good current. I must wait in this port for the shipments I need to be ready."

"My batteries will be available when the tide comes in. If you can wait that long, the power source is yours. I won't take any more of your time." I gather my case and stand, leaning over to shake hands with him, and an imperceptible thread of energy is woven between us. I feel the momentary rush of guilt, as I know then he will sign my contract, regardless of his own doubts on the matter. "My contract is here," I say, placing the parchment and ink on the low table.

I glance at our mediator for a moment before exiting the room. As before in recent days, I continue down the dark corridor to a similar but smaller room to await her appearance with the signed contract. I don't know exactly what she will say to him, but she is an intermediary link and he trusts her, not knowing that he is really trusting me.

The sea is visible from this room, too, a broad dish of boats, islands and empty space. I imagine the serene crafts I see wafting in the swell may belong to any one of the sea traders I've already met with. They look peaceful and natural, as if made of kelp and driftwood, anchored on lines of dark cable to the floor of the bay.

I would never be anchored in these ocean waters. The trader in the other room is of the massive, wide sea, while I am of the water's clear sources, high in the upper reaches of the continent. No wonder he is suspicious of me.

A figure appears in the doorway, shadowy after the brightness of the sky and water. My ally has brought the contract bearing the sea-worn signature of the trader, and I sign it as well. Her signature is last, that of the witness, and she adds to it her sea turtle seal.

"All the traders have signed on now. I'm most grateful to you." I offer her my hand and the shake is strong, but her eyes are wary and veiled.

"They feel you can offer them a fair agreement," she says, and leaves any other thoughts on the matter unsaid.

"We will be contacting you soon," she says, then, in closing. I incline my head in answer before turning to the door. When I glance back, she has turned to face the sea.

The day following Kyra's arrival in Waters Rising she walked with Eson on the waterfront and soaked in the sea air, so different from the dryness of the Glass City. The lattice work of entanglements that had bound her were washed over in newness, and while she knew she couldn't simply run from all that was boiling up there, she felt submerged in a rush of relief to be away for a time.

The markets and docks that ran the main length of the waterfront were relatively dormant, given the current low tide. A massive swath of sand stood between the city waterfront and the distant edge of the water. The city was raised high above the sand bar on an artificial cliff that she understood had originally been a steep slope of sand and rock. The docks too were high above the sand, resting on reinforced metal supports that could withstand the barrage of the tide. Further out, where the water shimmered, there were islands, rocky and severely angled.

She'd gone out early in the day, borrowing a guidebook from Eson's shelves while he and Jado still slept. He'd met her later in the day, after she'd had time to explore some of the city. She briefly relived her initial time in the Glass City, and when she came to the sculptured fountain they'd agreed on in a square overlooking the water, she felt an echo of their first meeting on the monument. There was no dust this time, though, and this fountain coursed with abundant water, casting a cool cloud into the air, no errant roses straining in the clear basin. There were, however, flowers growing in profusion around the edges of buildings and walls, which were of stone, wood, or painted metal paneling. The humid air caused rust to form on the metal of some buildings, and the patterns reminded Kyra vaguely of the glass patterns to which she'd become accustomed. Here there was variety and botanical chaos, and the motion of air moving off the sea was constant.

A bright flash passed over Kyra, and she assumed it was the vision bird, then remembered she had left the bird in the Glass City, positioned so it could watch over the suite as if guarding it. The bright flash was a real bird, small and colorful, that landed on the edge of a wall and let out its echoing, natural cry.

She thought of Neriv, and then wished she had brought the vision bird so she could have made an orb of Waters Rising for her. She'd seen her before catching the train to the edge of the continent, and her friend had been both relieved that Kyra was going to a safe place and sad that she was going away.

As for the debtors and for Sarah, she felt a mixture of curiosity and fear. It was likely they would try to draw her back, and that Sarah would persist in trying to influence her. They couldn't break into Eson's suite and steal the contract, but if they were beginning to draw energy out of the dry fountains they would be unpredictable, and could try to reverse or undo Eson's power over them.

Of Eson and of his power, her doubt was mixed with her loyalty, and the two combined into a heady potion that wrapped around her when he appeared, as if casting a translucent film over them, powerfully binding her inward.

Upon seeing her he had embraced her and swung her off the ground a bit, further evidence of his carefree mien in Waters Rising. She pointed out the bird to him now. It was upside-down, gripping artfully a twisting branch and reaching its beak toward a cascade of flowers on a metal wall.

They stood knotted together by the clear fountain, watching crowds pass as they had done on the monument. The clear water was in sharp contrast to the dust that had surrounded them then. "Like the divining pool in that painting of Sarhul," she said. They'd spoken for a long time the night before, though Eson had been somewhat drunk. She had told him of the gallery, but omitted her meeting with Sarah. She'd spoken also of the club and of her discovery of the fountains, but had not yet mentioned the debtors. She was cautiously leading him toward truths, gauging his reactions to what she revealed. He hadn't been upset that she'd gone to the club, and was delighted that she'd seen the old-world paintings and fountain room in the gallery. They'd slept soundly in each other's arms in the highest room of the coast house.

He now spoke to her easily of the sacred water conduits. "Yes, this fountain is clear, like the springs that I still miss, and like the pools in the old world."

"I saw someone in the painting of the hunt scene that looked so much like you," she went on. They spoke quietly, leaning together on the edge of the fountain.

His voice was soft and a bit distant, unusual for him. "You saw the original Eson, then, hunting on the ancient landscape of the old world. They hunted to live, and held were-creatures at bay. They defended the people around them, and yet they were persecuted."

"And you still hunt, though in a more civilized way, with parchments and signatures—"

He became more alert, but still spoke gently, fox-like. "Do you find yourself in conflict about the people in those contracts? About yourself?" He spoke so fluidly that she was set completely at ease, and felt that perhaps he had even guessed already about her meeting with the debtors. "Look at Jado. He is named in my contract, but his life here in my orbit is fine. I'm helping him to create something that will change his entire life." He was soothing her, was only mildly defensive in his tone. "You had a chance to leave me, but you stayed, because this is what you want. Has that changed now because of them?"

She was certain now that he knew of her meeting with the debtors. Did he know then of Sarah, of how close she'd come to being swayed by her? The enchanter was reworking his spell, enveloping her more deeply. She felt a comfort and refuge, his protecting arm encircling her shoulders. Here with him, she didn't have to think about the others.

But she couldn't resign herself completely.

"They're interested in the fountains in the Glass City. Do you think there's a way to make those fountains work again, to appease the debtors and make them feel like they're free, without damaging your interests?"

He seemed to resign himself to her hopefulness, but clouded his acceptance with cynicism. "Go ahead and help them, but remember that your connection with me is stronger. You're safe with me. Do you think you would be safe if you were with them? Don't risk what we've made together, and remember that anything you offer to them really belongs to me." He fixed a deep look on her, his voice still gentle but his eyes dark and a bit sad.

How a fox can look sweet, if one ignores the trail of feathers leading to his den.

"I don't think they can reactivate the fountains, anyway. There isn't enough water under the bedrock anymore." He added this as if trying to dissuade her from the notion, yet he sounded too as if he wished the fountains could be made to flow. She knew he couldn't deny his instinctive fascination with water sources, given the history of his lineage.

She hadn't been seeking permission to interact with the debtors, but in a strange way, she now felt she had it. Though he didn't bless her actions, he didn't forbid them either, and she felt she had the strength to reconcile with the sense of conflict that she felt. Oddly, the knowledge that he was able to intuit her activities absolved her of a need to confess. If he knew she had visited the debtors, she was relieved of having to tell him. She left the issue of Sarah untouched.

She looked out beyond his shoulder to the landscape before them, and the sea expanded outward and the sky upward with her sense of safety and rightness. Surely there was a compromise somewhere in the balance between Eson and the debtors!

By tacit agreement, they closed off their heavy discussion and stood up to roam along the waterfront. The ocean was dazzling, and the echoing birdsong and breezes invited the wanderer to explore further in this maritime city. They bought flowers and seasoned fish and maps of the city, reveling in the fresh possibilities of pathways free of constraint. The fish was eaten on the sweetened leaves of a plant from the south coast, and followed with a refreshingly dry local tonic. They bought an extra piece wrapped up to take to Jado and enjoyed the peace of each other's presence, as they had come to expect that moments of ease were savored islands in a murky and uncharted sea.

By the time Kyra and Eson returned to the house on the hillside, Jado was drowsy and satisfied from having spent most of the day in intense concentration. He'd finished all but two of the batteries, and was looking forward to taking the next day more easily. He heard them come in, but it was several minutes before he put down his work and ventured out of his second-floor retreat. By then they'd disappeared up the staircase for an afternoon rest and Jado found the large room on the main floor empty, the late afternoon sun filtering in through the high windows. In the kitchen he found a note telling him of the fish that awaited him in the fridge, and asking if he could make a trip down the road to the exquisite, small deli that served the hillside neighborhood.

He set out, slowly readjusting to being outside in the real world after his intense work. The neighborhood appeared much different in the light of day, the houses solid and real and owned by other people, the gardens streaming with light, and he felt comforted and revitalized by the newness that surrounded him.

He returned to find Eson and Kyra relaxed in the main room, a wall panel open to the garden, and they helped him to set out the foods and drinks he'd bought at the deli. It was the first time the three of them had all been together, and he found his emotions conflicted.

When Eson had called and told him they'd be going to Waters Rising sooner than planned, he had despaired of ever seeing Kyra again. Now she was here, and completely inaccessible. It was a difficult thing to bear graciously.

He tried again to put it from his mind. She spoke freely with both of them, and seemed set at ease by Jado's presence. She seemed able to act as intermediary between himself and Eson, and despite his wounded emotions he was glad of her involvement with Eson for that. If she could be so close to Eson, too, it meant Eson was only human, less of a mystery—or had he put her under some kind of enchantment, too?

He kept his manner reserved and honorable, refusing to let in on his inner conflict.

After an indoor picnic around the low table, he and Eson listened to the recordings made by the listening device while Kyra took a phone call from the Glass City, disappearing into the garden. The mouse had recorded three conversations between the tidal power administrator and a guest who had visited his home office that afternoon. It had also recorded some discussions with his family, which they skipped over silently and then erased, feeling a shared guilt. Jado noted to himself that when the more unsavory aspects of their doings were brought forward, he and Eson became equals, both in the wrong.

The recorded conversations had an echoing, distant sound, as if they listened to a radio program from the past. They had to listen to it several times to catch the information they needed. The high tide would come in at an exact time in the morning in three days. Estimating how much power was to be gathered, they fine-tuned the settings on Jado's battery collectors.

There was something intriguing in listening to the low-voiced conversation about the sea and its science, the calm turn of the tides on central nodes in the sea, the elegant simplicity of the movement of water. The voices themselves sounded elemental and oceanic emanating from the small silver speaker.

They eventually switched it off, and looked up at each other as if to seal an agreement. After a moment, Jado said, "I'd like to bring the listening device back, now that it's finished in that house."

Eson nodded. "Of course. Only be very careful. Can you do it without any wall-jumping this time?"

"Yes, it can burrow under the garden wall to get out. It was too risky to send it in that way."

Eson nodded, and while they sat thinking about the logistics of what they would do Kyra returned from the garden, giving them each a pleasant but preoccupied smile before settling next to Eson on the low seat.

Her face was serious as she said, mainly to Eson, "I have to go back to the Glass City. A friend of mine needs me to be there."

"But you've only just arrived! Do you really have to go?"

"It's important. I'd like to stay here, but I'm needed by Neriv."

Jado felt he was hearing things that were not his business, so he stood and went into the kitchen to refill his glass. The light filtered coolly into the window through trees that framed the side of the house, and he thought of the ocean, and of the islands where the majority of the Niyali still lived, and of the shift in tide that could take him there if he had a boat. The drink in his glass was a cool sea in itself, and he shook the glass lightly, creating a minute, quick tide from one side of the glass to the other. He leaned to the window and looked out before returning to the living room.

Kyra and Eson were sitting a bit apart, but appeared to have resolved things. Eson was saying, "If you must leave so soon, then we should enjoy this evening." He looked up as Jado entered the room and courteously invited him back into the conversation. "Jado, do you have some music that would suit a celebration of us all being together and of your success with the batteries?"

Jado nodded and went to forage through his music collection, returning with a set of Niyali love songs that spoke of night beaches, of fires burning on distant islands and lovers separated by the sea. The words were in his language but the music was universal, and he told Eson and Kyra the meaning of each song. The two danced together, inventing their own slow steps, while Jado closed his eyes and mouthed the words to the ballads. The evening deepened, and they lit tall candles that framed the center of the room and the garden, where they took in the cool night air. They fell into telling stories and mixing drinks until long into the night.

The first sound to awaken the sleeping house the next morning was that of the gate chime. The only one who heard it was Kyra, and she moved down to the front door, trying to rush but still slow-moving with sleep. She answered the intercom, and a sharp voice said, "Courier," followed by an electric buzz. She opened the gate and then the front door, walking barefoot into the bright morning. A delivery woman hidden under an industry cap was pushing a large box on wheels with difficulty up the gravel path.

She wondered at the size of the package, and ran to intercept it. Together they maneuvered the box into the house, and she signed for it. When the courier had left she loosened the lid, and couldn't resist smiling at what she found. Inside was a canine counterpart to the vision bird, a sleek metal dog that could pass for an artpiece, or at a glance, for a real creature, perhaps a greyhound.

She began to prepare a small breakfast, thinking ahead to what she would do that day, since she'd found she could return to the Glass City no earlier than the next day due to the train schedule. Eson and Jado had planned to go to the shore as soon as Jado was completed the batteries, which he could easily do that morning—so they'd likely go to the shore that afternoon, and she could go with them. The day spent out in the open air would give her time to plan what she would need to do when she returned to the Glass City.

Jado set his bare feet on the cool sand, dampened from beneath by water. Kyra and Eson were descending the stone stairs behind him, also barefoot, and the dog trotted beside them. They seemed ordinary people among the others scattered across the tidal shelf beside the large wall that kept the city safe from the sea. The dark sheen of the sand reflected a luminous glow, and other people appeared giants on the horizon, which was closer than it seemed on the immense flatness of the sand. There were no convoluted pathways or constraints written into this natural flood plain.

"Very powerful, these places that are part of both the land and the sea!" remarked Eson. Kyra ran skipping away on the sand and threw a branch for the metal dog. The sea air floated them into a state of excitement, though each had been weighed down by their own concerns before descending to the sand. Eson had been a bit out of sorts that morning, which was understandable, considering Kyra would leave them again soon. He and Kyra had spoken for a long time in low voices while Jado finished the last of the batteries and set the final details on the set of ten. There was something else going on between them, too, that Jado couldn't surmise.

But now, crouching on the sand, Eson coded some instructions into the dog using a pocket-sized control disc. "Good dog," he murmured, clearly in admiration of the incredible work of technology he'd managed to acquire. Jado was surprised to see him register affection for an animal, especially an inorganic one.

Eson stood up and pointed outward over the sand. "It will run over there to the generator you can see, and to the others beyond it. It won't take long. We can go for a walk while we wait for it." The dog would carry the small batteries cleverly on its back, and could dispatch them onto the generators on its own. It would make two trips out along the tidal flats, to generators in a line along the shoreline.

"I'm going to run with it for a while," said Kyra, suddenly looking eager to enjoy the freedom of the shore.

"We'll see you back here, then. Jado, we should go and see that structure over there near the city wall. It's the breakwater the batteries need to be activated from."

Kyra and the dog ran in one direction, and Jado and Eson walked in the other. The temporary imprints left by their feet were added to the collage of the many footprints that crisscrossed the tidal plain.

"This will be completely submerged in water within minutes of the tidal flow," said Eson when they arrived, gesturing to the breakwater that stood as a monolithic rampart in the sand. "The activation element needs to be in contact with water almost immediately in order to send the energy wave out to the batteries that will start them up." The activator was the one aspect of the technology that Eson knew more about than Jado. It was a small stone module that had arrived in a package several days earlier, rushed from somewhere far away. "It fits seamlessly into the iconography on the side of the breakwater, here." They were standing right next to the rock structure, and in its etched surface, Jado saw an indentation similar in size to the stone module Eson held. "One of the sea traders we met had the skill to modify the iconography just enough to allow the module to fit. Next to it here, you can see a carving of a sea turtle. If you push on this, a passage will open in this stone, and you can make your way back through to the city waterfront, surfacing in the boat-makers' yards. But of course you won't need to do that—Gerson or Carstell will be the one to place the module here. You can watch from above, in no danger of the incoming water."

Suddenly Eson was speaking of these events as though he wouldn't be here himself. Jado held his tongue, for the moment.

They walked up the stone staircase that led to a platform above, and he saw that the breakwater was connected to a walkway leading back to the city. This was the high tide method of access to the breakwater. The breakwater itself continued solidly as a support for the walkway, and he could easily imagine the other passageway leading through to the city from below.

"Yes, I'll be happy to watch from up here," he said, imagining the water flooding in and covering the sand below them. "And where will you be?" he asked, finally.

Eson answered with hesitation. "I haven't told you or Kyra yet, but I'm planning to return with her to the Glass City tomorrow. I only decided this properly as we were walking now across the sand. There's really nothing I need to do here. All you have to do is watch what goes on when the tide comes in, and make sure nothing goes wrong. Gerson and Carstell will take care of everything else."

Jado felt doubtful, but didn't question him. It was natural that Eson would want to go with Kyra, but in a way it was surprising, and irresponsible, that he would leave the coast before events were finished here.

Eson spoke as if in answer to his thoughts. "I know it's strange, but there are many things compelling me to go back, and I only just felt the full force of them this morning when I woke. We're having good times here, but I'm neglecting my interests in the interior, and I'm simply too far away from my springs in the mountains. I feel cut free here, and at first, that was wonderful, but always there's a counterbalance. To be carefree and away from the past is good, but only for a while. When Kyra told me she needed to go back to the Glass City, I realized how much I'm tied to that place and even more so to the mountains in the north. The places that bind to you will only let you escape them for so long, and then the floor of meaning is swept from beneath you. You're empty if you don't return to the places that are part of you."

There was really no way for him to respond to this spontaneous confidence, so he only nodded and looked seaward, focusing on an island in the distance that looked ready to topple into the sea. He felt the places he'd spent his life as part of him—Five Gardens Meet Above a Square, Glass in the Pattern of a Celestial Calendar, Vines Creep Along a Wall, dozens more—and he felt them beckoning to him now.

Lowering his eyes onto the nearby sand, he saw the small figure of Kyra, walking now instead of running and without the dog. Kyra and Eson would both leave, then, and he would be alone in this city.

As soon as the tide had come in, he decided, he would return home to see his family for a time. After that, he wondered, could he travel across the sea? He wanted at least to explore the islands that floated so sublimely in the ocean before him. Looking toward the city, he could see great colorful sails raised above a boatyard, where ships and sails under repair were marooned during the low tide. He and Eson walked back down to the sand, met Kyra, and settled onto a patch of rocks to await the dog's return.

Everything is set. We've brought the dog back, and its record of actions show each battery was placed as it should be. I'm confident that Jado can see things through on the crucial day, and my own absence shouldn't matter at all in the end run. The traders are secured into my deeds, and the power they consume will be small compared to that which I will gain from their bond to me. The siphoning of the power is a necessary game for me, variety, a new way to expand my holdings and enhance my circle of control in the world. I'm beginning to doubt the true worth of these games, though, and feel that I've overstepped my bounds this time. The springs are unhappy with my distance from them, and are asking me to focus my efforts inward, so I must go back to the more familiar territory of the Glass City. Though it is physically more restricting in that city, I think my spirit will benefit from being closer to the springs, on ground I've already covered. There will be difficult people to negotiate with, but I will at least feel grounded in my past.

Kyra and Jado were both surprised when I told them of my decision, though Kyra's reaction was of course more positive than Jado's. He'll be all right, though, and will see that he can do things for himself without trouble. Gerson and Carstell will look after the difficult part of the action. And besides, I will leave him with enough money that he can outright buy the solar generator he has been wanting.

Kyra, on the other hand, was relieved I would go back with her. I think there is some entanglement with the debtors, and with her friend from the nightclub, that she is not ready to tell me about. How odd it is that we are now fleeing back to the place that we thought of as a cage.

That evening in the spacious, cool house, Kyra found a chance to speak to Jado about the debtors, and was surprised to find how little he knew of them. She noted he was reluctant to talk about them, as if mentally distancing himself from their circle, and he looked a bit mystified that she was asking him about them. He knew little about what they were capable of doing, or what they would do, if anything. "Sarah and I both stay away from them," he only said.

Though he clearly knew his relationship with Eson was different from the others in the contract, Jado wasn't drawn to them the way she was. He just followed his own pathways. She let the matter fade, and they spoke about music, and about the coast and the alluring people who streamed along the walkways of the cool waterfront, solitary or in packs. When she asked him if he had met anyone in Waters Rising, he just smiled and shook his head, closing his eyes as he did so.

His silence made her think, for a moment, about the conversations they'd had in the tea shop—that he may have thought of her more seriously than she'd realized. He was both an ally and a friend, and she was glad to see him in Waters Rising, but could only guess at what emotions were hidden behind his youthful and reticent face.

The train ride will take us through beautiful country, and to travel into the interior together will set things right with us, I feel. Clouds stream over us, moving in the opposite direction over the green wilderness. Our train car is much sleeker and smoother than the ones that lead to the north and the local trains that ours passes by. They appear to stand still in comparison to our capsule of swift movement. I feel I'm never standing still. I'd enjoyed the sensation until, only in the last couple of days, a sudden sense of dislocation overtook me. I'd been outrunning it, but it has finally caught up to me, and I must answer to it.

It was hard to turn away from the coast, but there was little other choice. Communication links with the north are tenuous there, and while the tidal power plan will be profitable, I'm beginning to see a kind of pointlessness in that kind of worldly profit. I've been endlessly striving outward while ignoring the things that really support us: in my case, proximity to the springs. I only hope that returning to the Glass City will quench the restlessness building in me. While I wish I could be very near the springs, returning across the northern border would be political death for me. Kyra enjoyed the coast, and had spoken of returning there after she aids her friend in the Glass City. But that was before she knew I'd be coming back with her.

I've left Jado the promised sum, and have kept an indefinite lease on the coast house. Any one of us can return there when we want to.

The cool, smooth air of this modern train has lulled Kyra to sleep. The people around us are of all kinds, very few of them northerners, however. There are only a few of us who stray outward over the borders as far as the Glass City, and fewer still who venture further out to the coasts or the southern territories.

The other night I dreamt of the hunting party Kyra mentioned from her trip to the art gallery. I was in riding in place of the youth that resembled me, and the party rode under our family banner. My horse and I somehow strayed from the party and became lost in the twisting dark fields of bramble, and were soon boxed into a narrow canyon under the shadowed sky. Terrible creatures lined the hills above us, but the horse and I had drunk from the divining pools and were kept safe, the creatures of the hills guarding us against all ill instead of devouring us.

I'd woken from the dream feeling ill at ease, conscious of the vast miles separating me from my springs. I was relieved when I came downstairs to find the robot dog I'd ordered from the old world had arrived and was standing in the living room! It was a beautiful machine, cut from the same mythical block as the vision bird, and in good working order. Jado was already at work completing the batteries, and we could place them on the generators that day.

This morning, I decided to leave the dog with Jado, asking him to return it to me in the Glass City when he comes home, and wishing him luck with the next few days. For much of this time, all he has to do is wait. He might even enjoy being alone in a foreign city without anyone to tell him what he should and shouldn't do.

As to what Kyra will do in the Glass City, or what I will do, we will determine when we arrive there in a few hours. I've ordered another drink from the attendant who passes by our seats every few minutes. We've passed two borders on this trip, but no one has asked for our identification. The countries here are fused together while the Steam Territories are disjointed, at odd angles to the rest of the continent.

I soon nod off to sleep myself, thinking of the colorful blossoms we'd left on the table in the main room and the lush garden beside the house, where we'd lit the candles at night. Over the garden wall, the neighbor's bees lived in squat towers, skyscrapers in a hive city, where the odd honey we'd come to enjoy was their currency, food and fuel. Much more efficient than our lives, perhaps.

While Kyra was strengthened and elated by Eson's decision to return with her, she was unnerved by his being in the Glass City, in proximity to the people he was linked to by the deed. Neriv had told her the debtors were trying to activate the fountains under the cover of night. They hadn't succeeded yet, but Charis had told Neriv the debtors had felt a power building when they'd each stood by one of the fountains at night, having acquired a stone module that fit into one of the niches. Having heard of this, Kyra was little surprised when Eson began to seem weighed down and distressed. If the debtors were mining power from the ground beneath them, then Eson would conversely be losing power. They really *were* drawing their energy from him, as he'd been doing to them since they'd fallen under his influence.

His elation and excitement over the tidal power plan and the new debtors he'd acquired through the coastal contracts seemed to evaporate into restlessness. He now expressed a satisfaction and solace in speaking of the springs, as though he hungered for them and could be recharged by them.

She now knew what Sarah had told her was at least partially the truth, and a fierce need grew within her to protect Eson. She could insulate herself and Eson from the debtors by intercepting them, remolding their ideas, and binding them to herself. She would be the breakwater that protected him from them. He was powerful, but the debtors were his blind spot, and she would be the barrier needed to make him impermeable to their menace.

Charis had spoken to Neriv, had confided in her and warned her. Charis was the vital link with whom she must fuse in order to forge a connection with the group. Kyra nearly swooned with gratefulness to Neriv, the guardian and watchkeeper who had protected her from the debtors, who had summoned her back to the city. Neriv had a directness and genuine charisma that drew people to her, a beacon on dark seas. It was natrual that Charis, with her thin look of spiritual hunger, had confided in her.

Eson seemed to her relaxed on the trip, though lost in his own thoughts. "You understand why I have to go back, don't you?" he asked. "The springs decide what's right for me. I can't deny their authority."

"Of course. I've been to the springs. I know."

Still, he looked at her doubtfully, as though she could not really understand. She changed the subject to her own reasons for returning to the interior. "A friend of mine has spoken to one of the debtor's circle. She thinks I should try talking to some of them again."

"You needn't worry much about them—but be careful."

He was reluctant, in the end, to accept that they might have any power over him, and dismissed her worries that they were sapping his power. By doing so he gave her an ambiguous blessing; he took an oddly remote stance on the issue, almost as though delegating it to her. He even seemed distanced from the endeavors he'd been working on in Waters Rising, the batteries, the clandestine spying and deed-signing. She'd met none of the traders with whom he'd set up deeds, and imagined hardened seafarers, salt-worn, with vigilante codes of conduct.

Surprisingly, she felt little oppressiveness in the Glass City when they arrived, and was enchanted again by its antique, sepia-washed character after the modernity of Waters Rising. While the air on the coast had been tinged with moisture, the air here was dry and slightly hazy at any distance. The glass tiles reminded her of the ocean's water. Here, stones surrounded glass oceans while on the coast the ocean surrounded stone islands.

Entering the warm, small suite, where tinted light poured in, Eson sighed in relief, but quietly, as if only to himself. She sensed that his emotion was his alone, and not meant to be shared with her. With the walls of the apartment wrapped around them, he whispered to her his gratitude for her understanding. "You're a refuge for me, like the waterfalls that provide for the springs." He stroked her arm, lying next to her.

She felt her love like an underground cascade and had the sudden sensation they were falling over the precipice of it together, floating in the cataclysmic waters. They blended together and their concerns fell away, washed out into a labyrinth of subterranean caves.

Neriv met Kyra the next day on the monument, under the strangely burnished light of a cool, dry day. They met in the smaller, upper arches of the structure where the stonework was more delicate, but still insulated visitors from the winds and open sky of the hilltop. A group of architecture students were sketch-

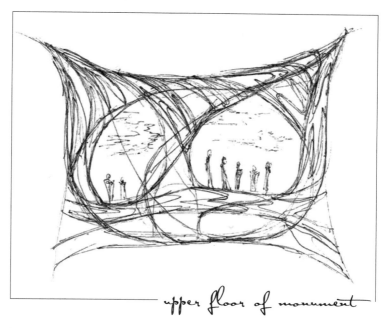

upper floor of monument

ing earnestly, occupying many of the seats around the monument, so the two walked most of the way around the structure before finding a stone alcove to lean in. She told Neriv of the rough beauty of the coast, the exotic house, the immensity of the tidal plain. Neriv was envious, and they made plans to travel there together, though in a future that was too uncertain to plan. Neriv's face was animated, her hair glowing in the copper light of the stone monument. She looked out with satisfaction over the city before becoming more serious.

"Charis is very eager to speak to you again, and a couple of the others have also asked about you."

Kyra nodded. "Loken and Illusia, I would guess. They and Charis are the most amenable of that troop." She couldn't keep a note of sarcasm from her voice, and Neriv reciprocated with a knowing look. "They're all bound to Eson, and could damage him if they're left on their own. If the fountains are to flow again, it will be under my seal and signature." From her shoulder bag, she brought out the small satchel that held the parchment and ink Eson had given her. "I may use this for the first time."

Neriv knew of the contracts Eson possessed, but couldn't seem to hide her alarm. "You always were a mysterious girl," she said. "I shouldn't be surprised you'd have tricks for dealing with the rough knocks of the world. But it seems archaic, feudal, even! Do you want these people to be your vassals?"

"No!" Kyra gasped. "I only want to do what's fair for as many people as possible. The deeds that I would make up would be... equitable." She paused. "You're looking at me as though I were a monster."

"Just give me a moment to take this in. I believe you, but I can't reconcile with what you're involved in. What is Eson, a kind of vampire?"

Kyra sighed. "No. He's just the end product of many generations. They used to gather a type of energy from deep-water sources within the earth. There are other families like his and they live around the springs in the mountains. He's mortal like the rest of us." She shrugged—but as she said it, there was uncertainty. The inscription in the alcove above the springs, the paintings of the divining pools, the servant, Sarah... "They believe they're blessed by a goddess of the old world, who protects them."

Neriv shrugged, half dismissing, half accepting. Kyra was relieved when her friend touched her arm reassuringly, with a look that said she was passing no judgment on Kyra. The bond of friendship was strong.

"At any rate, Charis told me where she works. We can go see her today if you'd like," Neriv said, quite casually, moving away from their more heated discussion.

Kyra smiled, relieved. "That would be wonderful, but we may

have to take a special route to get there. Can you find the place on this map?" she asked, bringing out the worn map Eson used. The days spent on the coast had been just enough to relieve her sense of being trapped in the Glass City, and the inscribed pathways no longer felt like rat's tunnels now that she knew the city could be escaped from, could grow smaller in the window of a train car.

The stone pavilion arched over them and captured their voices along with those of the architects as they walked back around the soft contoured walkway of the monument. The generator Kyra had seen when she ran with the robot dog was a similar, elegant stone structure, resembling almost a statuesque elephant standing on pillar legs in the sand. Having been in both cities, she could now notice the subtle similarities in design and atmosphere. Of the north and what she had seen there, she still couldn't reflect with comfort. There was something too foreign about the place.

They took a fairly direct route down through the city into the semi-industrial areas she had noticed on her first walk to the monument, during the dust storm. They came to a light warehouse that was also a storefront with metal-framed lamps, lanterns and windows stacked and arcing toward the ceiling. Stepping inside, they saw a workshop that opened into a fenced yard where people were working at welding, carrying and designing new lanterns and windows. She could see Charis and also Hesek, both working on a large metal frame in the yard. They both had lean, strong arms, marking brother and sister with a clear family resemblance. Neriv asked for Charis and they waited for a few minutes, walking between the rows of colored glass windows and lanterns, which were incredible in variety and in size. Some were designed as beacons for use in the desert or on the plains, others to light buildings and courtyards, others as decorations. The City of Glass was infatuated with color and light, and the cavernous warehouse was a treasure cache!

It was while walking among these rows of light that Kyra wove together the nebulous strands of an idea.

When Charis saw her and Neriv, she gravitated toward them. Kyra led the two out into the nearby courtyard to talk, Neriv walking closely behind her and Charis trailing slightly behind them. Charis sat lightly on the side of a short wall and spoke quickly, dark eyes flashing, with the slight accent of the plains. "They're going to make the fountains run again! But I don't think the others know what they're doing, and the whole thing could be a waste, ruining us and also harming you and him. You must do something."

Kyra spoke calmly. "You need me in order to make the fountains run. You know this, but the others don't believe it. You must help me to convince them." She waited until Charis tilted her head in acceptance, signaling her to continue, and used the soothing tone Eson had so recently employed with her. "Your group has a stone module that can make the fountains work, but this can only be done with the aid of a precise energy field only Eson or I can bring. If you want my help, we'll make a deed with all of your names in it, and mine as well. Your group will have most of the power and money that will come of the fountains, though you will not have any power over Eson, or over me. The others must forego any notions they have of doing harm to us." She paused again, this time while Charis looked away across the courtyard. Hesek was slouched in the doorway of the storefront, watching them.

She spoke quietly again, as if stating a simple truth to Charis. "If you accept my terms, the underground rivers that have sapped your energies will become the conduits for your success."

Charis listened, visibly musing. Neriv watched both of them calmly, ready to intervene, but waiting now.

At last Charis said, "I've always known we would need the help of an intermediary. I'll talk to the others, but you must help me with this. You must do this quickly. Some of them are impatient. Nobody has seen Jado or Sarah for some time, either. There's a lot of confusion in our lives, and when someone disappears, we don't know what has happened to them, or when they will come back."

Charis was playing on her sympathies, embellishing on the sense of threat Eson posed to their lives. Yet, she could appreciate the chaotic and haunted desperation of the deed-bound, and so spoke to Charis with sympathy. "You may not know this, but Jado has already been working closely with Eson and me on something else for the last while. I can contact him easily."

Charis furrowed her brow, clearly perplexed that Jado could be working with them on something, most likely at a loss imagining what the work could be—and Kyra became aware too late that the group might see Jado as a traitor for his collaboration. She hoped, with some alarm, that she had at least established Charis' trust with her honesty.

Before she could smooth it over, Charis spoke again. "Come with me tomorrow and speak with Loken and Illusi. They've been waiting for you, though Mersad and Carda have been putting the heat on them to make another shot at the fountains." She spoke casually and more slowly now, gesturing toward the doorway where Hesek still stood. "My brother and his girlfriend will likely come around. Then maybe the five of us can convince Mersad, Carda and Stas."

Charis had to return to her work, then, and asked them to meet her the next day in a crowded square below the monument. Kyra and Neriv agreed and made their way back to the center of town, where they separated, deciding to meet in a café before seeing the others.

Kyra walked home, glad that she had regained some of her accustomed anonymity. The conspicuousness that had come about with her return from the north had faded as she learned to focus her energies. She was becoming more like Eson, able to blend in or make her presence felt as she chose. The resonance she'd been able to pick up from other people was still with her, but had not become any clearer or more intense. She had been aware of Charis's inner motives, but not the details of her thoughts. She'd used Eson's techniques in persuading Charis but didn't feel she had been deceptive. Perhaps Eson never was, either. Perhaps Eson only used his power to convince people of what he saw as the truth.

She would tell Eson what had transpired that day. He had, after all, confided in her about his reasons for returning to the city. He hadn't been upset with her so far, so she felt more comfortable now in speaking with him. He'd come to treat her almost as an equal, trusting her judgments and actions even when not enamored with them. Still, she couldn't believe he would really loosen his basic bond of control over her. Part of her knew he was only allowing her to act freely, but would never allow her to be free.

When she arrived at the suite he was absorbed in one of the books he kept, which was written in a dead language and related to matters of the old world. Like the other, there were a few pictures that had given her a sense of the history and people, but beyond that she could read none of the language. Eson had said much of it defied translation.

As she came into the room he put the book aside and turned to her. "You've returned. And what did the day offer you?" There was no guile in his voice, only kindness.

"I met with some friends, actually. Neriv and I met in one of the upper courtyards. We spoke to someone else as well, one of the debtors named in your deed."

"Which one?" he asked calmly.

"Charis. She contacted Neriv and insisted I talk with her. She says the others are fomenting trouble and losing patience. They'll try to take your power if we—or if I don't cooperate with them.

Don't you feel your powers being drained? That must have played a part in your decision to return here."

"That's so, I admit. When you're bolstered by others, they of course have a certain impact on your life, a reciprocal force, though a limited one to be sure. It's what one must accept."

She answered in a compassionate tone. "They've already weakened you, if you really accept that. You've let the coastal plans slip away entirely." *And Jado and I both rely on you,* she nearly added.

"I've come to a new way of thinking about those plans. Really, there is more strength to be found if I don't stray too far from the springs right now."

"I should tell you, then, that I've agreed to meet Charis tomorrow, with Neriv and Loken and Illusi. I'm going to put the parchments and ink you gave me to some use by making my own deed and asking them to sign it."

None of this seemed to disturb him, and his reaction was almost detached. "I'm glad you'll be able to use those gifts. They're very old." He paused. "But I wouldn't expect much from that group. Really, it doesn't matter that much what you do, just don't put yourself in danger."

"I'm trying to do what I can to make sure nobody hurts either of us," she protested.

"That's true. But don't try to force the universe to comply with you. You can't make things work out for everyone, and it's not wise to sacrifice your own interests. But I can't involve myself too much. I've been neglecting my studies of history and religion with all these schemes I've been setting up. It's easy to get caught up with external ephemera."

She found it strange to hear him nearly renouncing ideals he'd so recently been impassioned about. "Don't you care about striving outward anymore?" she asked him.

"Not striving outward, but upward," he said, before picking

up his book again.

"You're becoming an ascetic, like the roses in the fountains here," she said. He only smiled at her distractedly.

He put his book down before long, though, and they spent the evening together. He held her for long periods of time, but always as if trying to reassure her. They spoke, but he had a detached and preoccupied air. They walked outside together, but he was watchful, and they soon went in again.

"Will you go to Waters Rising again?" she asked him.

"No, not for a while. You can go if you like. You had so little time to see anything. It's a wonderful place for the free."

She didn't ask him what he meant, only pointed out the shooting star that she'd just seen through the glass in the garden room. They watched the meteor shower for a while, sitting close with the glass around them.

Jado woke from a late afternoon nap on his first full day alone in Waters Rising. Kyra and Eson had left the day before, and the house and garden, the entire city had grown larger around him in their absence. He'd gone for a long walk on the harbor front that day, and climbed up a small lookout hill that cropped up in the city. He watched the people, who seemed more loose and relaxed than most in the Glass City, their clothing casual, modern and high-end. He'd delved into a massive shopping center, rippling with echoing sounds, and had been unable to resist spending a fraction of the money Eson had left on some new music recordings. Young women looked at him frequently and more openly than they ever did in the Glass City, and for the first time, he was conscious of his Niyali looks being exotic... even attractive.

Tomorrow he would go to a solar panel outlet and price out a model. He would perhaps also go to the beach again with the dog, as it would be the last day of the beach's existence for another couple of weeks. The day after that would be the day the tide would come in, and he would watch it happen from only a few feet above.

That night he planned to make a journey out to retrieve the listening mouse. It had tunneled its way out of the house at his instruction, and was now digging underneath the garden wall into the narrow alley, where he would be able to find it easily. He would possibly go out and look for a party after that if he felt unable to come home and relax, which was likely. He now felt he was on vacation on the coast, and had rarely felt more free, though his desire to see his family and friends was still strong.

He stretched and stepped out of his small room into the bright outer area of the second floor, realizing he could now sleep in Eson's upstairs room if he chose to.

For now, he stepped down onto the first floor and prepared a light dinner, heading out into the garden to enjoy the evening.

He saw the neighbor attending to her bee towers in the next yard and waved a hello. She was standing on a small ladder near the fence, braving the bees that hovered around her.

"How do you do that?" called Jado, his skin smarting at the very thought of having so many bees around.

"We all use a vaccine that prevents us from being stung. Otherwise it would be impossible." She smiled brightly as bees covered her arm. "I've seen you building some machines," she called, then. "Why don't you come down to the university one day? We need technicians."

"Sorry, I can't stand school." He held up his drink and smiled.

"You wouldn't have to study. You could just help out with the technical workings and be paid to do so. Come down anytime if you change your mind." She disappeared, and then the ladder did as well. Jado took another sip of his drink, shuddering at the buzzing bees over the fence.

246

Much later that night he was standing in the street outside the tidal administrator's house, combing the alley for the listening mouse. He had to move some boxes to get to it, and made a sound in doing so. He picked up the mouse and walked quickly away, aware that someone had opened the back gate of the yard and seen him moving away down the alley before curving out of sight. He felt suddenly very alone.

He stepped into a pub several blocks away to ease himself back into feeling like an ordinary person, and to ease his mind and conscience. Whether it was an unnoticeable amount or not, they were still stealing power from the country's electricity supplies. Though they likely could not even be traced, he felt a bit uneasy being in a foreign state and conducting something that wasn't legal.

He couldn't tell his family about the details of his work on the coast. These thoughts only occurred to him at night, when he felt most alone here. During the day, the vigor and excitement of the coast city carried him along, insulating him from any feeling of doubt.

The vision bird floated over the night city, its wings a near-silent sound of pulsing. Kyra was sitting up awake, curled in the corner of a wide chair in the sitting room. Eson had gone to sleep some time earlier, and she'd slipped away, anxious to know if anything would take place around the fountains that night. The bird had already sailed past the fountain nearest Eson's apartment, finding nothing near it, and it was approaching the next fountain over the top of the patchwork of roofs and walkways. She was jolted by memory when the bird passed over the same ghostly-lit courtyard she'd been escorted through by the Heiress's agent long ago. The entire city was lit with a spectral glow, the lightest of the stones chalky, the glass patterns forming liquid, obsidian lakes and rivers in the stone. The bird's flight was as smooth as the paths of the meteors she had seen earlier in the evening.

The bird came up on the vicinity of the next courtyard, and she inhaled sharply, seeing several figures approaching the area, one clutching something close to his chest. She waited, keeping the bird perched silently on the edge of a house.

She looked up when a light suddenly came on near her in the suite. Eson walked toward her, curious that she would be awake. "What's happening?" he asked softly. She motioned him to come over, and passed him the orb. On it, the group was disappearing into a portico leading to the courtyard. He took the scene in with little distress. "They don't know what they're doing," he said, and gave the orb back.

Several long moments later, a glow flared from the vicinity of the courtyard, then extinguished completely, taking with it the light that emanated from the windows and lanterns in the nearby streets. She directed the vision bird's eyes up, and could see the electric power had been shorted out for blocks around the fountain.

Several figures reappeared, taking flight into the shadowed streets.

"They don't know what they're doing," reiterated Eson in a slightly pitying tone of voice. "Are you really going to meet with these people? Do you think there's any hope that can be gleaned from them?" His voice was now a bit mocking.

"I'm only going to meet with the reasonable ones. I'll find out what is possible and work from there." She spoke in a low voice, without pretension, diffusing his arch tone instead of competing with it. She felt freshly aware of the divide between them, aware that his privileged upbringing was an inescapable aspect of his being.

"Give up on them if you want to be part of what I am," he said, and she could hear the cold threads of old-world hierarchies in his words, though his voice was now genuine and bare of irony. He placed his forehead against hers gently and they stayed close together quietly, until she kissed him. They sank into each other as they had done when immersed together in the springs, surrounded by rocks and vapor. The dry air of the city was cool around them, and they found warmth in each other.

The vision bird sailed home, its dark eyes reflecting all that it saw as it crossed back over the city.

The two friends met on a cantilevered platform that jutted out over a lower courtyard, beneath the stern facing of a stone mural. They were below the hill on which the monument stood, and were at that time of day in its shadow.

From a café terrace across the court, a waiter beginning his midday shift saw two young women, one small with dark hair and carrying with her a sleek, patterned case, from which she brought out an archaic sheet of parchment. The red-blond woman shook her head and reading over it, appeared to question her companion before the two began walking slowly back along the platform, disappearing up a staircase into a more crowded courtyard above. The waiter turned back to his tables, wondering vaguely what secrets and details governed the actions of other people.

Kyra and Neriv circled the courtyard, which was swarming with people in the late morning warmth. They could see Charis leaning against a wall some distance away, like a graffiti artist's tag. Kyra held close to her a silvery, thin case containing the deed she'd written that morning. Eson had left the suite before she woke, and she'd composed the deed alone, looking over some of his contracts and borrowing the deeply permanent and oath-like language he used in the deeds.

They approached Charis, who stood up and loosely swung her hands together, looking relieved but edgy. There was a similarity in her movements to those of Loken, a sharp and nervous energy. There was likely a deeper involvement between the two of them.

Charis fixed them with a cool, solid smile and said, "The others couldn't make it here just now. They'd like it if we could meet them at the glass tower as soon as we can."

Kyra exchanged a look with Neriv. The glass structure was nearby, but was more difficult for anyone to access than this court, being at the top of a hill. Was Charis hiding something?

"They thought it would be a more peaceful place to have our discussion. Fewer people around to overhear... " Charis trailed off, as though the implications of this should be obvious.

Kyra answered in a low-key voice, "They're fond of secrecy, aren't they? Last night's gathering, for example. Nobody was to know about that, I assume?" She waited for Charis to answer. Neriv tensed her brow, taken aback slightly at Kyra's ensnaring tactic, but clearly judging it fair given Charis' deception. Kyra had filled her in about the events she and Eson had witnessed the previous night. "A fools' parade," Eson had called it.

Charis remained cool, but was still caught off-guard, looking warily at Kyra. "I tried to stop them," she said calmly.

"I'm sure you did," said Kyra in an understanding tone, "but you didn't want to argue too harshly with Loken." She was aware now of having the effect on Charis that Eson often had on her, when he seemed to know things through hidden means. He guided people along paths he'd made ready for them, delighting in the control he could have over the bemused follower. He was a fox running down trails in the tall grass, eluding hound and hare alike. She, his fox-wife, had learned from him well.

Charis seemed to give in to her soothing, knowing demeanor, to seek acceptance from her as so many did with Eson, though those same people found him disquieting and unfathomable. She spoke with obviously mixed emotions, succoring but also keeping a reserve, as one who holds reserve toward a magician while still marveling at the trick. "Loken will help us, I'm sure of it. Some of the others are already angry with me, so I was caught between a stone and a river's current. I couldn't keep out of their actions without fracturing myself from them dangerously. Loken and Illusi feel the same way, though they are accommodating and more easily swayed by the others."

Kyra listened, believing her words but still not fully trusting. "We'll come with you to the glass works, but no one must harm us," she said. "If something happens to me, Eson will be angry, and he will know who's responsible."

Charis looked chilled, and glanced over her shoulder, but agreed. She gestured to Kyra's case. "The deed you spoke about?"

The glass structure was as otherworldly and celestial as Kyra had remembered it. As they walked through and up, they could hear the voices of the old city reverberating through the meteorite glass corridors. Certain old echoes had been set onto airwaves that still hadn't died out, repeating eternally as a mantra. In outer passages they could see out over the city from an amazingly high vantage point, everything set into sharper angles, even the plains appearing steep. They walked silently, as if afraid to utter a sound in a place where any word could be made permanent. Charis led them to where Loken and Illusi waited in an upper gallery of the structure. There were other visitors, but far fewer people than had been visible in the courtyard.

In moving upward through the glass works, Kyra became

conscious of being distanced from the pulsing power of the planet, of interfacing with a different energy, that of comets and meteorites fired into glass. She wondered absently if she could pull energy from space above that was not claimed yet by Eson and his clan, hers to take hold of and shape.

Loken and Illusi were standing like errant shards in the sharp line of a high-framed doorway in the glass, their blade-like hair seeming to integrate them with their surroundings. Charis and Loken greeted each other with a subdued affection, he tracing his hand lightly along her tattooed arm. "She knows about last night," said Charis, at which Loken and Illusi broke into giddy, half-sly laughter.

Illusi said to Kyra, "You can see through walls, no?"

Kyra smiled with a devil-may-care shrug. "It's no secret when the circuit blows on half the city."

"The blackout was limited to a ten-block radius around the fountain. Only a few scores of homes lost power," said Loken with a mock seriousness that underscored the cynical hilarity he and the others had used to make peace with the situation. They broke into cynical, off-beat laughter, even Kyra and Neriv, and the sound rocketed around the chamber, bathing them in a collusive, tension-diffusing auditory haze.

Kyra noticed Neriv looked slightly out of her stride, seeming thrown off by the ascent into the meteorite tower. It was as though they'd temporarily stepped off the planet onto an anchored satellite, a stationary moon. Neriv needed the solid ground of the planet beneath her feet. Kyra felt guilt at having involved her friend with the debtors, but Neriv gave no sign of wishing to leave her to face them on her own.

Loken craned his neck to look into the corridor behind them. "He didn't come with you, did he?"

Illusi answered him instead. "Not likely that he'd ever come to meet with his debtors after he has what he needs from them."

She turned to Kyra. "And what about you? Will you only take what you need from us, and leave us to our fates? Will your agreement be as one-sided as his?"

In answer, Kyra opened the sleek case and held out the deed. "You can decide what you think of it yourselves."

Charis came forward and accepted it with careful hands, stepping back to where the others stood. The three crowded close around the parchment, their energies condensed into a small knot. A couple of other visitors filtered past, giving a curious look to the three of them, and to Kyra and Neriv, who stood a few feet away. The visitors turned a corner, and Kyra could hear them resume their conversation. Following with her senses, she could intuit the energy trails of others in the nearby passages, hidden behind prismatic walls. They were familiar to her, as they were recognizable as the other debtors. The three before her must have been knowingly deceiving her, pretending they were the only ones present in the glass works.

In the air currents that slipped past, she could hear tangled remnants of old conversations, incantations, arguments, laments, threats, as if the meteor had fallen for the purpose of collecting and reshaping the spoken word. Only the written words of the deed could go undetected in this place. Charis, Loken and Illusi were mouthing some of the words to themselves as they read, and after a few moments, looked up again at Kyra.

Loken said, "We want to take it away and discuss it for awhile."

"No," she answered, aware of the dangers of those hidden behind the walls, "It doesn't leave my sight unless it's signed. In light of last night's transgression, you must regain my trust."

"All right," said Illusi, speaking a bit too loudly, "we'll sign it here, then."

She could sense something in the air behind her. She turned and stepped to the side, and a large form appeared from the passage: Mersad, and behind him Carda. Kyra turned to Neriv, who looked surprised but composedly motioned with her eyes to an upper ledge in the chamber. She climbed up onto the ledge with Neriv's help, then sat there facing the group. Neriv also faced them, her arms crossed, standing in front of the ledge.

Carda and Mersad added much to the mass of humanity in the gallery, and the geometric room was almost crowded. An instant later, Alon and Hesek moved out from another entrance, and the room suddenly was quite crowded, with the debtors congregating around the parchment, which Carda took from Loken's hand.

Mersad looked over at Neriv with amusement. "Are you going to order us to leave?" he challenged her. "Last call!" he cried a high, fey voice. He and Carda began to laugh in low tones, while the others stood by coolly. Neriv merely shrugged.

Mersad looked around at Loken, Illusi and Charis. "Not very funny, eh?" he muttered to Carda. "That's what we get for taking up with two yuppies and a new-age glass worker." She gave a rough sound of agreement, but was focused on the deed. Alon and Hesek looked like the nocturnal creatures they were, dragged out of bed too early into the light of day. Loken, Illusi and Charis were coalescing into a separate group, stepping away from Mersad and Carda.

"I'm going to sign, anyway," said Charis decisively. She held out her arm and Carda handed it to her with a derisive motion. On the ledge, Kyra began preparing the ink Eson had given her, its flowing darkness and slightly cloying aroma putting her into a trance, as a shaman who prepares herbs and incense.

Neriv watched Kyra, interpreting her actions to the others. "She's preparing the ink," she said. Loken and Illusi watched her as well, mystified, then looked at the parchment, nodding.

Carda and Mersad looked at them incredulously, while Alon and Hesek looked only at each other, affecting a veneer of boredom. "What about you two?" Charis asked, and they shrugged,

the signing of a new contract

pulling their shoulders up defensively.

Kyra felt a strange clarity as she finished preparing the ink and passed it down to Neriv, who met the debtors in the middle of the chamber. The words of the glassy rock around her resonated a truth. She had a vision of the meteor as once part of another planet, streaming with life, and then how it had traveled through space and landed in the desert near this city, to become part of the life of this place. She heard something suddenly, words in a low voice that passed by and vanished. It sounded like, "The rose fountains... again."

It didn't matter. The moment had pased. With power electric in the air around her, she watched the others as they began to sign the deed.

Charis signed first, with an ardent resolve, then Loken and Illusi. They passed the parchment to Hesek, who unfolded his arms slowly and stretched out with nonchalance before placing the deed against the wall to sign it. He held the parchment there while Alon signed with a noncommittal grace.

Neriv watched with fascination, moving her gaze along with the parchment as it was passed. Only Carda and Mersad remained. "What about you?" asked Loken tersely, as though he would be happy to have done with them forever.

Mersad smirked. "We can't make matters worse."

"There's nothing left to risk," Carda agreed. "The enchanter's already taken everything from us." Their laughter was bitter with dark ichor as they placed their signatures on the parchment, handing it back to Neriv dismissively. "This won't do anything," Carda added. "Besides, Stas hasn't signed, and the other two are missing without a trace."

Kyra shook herself from her trance, "Only Stas' signature is needed. Jado I can find, and I can fill the tenth space myself."

Mersad said, "Stas won't listen to you. But he might listen to his favorite bartender... " He and Carda ricocheted a dart of laughter between them.

Neriv looked at the edge of her patience, and was flexing her strong fists under crossed arms.

"It's true," said Charis, facing Neriv. "He does like you. But you've taken enough trouble on yourself."

Kyra shook her head at Neriv.

But Neriv said, "I'll talk to him, if you think it'll make a difference." She turned to Carda and Mersad. "But I'm not going anywhere with either of you in the picture." The two made expressions of mock fear, but turned away and began walking down a passage, snickers erupting from their disappearing forms.

The atmosphere in the gallery lightened with their leave-taking.

Hesek and Alon began to stir and get ready to leave, and Kyra addressed them. "Thanks, you two. Within a couple of days we should all be free of this."

"I hope so," said Alon as she left, looking Kyra in the eye for the first time.

"The four of us can go track down Stas right now," Loken volunteered, and turned to Kyra. "It's probably better if you don't come. He thinks you and Eson are one and the same."

"Not exactly one and the same," she said, "but there is something of him that works deeply on people who fly in his orbit."

"We all know that much," said Illusi.

Neriv said quietly to Kyra, "Contact me later."

She agreed, then said to the others, "Today was only a rehearsal for the real action in a couple of nights or so. It may not work, of course, but the chance must be taken. The water courses of the planet have the power to liberate all of you." *Without damaging Eson*, she added to herself.

She felt a satisfaction and anticipation at what was to take place around the fountains. But what were the consequences of allowing power to be held by each of the members of this uneven group? Was her deed enough of a safeguard to keep them under control? Had the two factions in the group even been friends before Eson's deed, or had they been brought together unwillingly by the folly of their mutual friend?

She had no image of the mysterious Stas, but imagined he was of the same rough type as Carda and Mersad, while the others struck her as more peaceful—freethinking folks with an alternative flair. She could even think of them as potential friends, if she ignored their earlier deceptions.

The three debtors looked almost elated as they shook hands with her and led Neriv away around a curve in the passage. She felt a sudden exhaustion and surrender to the sublime atmosphere of the glass gallery. She'd put them under an enchantment with the deed and its ink, but it was not an enchantment of deception, in her mind. They would all be set up with minor power sources, and likely even their descendants would benefit, she assured herself. Power was something that could be created, tapped into, without necessarily taking it away from another person. She was almost certain of this.

She imagined herself on the coast again, with the waves of voices around her in the tower like the sound of small waves on the sea. The meteor glass structure was like a translucent island above the city, as though the continental plateau were no different from an abyssal sea plain, and she sank to the floor beside a wall to contemplate the many feelings she had, among them extreme gratitude for Neriv.

After a time she got up and returned down through the structure and then the city, feeling like a glass marble fed through a contraption of chutes and gates made of the rocks of meteors.

Kyra is enjoying a much greater success here in the old city than I am. She came home today with a radiant elation that was tempered by exhaustion from some effort or other. I remember when I was first developing into who I am, feeling a similar kind of exhaustion on the completion of a new deal or venture. This thick feeling has been eroded with the completion of many such successes, so that I feel only a shadow of the former intensity. I think the project on the coast may have been the last time I could feel any passion for my success in the outward stretching of the entrepreneurial. I am aware of my new debtors as small additions to the threadwork that encompasses me, but there is little of the personal feeling of power transference I've come to expect on the formation of a deed. Perhaps they are simply too far away, and I've overestimated the spatial range that my influence can cover, but I think there is also some fading away of the kind of life I've been connected to. All of my oath-bound are tied to me as roots that feed life to a tree, but there is an element now of enfetterment. I long to escape them as many of them must long to escape me.

How did this come about? It has been happening gradually, but the change did not accelerate until quite recently, during our last days in Waters Rising, and now here in the Glass City. I returned home today with only a need to purge myself of what had occurred this afternoon and the previous day. I haven't the heart to tell Kyra much of this, as I know she is wrapped in other concerns. She feels she is helping me with her actions, but I don't see how this can be the case.

There must be better ways to serve Sarhul and the ancient watercourses of my ancestors than the accumulation of petty power interests. The events of the last two days have convinced me of this.

I left the house early yesterday morning for an innocuous lunch meeting with one of my links to the north, an energy dealer who helped set up my lines of steam power distribution through the north and into other territories some years ago. He has been helpful in innumerable ways and continues to keep me networked to events in my odious home country.

We have a tradition of drinks and flaked Rhiso branches at

an authentic Lidvun Islands-style bar in the northern quarter of the city. Above the clanking of glasses you can hear the delicate flaking process of the still-smoking branches, which the cooks hand directly to you over the bar. The branches crumble as you eat them into richly flavored pieces that are unequaled in the cuisine of this region, and they are imported to this bar alone of all in the city.

This contact, Lonred, is someone with whom I can speak clearly about important strategic matters. I thought all was well as I met him at our accustomed table and the smoking branches were placed between us on the polished surface. He is small and usually of a jovial kind of expression, and seems always to convey the sense that things are all right. It was not until we began to speak of more serious matters than food that I learned something was amiss.

"I'm lost my river station," said Lonred. "It was to begin experimenting with clay power in the northern plains when there was a falling out between my researcher and one of the outsourced liaisons. The foreign company pulled their people and resources out, leaving only two of them and the remains of the structures on the riverbank. I'd invested a lot in that project. It seems there is trouble these days with the international codes for these things." He crunched thoughtfully on a branch while I struggled to understand the implications of what he was telling me. The drinks on the table went cloudy pale as they reacted with the air around them. He continued, "The foreign company liaison had received some veiled warning about an investigation into an unscheduled research project. My researcher claimed there was nothing questionable about the river station, which was true. It was only to be studying the feasibility of clay and algae conduction. The liaison said no more about it, but several days later confronted my researcher, saying he could not participate if the warnings he had received held any water. My researcher and I are sure they don't. Still, it is a worrying trend." He paused again, swirled the cloud in his drink while I wondered what he was getting at.

"I'm sorry for your loss. It would have been an interesting experiment. Do you need any support in starting off something new?"

"No, though I thank you. I have other businesses running smoothly at present. I'm telling you this not because I want to share my misfortune with you. The warnings the liaison received, the references to cross-national investigations, I think were meant not just for me, but for you." His little face peered at me seriously, and I looked back at him with frank surprise.

"Veridi is involved. Someone who knows of several of your business deals is stringing them together in a chain, linking you with some questionable patterns. I think they wanted to know if I was a direct lead to you, or only a casual acquaintance. I wanted to warn you to tread carefully."

I nodded my thanks and casually ground one of the branch ends into a charcoal-like powder on the stone dish. I thought of the meeting I'd booked at the high bank the next day. I wanted to check in on my interests stored there. There's an account room there that only few are admitted to, and I am one of those permitted. I would have to be cautious, I realized, and not only the next day, but from that moment onward.

Lonred was gently asking me about how I had fared on the coast. I replied, "Nothing came of it. The deals didn't go through, and I struck it off as a lost venture. I've returned here to lie low for a while."

"That's just as well. It doesn't do to take too many risks right now, with the political climate in the north, and with cross-nationals and the watchdogs in this province paying more heed than ever to the steam officials."

He provided me with this information, but I told him as little as I could. If the government here were to become suspicious of me, I could end up fugitive from this beautiful city, as I was from my own inherited place in the Steam Territories. "How is Veridi involved?" I asked, nearly grimacing as I uttered the name of the one who'd caused me no small degree of misery.

"She appears to have more information about you than you might care to imagine. But beyond that, I don't know how she is connected, or who is involved. I only wanted to warn you before something occurs."

"Thank you." Here was cause for concern to me. The small-time debtors of this city I knew could not really undo me, but entire networks of officials from the north, the Glass City and other places could. It is for this very reason that I usually choose my debtors and oath-bounds from among the less significant quarters of society. I'm not omnipotent, and to go against higher powers would invite risks. I'd made an exception to that in Veridi, and that had perhaps been a mistake, I now think.

"This is a bit of gossip," he added to me, regaining his usual impish composure, "but did you know about Veridi's current lover? He's the sly watchdog who runs mercenary missions for the top banks and power companies. Watch out for him."

I chilled internally. I knew of Veridi's habit of strategic affairs, and even suspect sometimes I may have been one, just a way for her to gain influence in the electricity sector and northern interests. That she and the watchdog might be in league could do me no good.

We finished our branches in companionable near-silence, talking about insignificant matters. There was a cry of amazement from some patrons at the next table, who were experiencing the smoking branches for the first time. We inhaled the smoky scent and downed our drinks. He told me the situation in the north had not changed appreciably, except that my punishment if caught would be house arrest in the mountains rather than in the capital. There was a popular following in my favor that had somehow erupted in the poorer districts, of all places. Many people must remember the fair distribution act I'd lobbied for in the capital. Maybe there was some good to be had. But for now, I decided I would take Lonred's advice. I considered him one of my most trusted allies, though I'd been cautious in telling him about Waters Rising.

But the events of my second day in the Glass City would bend that trust to its limits. Kyra knows nothing of what has happened, but when I tell her, when the moment is right, she'll understand completely my actions.

A trip to the bank is normally no traumatic experience, especially not for one in my position, but this day will rest forever in my memory as the dissolution of my faith in a place to which I'd long been loyal.

The bank is a high building, angular and light, and is one of the few examples of partially modern architecture in the city. It is one in the circle of structures that bow reverently at the foot of the great old monument, in concert with the gallery, the amphitheater and several other bastions. While it is of old stone like the others, the bank incorporates squares of green glass and square forms on all its surfaces, with sliding glass panels altering the configuration of the building according to the financial climate of the days. As stocks rise or fall, the panels are slid in requisite patterns, signaling the prosperity or temporary decline of the city in world matters. A picture will appear in the news on the day that some shift of great portent occurs in the bank glass. No one will forget the full-scale lowering of the glass that heralded the last recession. I don't think any other city has such an idiosyncratic or charismatically gripping way of displaying its monetary tides. Today the panels were suspended at heights and intervals that succor the spirit with their stability and appearance of permanence. I took solace in them as I made my cautious way

the high bank

along side routes and the edges of the wide avenue before the bank. There was a nervous lightness to my step as I ascended the shallow marble stairs and came through the doors of the great edifice. I was conscious of this but unable to control my nerves; I'd been set on edge by Lonred's warning.

Once inside, one is contained within a high chamber of green glass squares set in light stone. The green squares give onto fragmented views of inner offices and rooms, showing only disembodied scenes of feet on stairs, hands passing sheets of free market capital. There is a sound like waterfalls, and it is the sound of money being moved. The lightness of this free-world bank is always striking to me in contrast to the heavy, oppressive quality of the steam capital's official places.

I approached the small wicket reserved for patrons like myself and felt a momentary stab of panic as I mistook the young clerk for one of my low-level debtors, a certain Loken Birch. But the clerk was only a doppelgänger who viewed me with as blank and unsuspecting eyes as any other patron. He directed me to a side staircase, where I ascended into a higher arcade of rooms, gravitating toward the chamber I usually take my appointments in. The illustrious bank officer was occupied, so I was to wait momentarily. I'm not of the class of individual who must hurry through their transactions, and to show a genteel patience with material affairs is a mark of honor in my lineage.

I felt my calm sense of security resurfacing as I lounged in the silent antechamber, lit from above by small skylights. There was an aquarium, replete with the restored rarities of a prehistoric ocean, a murky window into the deep past. There were trilobites, circular fronded plants, and an *Ichthyic horribilis* with a hugely under-slung jaw, a monster that haunted the shallow primordial seas. I watched it scour the floor of the aquarium with a looming, rushing motion, and I began to wonder how long my patience was expected to endure.

Suddenly there was a patch of light, starting as a small square reflected on the tank in front of me, and extending outward to the edges of the room. My own shadow stretched forth onto the now illuminated aquarium, and I felt aware of a larger space of air behind me. I turned and saw the wall close behind me had slid away, and that I was now incorporated into a larger, higher room, a room that was entirely glass at its opposite end. I had never seen such a metamorphosis of this usually unremarkable chamber!

More shocking and worrisome to me was the row of figures, framed by the natural light of the window. They were arrayed above and before me at a high, long wooden desk like a judge's seat, with the sky behind them.

My eyes were some moments in adjusting, and the figures seemed to wait for me, for my eyes, for my acceptance of these vastly unprecedented occurrences. They were anonymous and silent, and must have watched me with near ridicule as my eyes strained to assimilate them against the harsh sky. My only precise sensation came from beyond the ordinary five senses: I was aware that the furthest figure at the end of the row was reeling my energies greedily inward as though I were a spool of thread and he were a mechanical loom. I felt I was under attack by this subtle, undermining presence, and then felt another echo of threat as I recognized the magnetic pulses of the figure beside the energy drainer. I recognized the pulses on a most immediate level, and knew that I was finally getting my chance to meet Sarah.

As my eyes finally came back to me I was fixed on these two figures, and saw the all too familiar face of Sarah, a mask of similarity to Sarhul. The figure beside her, the one who threw me off with his very presence, suddenly became known to me as I remembered a chilling anecdote I'd once heard from a relative. He was known as a Domain Chaoser, which is a person who interferes with the magnetic field transactions and energy trails of others, particularly of those like me, who rely on the magnetic fields of the planet to maintain strength. A person like this could track my energy trails and entangle them with those of others, undoing any advantage I held. Sarah must be the perceptive agent who helped him to intuit these trails, who led him to my connections and hiding places. They were a dangerous pair.

Beside them was the also familiar form of Lonred, looking away from me as I fixed my eyes on him. I realized I'd been routed here by a matrix of betrayals, and that the blueprints for this encounter had been set long before today. I'd no idea what was to happen, or how great a threat there was to me. To gauge this further, I looked to the other three figures before me, and the resulting prognosis was not good.

Beside Sarah, Lonred and the Chaoser at a raised section of the desk were three officials of grim character: a minister of northern liaisons, a watchdog of the power corporations, and a banking magistrate. I'd been surrounded as if by hounds, in one of my most sanctified dens. The northern minister was an authoritative if physically diminutive elder, one of the conservative old guard of relations with the north, who would be cognizant of the fine details of my recent flight from the north. The magistrate was a formidable judge with a terribly perceptive look, whose concepts of justice and of financial ethics would clash terribly with my own. She would have the capacity to make me feel like an insidious rogue.

Worst of all, perhaps, on a biting personal level, was the black-haired and rugged watchdog, of an age just enough senior to my own that he was intimidating without losing an edge of shrewd modernity. He was Veridi's lover, and though I don't envy him that, I felt that my inner life had been trespassed somehow by his involvement. Lonred sat below his elbow, nearly in his shadow, the creeping invertebrate! The watchdog was sleek and understated in a gunmetal gray suit. In contrast to him, the Domain Chaoser looked like a garish carnival trickster, and Lonred like a soft doll of a person. The judge and the northern minister were suitably venerable and sedate, while the mere presence of Sarah annoyed me and contributed to my feeling of invasion.

It is amazing the speed of the leaping mind when confronted with alarming things. I had less that a minute to formulate these emotions before the judge called the meeting to order. It was her right to do so, as the bank's host official and legal authority. She addressed me with a voice of rational efficiency. "This will not be your usual transaction," she warned me, and gave me a few seconds' grace to embed myself in the knowledge of this. "We have worked in conjunction with these others and performed an audit on not just your monetary transactions, though those alone would be enough to cast doubt on you: a history of numerous small deposits transferring in, as if from nowhere, under your account name." She spoke in drawling and urbane fragments, with the grace of the Glass City's highest echelons. "But it is only the beginning. They've found strings of people harbored under your family name, bound by oaths that are barbaric in their feudality... and power cables buried under the mountains, with other breaches of power distribution codes." She paused at this, and the elder took up, in a heavy northern accent.

"There was scandal enough about you in the north, a disgrace to hereditary dignity." The northerner of course cared less about the old-world nature of my deeds, feudalism being an accepted mode in the north. But his indignation at my expansive opportunism and code breaches was clear. I felt the need to defend myself.

"That's not what the poor boroughs of the steam district believe, if my sources are correct," I said sharply, casting a beam of accusation at Lonred, who looked increasingly wilted. The Domain Chaoser and Sarah were fixing me with subtly wry looks, as though I entertained them greatly. The Chaoser basked in his immediate proximity to me, glowing with the acquisition of my power. There was a chair in the room near me, and I wished for its support, but would have appeared weak in sitting down at this moment, so I fell to pacing. I noted with relief that the movement thwarted the Chaoser's attempt on my stores of energy.

The watchdog had been solid and inert until this point, nearly android like in his stillness, but now he spoke with a clear and controlled voice that conveyed clean impermeable superiority. "We have tracked you successfully and completely. That part of it is done, so don't hope for any further secrecy in your actions. And do not be mistaken: we mean not only to track but also to obstruct further action on your part. To this end, we have employed the gentleman at the far end." He gestured toward the Chaoser, who tilted his head with a mean little smile. "We offer you the following ultimatum."

He paused, and looked at me in a way I didn't like, as though he had recently discussed me with one whose opinion of me was unflattering and wrongfully biased. I had a sickening image of him and Veridi couched together, extolling my shortcomings over vintage liqueurs. In a perverse way, I desired the simple company of those I could overwhelm, the easy nights at low-end clubs. Beyond that I wanted the freedom I'd felt before coming back to the city, though I knew returning to the coast would be impossible. I was far enough away from the springs... Had I ever been free?

He was speaking again, with his mask of superior opaqueness. I now felt flashy and immature in my designer clothes under the metalloid glare of his clean-cut suit. It is rare for me to encounter someone who puts me in awe, let alone awe mixed with revulsion. He said, without friction entering his voice, "A colleague of mine, whom you may know, once sent a low agent in hopes of tracking you. That was some months ago, and the agent simply disappeared, though we later found she'd been absorbed into your network. At any rate, the colleague has not given up in her avowal to undo the deed that binds her to you. Do you know the one I'm speaking of?"

"Veridi," I uttered with difficulty. It was an imposition that I had to be the one to say her name.

"Yes. She's prepared to take great lengths against you unless you deliver that contract. It is with her expertise that we uncovered the messy trail of your other transactions. So she, and now we, control the means through which you move in the world."

I was given a moment to swallow this, which I did with composure. I was not about to be bullied.

"If you'd simply been more accommodating to her, these other highly regarded people need never have become involved." He indicated the judge and the northern councilor, who looked at me with distant appraisal. "It is too late now, though. Much is known about you that can never become unknown."

The judge held up her hand. "Simply put, sir, we require that you give up your collection of contracts in their entirety. We in the Glass City won't stand for the archaic indenture of our citizens or those of other provinces. We don't like employing such... methods," she indicated the Chaoser with a glance, "but your oppression of our citizens must come to an end." The Chaoser looked shameless, or at least accustomed to being referred to derisively.

The balance of power in this situation was precarious. They could not bring someone to law on account of metaphysical deeds and transfers of wealth or wellbeing. There was simply no concrete proof that the deeds had a physical effect on the real world. The converse side of that fact was that the Chaoser could also act on me in insidious and destructive ways without fear of punishment. I could withstand him, of course, but he could be a constant draining nuisance in my life as long as Veridi was paying him to do so.

"It was not enough for you to be hated in the Steam Territories," added the councilor in an almost pitying tone. The three behind the lower portion of the desk said nothing.

I was tempted to refute the northerner again but instead weighed my position silently, not wishing to jeopardize it further. This assemblage was not a law court, so they were powerless to detain me, but they could indeed make a difficult matter of my life in the Glass City, and they could take the deeds by force, posing a danger to Kyra and myself if we got in the way.

I took the road of humility, which was only partly feigned. The panel of judges I was confronting genuinely cowed me. I motioned to the Chaoser, and said, "If you could ask him to back off for a moment, I could think more clearly," at which the watchdog gave the Chaoser a mildly enraged look. From this I learned two things: that the watchdog was the Chaoser's master, and that the others present hadn't been aware of his calm but voracious sapping of my energies. I chose the moment as a dignified chance to sit down.

If I had told them I would relinquish the contracts to their authority with my own hands, they would not have believed me. There was no easy way out through words, and I couldn't hope to wage a campaign of influence over this phalanx of strong wills. Now that I was sitting, I took up a disaffected stance, turning my chair slightly away from the full force of the panel. "What would you have me do?" I asked, with resignation in my voice.

The watchdog glanced at the bank authority and the northern councilor, and then recited what I imagined was a prepared set of instructions. I had most definitely been set up. Lonred shrunk away from the openly accusing glare I cast at him.

"This afternoon when you leave here, go home immediately. We will make sure you do this. At home, put all of the contracts on the desk in your living room, and leave them there. After that, you and anyone else living there, even servants, must leave the suite for the entire evening." He gave me a sardonic look, and I could only interpret his remark as a dig at my relationship with Kyra. Veridi must have told him the agent who'd been sent to spy on me had been a servant of hers. This fellow was expert at cutting to the very personal marrow of things and I grew to resent him further. "Don't return until late at night, or until we signal to you that you may return. Your house will not be a safe place this evening."

And so warning verged on threat. They had me cornered, and I would be forced to comply. Yet, the judge and councilor did not delve into these matters with their own mouths, and the watchdog stood as an intercessor between them and the unsavory mercenary Chaoser. I sensed the watchdog and Veridi were at the heart of matters, and the higher officials would only dip their hands so much in this affair. The governors of an important free state would not really go to so much trouble over an isolated entrepreneur, nor risk blotting their own record with much underground action.

These difficulties would pass, and I wouldn't really be harmed at the core. I would lose the contracts, yes. This would be a blow to me. I might have to leave the city, and that would also be a blow, as there is only one place I can go, and that is no easy decision. I would think over my options that night while Kyra and I were out in the city. At that moment I felt urgently the need to return home and make contact with Kyra, to get her out of the suite before anything happened there. Tonight would be one of abandon and forgetfulness, possibly my last for a while. I had no concept of what the coming days would bring.

To my relief, the judge addressed me again, this time a dismissal. "You may go, sir, but I'd advise you to curtail your conjurer's games." The councilor and the watchdog gave me grave looks, while the Chaoser eyed me with leisurely malice, and Sarah cast a cryptic look at me before passing her eyes onto the others. Lonred stared into the aquarium and I followed his eyes to the tank, where the *Ichthyic horribilis* had opened the hatch of its terrible maw and was trawling in a fleet of tiny fish, no doubt prey that had been added to the tank from above.

The others were also intrigued by that spectacle of nature, and I took the opportunity to bid the chamber goodbye, not meeting the eyes of any of the dreaded panel. Out once more in the larger hall of the bank, I hurriedly made my way out into the cover of the afternoon crowds, eager to gain distance from the building that had, for the first time in my life, betrayed me. I could not even go through with any ordinary diagnostic of my accounts, and left the bank completely flummoxed.

I went home and had a quick dinner with Kyra, who'd gotten

home only a short while earlier, though I know not from where. I impressed upon her the need to go out for the evening despite her wish to stay home and unwind from the long walk she'd had that day. "We must go out," I said to her softly, though I didn't let on to any of the worry I felt.

"Couldn't we go out tomorrow night instead?" she wondered, to which I replied firmly that tonight must be the night.

"We'll go in a steam-cab," I assured her. "We won't have to face the tram crowds at night. There's a special competition tonight at the betting gallery. If it's too rough there, we can take ourselves away to quieter spot." I felt a need for the comforts of a densely packed room that night, and the betting gallery would provide just the frenzied release I craved. As well, I planned to give up gambling completely after that night, as I would give up many things. So I convinced her to vacate the house with me, feeling greater ease as we left the suite for the darkening streets. I casually left the stack of deeds on the desk as the watchdog had requested. The steam-cab carried us into the riotous depths of the gambling district, and we entered one of the city's premier betting galleries.

Within minutes I was purging, partying wildly, betting, reveling in a crowded place full of streamers and rolling clamorous music. I handed Kyra the spoils of my games, taking none of it for myself, gleeful at being rid of it, but unable to stop placing bets when the tray-table came round. She kept awake and took in the place as if it were not really there. Toothed laughter and feverish largesse surrounded us, drinks sailed by, bets soared, and flowers were strewn at the feet of contestants who'd won. Losing contestants were chased about by ghoulish clowns with noisemakers and pelted with soft objects made available by the establishment, thrown by those whose bets had been lost. The projectiles hadn't always been soft objects in the past, but civilization rears its gracious head at last, this side of the border at any rate. (I won't set foot in the gambling houses of the north, and won't be in any such establishments at all after tonight, I feel certain.

We'd been there for an hour or more when my burdens re-enveloped me like a dark slough, and impressed upon me that the afternoon's ensnarement had not been an isolated or empty threat. After I uncharacteristically lost three bets in a row, I glanced across the wide amphitheater. To my dismay, I found the cause of my ill luck, and was not surprised, only taken over by a leaden feeling of the inevitable. On the opposite side of the vast room were two of the figures before whom I'd stood court that afternoon. The Domain Chaoser and his date for the evening, Sarah, were intercepting my wagers and setting off the balance of the competition, ensuring my losses and the ensuing feeling of defeat that accompanies a downturn in fortune.

Kyra placed a hand on my arm questioningly, and I subtly pointed out to her the ominous pair. She nearly shuddered at the sight of Sarah, and with good reason, for Sarah's identity is one that could not be stolen lightly or without detection. The two of them held us in thrall together, and we both pretended to watch the festivities without concern, our hands clasped tightly beneath the table. Luckily, the Chaoser was too far away to exact the toll on my psyche that he'd had earlier in the day. I was determined to keep the radius of separation between the him and my own person. I contemplated the wisdom of moving elsewhere, finding some insulated evening lounge where we could relax without menace.

Glancing across the rows of unruly salon patrons, I saw the Chaoser's invasive eye winking at me languorously from the opposite terrace. This was the signal I'd been told of, that we were free to return to my home—if that can really be termed 'free'. A fulcrum eroded within my core at the knowledge that my deeds were likely no longer in my possession.

In the next second, the crowd roared up from the tables all

around us at a scandal taking place in the central ring. A mass of cries belted upward, and Kyra and I rose to our feet fluidly and escaped the gallery through the trajectory of a hail of flowers, which adorned us even into the street and in the steam-cab.

She nearly slept against my shoulder on the way home, and I could only convince her to stay up for a brief nightcap when we arrived at the suite. I couldn't immediately face the emptiness of the space on my desk where I'd left my deeds, so was willing to plead with her to stay awake for even a minute.

I can't think what must have gone on today for her to be so drained, but she will at least sleep well tonight, while I may not. There is much to think about, and I must begin to heal the gash of having lost my contracts. The night is too far deepened for me to determine whether my bond with any of the debtors has yet been broken. My only wish is finally to be graced with sleep.

Jado dreamed he was on top of the stone monument in the Glass City, and the entire city lay submerged beneath it by clear, still waters. He could see the roofs of buildings beneath the surface, but no people. He knew they'd all left before the submersion. Eson was standing beside him, and Jado heard him say, "I don't think it was really worth it," before he walked away. He realized then that he'd helped Eson submerge the city, though he had no memory of doing so and wished he hadn't been involved. "Of course it wasn't worth it; why would we do this to begin with?" he asked with short breath, trying to catch up with Eson. But Eson was nowhere to be found.

He awoke at the moment of awareness he realized he was stranded on the smooth stone monument. He lay in the uppermost room of the coast house, a sublimely silent green square. The air permeated open panels in the walls, which were of a plant-derived material and so comforting to wake to. He stretched in the loose mess of cushions and blankets, his mind still on the dream.

This was the morning of the tidal influx, and if he hadn't felt much doubt in his waking life, the dream stood as proof of doubt in his deeper self. The dream version of Eson had appeared powerful, irrational and feckless. He'd also had sun-bleached hair and a strange seafarer's coat. In the earlier stages of the dream, there'd been a woman, not Sarah, nor Kyra nor any other that he knew, but someone else unknown and intangible.

He awoke fully into the day though it was early. He was to meet Gerson and Carstell at a fountain near the harbor, then go with them to the breakwater. He didn't know where the two men lived or much else about them, and felt little connection to them. He only hoped the interaction would be short, the battery plan carried out with speed and done with, allowing him to be free in the city again.

He looked out from the wall panel and saw a sky with high, immense fields of cirrus clouds that appeared to evaporate upward as he watched them, arcing over the horizon like huge whales disappearing into the sea. In the city below, massive, brilliantly hued sails were raised as warnings to those on land and far out at sea that it was the day of the tides.

He ate a breakfast of coastal bread lavished with cheese and berries, and hot, strong tea fortified with the honey from next door. He needed strength to go through with the day, though the risk to him would be minimal. Eson's words in the dream had really been his own, he knew; it was he who wondered at the worth of their actions.

He knew Eson needed the sea-traders' deals for his own satisfaction. The tidal project was his way of beginning to cast a net of power outward, but he wondered that Eson would go through so much trouble to achieve this. He thought of his own dream of solar power, of how it had evolved into a vision of crossing the ocean to the Niyali islands on a solar-powered craft. The works Eson carried out must have a similar inner meaning to him, he surmised.

He had a solar generator priced out at a dealer's now, but no hope of being able to afford a boat journey. He could use the money for the generator to purchase a boat ticket, but then he might never have the opportunity to possess his own power source. He momentarily considered taking their neighbor up on the offer of a job at the university, but couldn't bring himself to do it though he could hear his family jumping with pride at the offer if he were to tell them.

He drank the rest of his tea and prepared to take a tram down to the harbor, walking out into the cool, hazy day and along the curved road from the house. From the tram's window, then, he could see the distant water, which looked calm considering the surge forth it was soon to make. It was as though a crowd were gathering silently, pooling its force before moving forward. He could also see cranes raised up, preparing to lower boats into the water once the flood plain was submerged. Jado moved downward toward the shore in the smooth tram, and the flood plain flattened out before him, the city soon around him rather than below. He felt as though he were being submerged under trepidation with each inch of descent. The islands on the flood plain reminded him suddenly of the monument in the Glass City and of his ominous dream.

The tram slowed to a stop in a modern metallic station, and Jado moved through the crowds toward his meeting point with Gerson and Carstell.

The two men greeted him with terse nods and murmurs, but then communicated only with each other. Their conversation coursed through the middle ground between two languages, only one of which was comprehensible to him, so he did not bother to follow what they were saying. They had traded their suits for more innocuous casual clothing, and drank coffee from stylish decanters. Jado didn't register on their social radar, being from one of the interior states, backward and mediocre by coastal standards. They took little interest in him until the time came for them to draw lots on which of them would risk walking the tidal plain. He flipped a double-sided metal disc for them, and it was determined Carstell would be the one to place the stone module in the foundations of the breakwater. Gerson laughed his gloating relief, while Carstell shrugged off the loss with a sportsman's pride.

The three of them were soon standing on the breakwater, looking out at the sea. They were alone, as the tidal influx was a regular enough occurrence to be bypassed by locals, and the tourist season had ended many weeks prior. By the same token, nobody would think it odd that three people would be trekking out onto the breakwater to see the event. Jado handed Carstell the stone module he would use, and after some listless hesitation he made his way down the staircase to the flood plain below. Jado looked over the edge at him, but was disconcerted by the vertical drop of the wall, and looked up again to steady his vision. He and Gerson waited for several minutes, saying little.

"When he goes into the passage, he'll turn up over there," said Gerson distractedly, pointing into a boatyard on the nearby waterfront. Jado nodded in response. From the sail towers along the shore they heard a loud, clear trumpeting sound, followed by a slow bell toll. It was the signal to all that the tide would soon be incoming. Jado felt the breeze around him and looked out at the still distant, swirling ocean. The specter of Eson hung over him, warning him that the battery plan must go through in order for him to receive the rest of his payment. While it should be easy for Carstell to place the module, and Jado would not have to do anything himself, he also had little control over the outcome so he felt powerless, restless.

Jado looked over the edge again to check on Carstell, and saw to his vexation that the westerner was not standing by the stone alcove, but was gone. The stone module was visible on the ground below, left in the sand.

"He's gone!" said Jado to Gerson incredulously.

"Got a bit of the coward in him," said Gerson matter-of-factly. "Guess one of us will have to do it, then," he said, but made no move toward the stairs. Jado felt uneasiness building within him. There were still a few minutes before the tide began, plenty of time to place the module and escape into the passage. He felt he was in trance-time, with the universe suddenly moving very slowly. The small risk of descending to the flood plain himself was weighed against the large gain of his payment, the possible solar generator, or the chance to travel across the sea.

He ran to the stairs and began to descend almost as though carried by a force beyond him, his heart beating with fearful excitement mixed with a sense of destiny and half-crazed bravado. Reaching the sand, he found the ground soft underfoot as though seawater already permeated the sand, and ran with heavy footsteps to the place where the stone module lay discarded. He looked up at Gerson, who still watched him, but looked now a bit nervous. The bell signaling the tide still tolled and he could hear a vague rushing sound out on the sea, which was now almost above him on the horizon. To escape the resulting sense of vertigo, he turned away from the horizon and moved with his eyes on the solid wall of the breakwater.

Remembering the day he and Eson had walked beneath the breakwater, he began looking for the feature Eson had shown him. Within the etched detail of the stone rampart, there was the natural port in the rock that had been adapted by another contact of Eson's, that could hold perfectly the module that would transmit a wave of power outward to his batteries on the flood plain. His eyes seemed to fumble with the illusory sense of several such portals in the manmade rock and he held the module up to several points on the wall before discovering the right place, next to the turtle icon that he was to push on to create his escape path. Across the plain, he could see a thin movement of very shallow water pushing forth from the horizon. His heart leapt, and he placed the module in the portal, waiting for it to settle into the rock around it, then pushed on the turtle icon. Nothing happened. The thin line of water still moved toward him.

Looking up, he saw Gerson making a gesture with both hands, and so pushed on the wall with all of his strength.

The stone rampart fell inward half a yard above the level of the sand, and he followed it, pushing the rock shut behind him as the line of water he'd seen approached the foot of the breakwater, with increasing waters behind it. He saw the sand engulfed where he had stood, and closed the rock before the rushing waters reached the bottom of the rock door. The sound rocketed around for a few seconds within the passage, and then he was in darkness and silence. He felt his way up a set of stairs for about ten feet, wishing he'd thought to bring a pocket light with him. The stairs and the walls of the passage were made of light metal, and were mercifully soft-edged. As he gained the top stair, he saw a small spark of light nearly disappearing ahead of him.

"Wait!" he yelled, and heard Carstell's voice respond from the distance, though he couldn't make out the words. He felt his way along the dark passage to the place where Carstell waited.

"Threatened to get a bit nasty out there," said Carstell casually.

"It did get nasty, right after I placed the module," said Jado with an edge of ruefulness, though it was not directed at Carstell. He couldn't recriminate Carstell for not completing his task, given that they were all taking a risk that should have been Eson's.

He didn't care one whit, now, whether the tidal power scheme would be worth the trouble to Eson. The enchantment that had been fostered in the late-night glow of the tea shop had by now mostly evaporated. He felt that his own gains must be all that he should measure, as Eson's gains and visions were capricious as the electric bolts of a storm front.

With the help of Carstell's small lantern, they made their way along the passage and eventually up a spiraling stair, where they came to a door. The door was sealed tight, and no combination of their strength could force it open. Carstell refueled the lantern, which had burned out, while Jado rapped his fist rhythmically on the door, hoping he could be heard from the outside. They waited for several minutes, and then sat down on the smooth floor. They could hear nothing of the outside, though he guessed they must be in the environs of the boatyard Gerson had pointed to. It was logical Gerson would come to retrieve them, knowing they'd both disappeared into the passage.

Eventually they heard voices softly through the door, and then heard the door shift before it slowly opened, allowing in daylight and fresh air. He and Carstell stared out into the glare, gasping as they became aware of the airlessness of the passage.

"There's often someone here when the tide comes in," said a boyish voice.

"You made it," said Gerson rather haltingly, attempting to mask the tension of their positions, and sounding much aware of his own ineffectuality.

Jado's eyes adapted to the daylight, and he saw they were in an enclosed shipyard, where a crane was already preparing to lower a boat into the newly raised sea. A young woman, small and light-haired and dressed in men's work clothes, stood next to Gerson.

"Did you get a good view of the tide, there?" she asked him with humor in her voice.

"Next time I'll stick to watching from the breakwater," he said slowly, keeping up the pretense they had merely blundered into being trapped on the tidal plain.

Gerson and Carstell had regrouped as a unit again, and addressed him as if they'd been there to chaperone him during the tidal flow. "Okay, kid, we'll see you around," Carstell said, and the two began seeking out the exit from the shipyard.

Jado stood getting his bearings, and the young woman asked him where he was from. "We don't usually get locals in the passage on tide day," she said, without any of the reserved smugness he'd perceived in many of the coastal people. "You must be from some other locale."

"I'm from the City of Broken Glass, on the interior plains," he said. "I'd never seen the ocean before coming here, and it almost saw the end of me!" Now that he was out of the grasp of the ocean, he felt comfortable playing up the danger. He walked with her to the edge of the shipyard, and they looked out over the wall at the newly submerged plain. The ocean still surged inward, but the largest influx was past. The top of the breakwater was only a few yards above the water's surface. Light from the hazy sky reflected on it, creating the effect of movement where there had been stillness and sand—the water a light green color, the sand visible far beneath it. The nearly submerged tidal generators were barely visible, and the island now floated as ships in the water. The seascape had dramatically changed in only half an hour.

He and the woman, who told him her name was Rael, took a lunch together on the sea wall, watching boats being lowered into the water and set out into the deep. Rael seemed to enjoy his visible amazement at the tidal change. "The tide change is always wonderful to me, too, no matter how many times I see it," she said, looking out over the water.

She was the daughter of the boatyard owner, and close in age to Jado. After their lunch she returned to work in the yard, but they agreed to meet later on in the evening at a midtown bar.

He caught the tram back up the hillside, as he had planned to hike to the top of the hill that afternoon to see a grander view of the ocean. When he returned to the cool, airy house in the hills, he saw there was a message for him, not from Eson, as he'd been expecting, but from Kyra.

Kyra awoke very late on the day following the gathering at the glass tower. It was past midday and Eson was out, the house quiet. She must have slept soundly to miss his leaving, though it was not uncommon for him to leave without waking her.

Her spirit was stretched thin as gauze from the experience at the glass tower, and from the night's wildness at the casino. She half-wondered if some narcotic element had been added to the concoction she'd drunk. That Sarah had been present at the casino, with her unnerving companion who'd given Eson such a look of amused accusation, struck her as an ill omen. Like the inside of a carbonated bottle, the casino had effervesced with glamor and kinetic frenzy, threatening to spill over. She'd been nearly unconscious by the time they'd returned home, yet Eson had insisted she stay awake with him for a moment before sleep divided her from him. He'd looked wasted and vulnerable as he implored her, and her devotion allowed her to fend off sleep for a few minutes. It had been well past midnight.

Today she must call Jado. The debtors, who were not debtors to her but an entourage of co-conspirators, were impatient, and hoped to make their attempt that night or the next. She wondered if Jado would even want to come back so soon, being at leisure in the coast house. Today was the day of the tides! Likely he would be on the waterfront at this hour. She was eager to learn of the result of the tide plan, as it had seemed a mad scheme once she knew of the specifics.

She called the coast house and left a message, asking only that he call her in return. Since she couldn't go out while waiting for the call, she instead looked through Eson's books, searching for guidance she could use in the activation of the fountains.

The deed and the stone were still with Neriv, but Kyra didn't need to have the deed in her hands to be aware of each of the signatures, which coded the essence of each chaotic person into her own being. Their echoes within her were disconcerting but brilliant sparks of expansive consciousness.

In an ancient text that was all but coming apart, she found a chapter regarding the use of written oaths in ceremonies involving magical objects. While she did not consider herself an occult practitioner, she needed to know how she was to use the stone module the debtors had secured, along with the deed and the signatories stationed at each fountain. An archaic woodcut depicted a method of folding a parchment around a talismanic object. Another showed an intricate positioning of people around a power source, which was either meant to be a person or a rendition of one, but in any case reminded her of herself when she had been overseeing the signing of the deed from her high ledge in the meteor tower. She was drawn into a sense of calm in seeing that others before her had enacted the same kinds of oaths and agreements she was navigating now.

It was later in the afternoon when Jado returned the call, and his voice cut through a haze of silence that had hung over her day. Eson hadn't returned or sent word to her. She'd spoken with Neriv, who said Stas had signed the deed, though he'd done so with a sneer of cynicism. Neriv had then stayed out for a drink in a cushioned lounge room with Charis, Loken and Illusi, who were spirited and had keen senses of humor when they were relaxed. Part of Kyra would have traded the Dionysian histrionics of the casino for a mellow evening with soothing, low light and easy laughter such as Neriv described. She'd come to think of the group as the 'signatures', since the feeling of the word 'debtors' seemed off to her mind, to her ideals.

Jado sounded as if a godlike dispensation of peace had descended upon him, and to her it was as though a veil of totality and calmness were being provided to all but her. Almost as though he were relaying a joke or an urban legend, he told her how he nearly met the oncoming tide that morning. She was incredulous that he could sound unflinchingly easy-going after nearly risking his life—for the cause only of a personal and business advancement for Eson, and a one-time payment for himself—but she found herself elevated out of her malaise by his lightness of spirit.

"There was no real danger," he assured her. "Though the tide surges in fast, there are tunnels in the breakwater that lead back up to the shipyards. They planned ahead for people straying onto the floodplain when they built the system of breakwaters."

"Eson should pay you more for having taken that risk on yourself. I'll speak to him about it." She tempered her grave tone with one of admiring amusement, then. "But you don't sound at all shaken. What's the secret of your cool in the face of crisis?"

Jado said slyly, "The truth is, I've met someone here on the coast. Just today."

"Aha! Nothing matters once you've sworn in with the league of romantics."

"Yes, I'm one of you fools, now," he said in tone that walked the line between self-deprecation and veiled criticism.

She let the remark slide, as she and Eson might well seem foolish to one who'd observed them as Jado had. She retorted instead, "Who is the one that already commands your emotions so much that nearly being swept away is of no concern?"

"Her name's Rael, and she is a boat-builder, in love with the ocean. She'll never really be mine, unless the whole sea is drained and her attentions have to find an earthly obsession."

"But that won't stop you from trying?" she teased.

"Of course not! We're already talking about the countries across the sea, and how we could go to them ourselves."

"Be careful when mixing travel with strong, intoxicating emotion," she said, thinking of her impulsive flight into the mountains with Eson.

"Mixing potions was my job at the tea shop. So I at least know how to keep out of boiling water. But I'll have a few days to cool down, anyway. I'm going to come home for a little while and see my family before returning to the coast."

"I'm glad to hear that. Actually, I was hoping you could help me out with something that's going on here in the Glass City."

The conversation took place against a backdrop of soft gray, the rolling landscape of the cover of the suite's bed. A desert breeze floated in the open window, an invisible coolness across Kyra's face. Both Eson's words and hers were colored with the stark and leaden innocence of long hidden honesty. She'd been about to go to sleep.

"Kyra, are you awake?" Eson's voice settled over her in the near-darkness.

"Yes, I was just here with one of your books. Where are you?"

"Kyra, I'm far away."

"You've gone back to the coast?"

"No, I've gone north. Back to the Steam Territories. Back to my springs."

"How is that possible? Aren't you under arrest there?"

"Yes. I'm confined to this house. There are guards outside the door. They arrived shortly after I did."

"Why? How could you go back there after what took place in

the capital? Aren't you terrified of imprisonment?"

"As you once said, dear, they are many kinds of freedom. Inside this house and with the springs near me, I'm free from threat, free from motion and chaos. They can't come in here."

"But it's madness!"

"As long as I'm near my springs, I'm powerful. I had to go all the way to the coast to come to that awareness. I couldn't have kept myself intact much longer in the Glass City. I'll explain to you in time the details. When you come here."

"I can't. Not yet. I'm needed here. The circle of signatures needs me."

"No, I wouldn't want you to come yet, anyway. I need time to fortify myself here. But you're still making deals with my debtors?"

"They're mine, now, as they've signed my oath. But I don't think of them as debtors. I have an equal relation to them."

"I'm sure it appears that way. Equal as a mathematical equation, except eight of them is equal to one of you. It is never equal. You'll do better to learn that now."

"I learn as I go. But what about your contracts? You have them with you, I assume. Won't your government confiscate them?"

"They're not my government and never have been. But for the record, I don't have them with me, so the steam officials will never lay hands on them. They will not cross the border again."

"Then where are they? They aren't here and you don't have them! Where are they now?"

"Veridi has them."

She burrowed deeper into the cover's gray folds at the mention of her old mistress. "Won't she destroy them?"

"No. They're worth too much. She can make her own use of them while the governments turn a blind eye. I came up on the wrong radar and lost the cover of impermeability I'd sheltered under. My ancestors and the springs can only protect me if I show them the respect they need, and their needs transcend any modern notion of politics or borders."

"So you had to return to them, regardless of the political risk."

"Yes. There's more to it than that, but I'll explain in due time. I'm exhausted."

"As am I. How did I manage to sleep through your leaving, again?"

"I helped you to sleep, to protect you."

"You really did put something in that drink I had last night!"

"I wanted you to sleep well, insulated from all this."

"You gave me a narcotic! Maybe you really are as horrible as they say."

He ignored this, but persisted in his justification. "Did you sleep well?"

"Deep and dreamless."

"Was it a relief?"

"Yes."

"There's more in the blue cabinet, if you need it."

"I won't." She paused. "You said it is never equal? Even with us, then, it was never equal."

"Kyra, you knew that from the beginning. I'm in a different stream from others, even you. I can allow you access to that stream, but it will never really be yours. I could dissolve your agreement with the debtors if I chose, because I'm the owner of all the parties signing. If that bothers you, you must leave me."

"I might."

"Please don't. I encourage your accomplishments because I want to see you happy. I won't be forging any new oaths anytime soon, and it may become unsafe for you to do so in the near future. Take care in how you allow yourself to become involved."

"The time is long past when such advice is of use to me. I would have steered clear of you if I'd taken that advice from someone else."

"It's painful to hear you speak that way. I've already lost so much in the last days. I can't lose you as well."

"You won't lose my loyalty."

"Come here in a couple of days. The authorities can't do anything to you, and don't even care who you are. My friends will be arriving soon, and they would be glad of seeing you again."

"I'd like to see them, too. I'll come to the mountains, but not before I'm upheld my side of the oath I've forged with the circle. I have to do this, to maintain my sense of who I am."

There was a pause.

At last Eson spoke again. "Our voices are dreary. I've disturbed your rest. By the way, did you speak to Jado? He'll be alarmed at this, no doubt."

"I spoke to him today. He's doing very well, though he nearly put his life in danger on your account. And now you've let the contracts go to another hand."

"I've told you, I was given no choice. I don't rule all the hands at the larger card table. Retreat into solitude was the only option. Is Jado all right?"

"He's fine, but he ended up on the tidal floor just before the influx. Those westerners you enlisted let him take the risk! You should give him some compensation."

"He may use the coast house for as long as he needs. That will be his compensation. And you can visit there if you like, though I'd prefer you came to the mountains first."

"Yes. Can I call you the day after tomorrow? I need time to settle my mind. You've given me more than I can handle."

"I do love you, Kyra."

"I love you too."

"We'll speak again soon."

Against the gray landscape of the cover, her wakeful mind welled up images of Eson in despair, of northern prisons and cold escapes in unsound mountain vehicles. She didn't truly sleep until close to dawn.

Jado and Rael went separate ways on two late-night trams after seeing an extravagant but terrible western film and eating a takeout dinner together under the torchlight of a fountain square. His tram circled upward along a ridge, passing closely over the university: a mass of dark forms, lit sparsely as a freight ship. Its cool monoliths were less defined in the night, empty of people and the oppressive aura of schoolwork. He might look around it the next morning, he decided, if there was time before his long train trip. Otherwise he could do it when he returned to the coast. He would be coming back to see Rael, that much was certain. A calm surety mixed with excitement had enclosed him. He was free in the world, and all the ways led him forward.

The next morning he awoke late and had to hurry to catch his train, the robot dog at his side. To observers who asked about it he replied, "It's an old-world breed, very rare. I'm taking care of it for a friend." The journey passed through a landscape of jutting rocks and small waterfalls before evening out into deep forest, and then rolling hills. For the first time in his life he was making a journey lightly, with enough money to buy a return ticket whenever he chose. The acres of ground passing beneath the train were not miles of impossible obstacles, but an unfolding map of possibilities.

The hills flattened eventually, and on the plain ahead he could see the Glass City, first pale against the light sky, then growing in intensity as the sun lowered in the west, setting the plains and the city alight. By the time he arrived, the lights of the city against the deep blue sky were like a galaxy, as if he were returning from a journey through the cosmos, and then the city he'd known since his life began surrounded him once more.

After the tumultuous night Kyra slept most of the next day as though drugged by the shock of Eson's decision. The concept of the Steam Territories rose as an unfathomable wall before her reeling consciousness. She felt dwarfed by the gravity of that wall and by the knowledge Eson was enclosed on the other side. He'd chosen to imprison himself, had given up his contracts to one he and she both feared. What could have happened that would induce him to act so?

She was awakened from her brooding trance by Jado's call from a phone in a busy shop. His voice was easy and light, and she agreed to quickly leave the suite and meet him in town.

She called Neriv, who had scheduled her day off. The circle of signatures was poised for action. Neriv would simply give the word to Charis, who would pass it on to the others. They'd make their way to the fountains scattered across the city and wait for the right moment.

Neriv had a kind of excitement in her voice that reassured Kyra she was involved in the plans by choice. She didn't tell her about Eson's flight from the city.

She and Neriv rested on the edge of a dimly illuminated fountain while the night breeze waved silently through the roses, setting them into a dark flurry of movement. The spectral illumination of the courtyard's stones was as it had been on the night before the dust storm. They'd met with Charis, Loken and Illusi, and were now allowing time for the circle to arrive at the various fountains. Kyra knew she would feel an instinctive solidity, a certainty of energy domains, when this happened.

Jado had been the last to leave. She had told him only that he could keep the coast house for his use, and that Eson was appreciative of his risk-taking. There was much more to relay, of course, but she hadn't wanted him to be distracted while the revival of the fountains was taking place. He'd left with an assured wave of his hand.

A window closed in a house near them and a light was extinguished. Neriv had given her the stone module, a sleekly carved geometric form with the look of stone smoothed and eroded by a fast river, and she pressed it between her hands now.

Against the backdrop of a high wall striated by years of dust and wind, Neriv's strong face observed her with concern. "You were exhausted after the gathering in the tower, weren't you?" she asked gently. "It takes a lot of determination to steer the wills of a mob. You were like a shaman or a medicine healer."

"A shaman dances, and spends a lifetime amassing knowledge. I only turn into a mirror and reflect onto people the beam of light that will bind them to me. Sleek tricks that can be picked up in a matter of months from one bred to it, as Eson is."

"So it would appear. But you have your own way of doing

things, I'd guess."

Kyra accepted her admiring remark with a smile, then tentatively began stepping over the conversational branches that would lead to her fully confiding in Neriv. "We spent that evening out in the city, at one of those real old-town betting houses, with the spinning betting trays that rattle, and flurries of flower petals that rain down out of the garrets. There were some other guests making a nuisance for Eson, though, so we had to skip out of there in a hurry. Eson was winning until a slithery-looking card shark began trouncing all his bets with nothing more than a glance."

Neriv raised a brow, but waited for Kyra to go on.

"You have to be registered in order to bet there, of course. They don't let just anyone into the games, and all I am is 'just anyone' in that strata. I'm amazed the carnival grade huckster who guttered up Eson's signals was allowed into the establishment. He must have had somebody else's name in his entry papers, and I don't think he even placed his own bets, only fed carnivorously from Eson's numbers. And if all that wasn't enough, he had Sarah with him as his date! So, Eson's been taking flack from some forces beyond the ordinary power wardens."

"Was he keeping that from you?"

"I don't think he knew until that day. He gave me his pocket winnings, though. He must have known I'd need them." She gave Neriv a leading look.

"Why would you need them? Doesn't he share his money with you daily as it is?"

"Usually, yes. But now it's going to be different for a while." She paused, finding difficulty somehow, as though she were confessing to an action of her own, not Eson's. Neriv looked at her, seeming to intuit that something of leaden weight was about to be cast into the verbal ether.

"He's gone," said Kyra, quietly and with slight despondence, but with definite, final clarity.

"Gone," Neriv repeated, as simply as she had said it. She waited silently for Kyra to elaborate further.

"Gone back over the border, to his ancestral home." She spoke more quickly now, tossing the words as snow down a mountain slope, gathering momentum. "I'm afraid for him in that wild land. He had to leave the capital in fear when we were together in the Steam Territories. He claims he's safe in his ancestors' home, with their deep wellsprings. He's guarded, now, kept prisoner in those dark, cold mountains. He has retreated from everything here and everything he'd built up on the coast. There was some trouble here in the city, with an angry oath-bound and a conspiracy of which I know very little. I'm going into the mountains myself tomorrow. I need to find out what has happened."

"You'll go back to the north to find him? I'm afraid for you," said Neriv quickly.

"I have to. My role is to be there with him. Maybe he's discovered something I need to know, and must hear from him personally, under the warmth of the protective springs. I'm needed."

"Can I tell you a story about one of the guys I met when I went into the foothills?"

"Of course."

"He actually came from the coast, but left everything there to come to the interior."

"And take a job here? Why would someone leave a life on the rich coast, to come and earn our small money? Are you saying he's like Eson in going away against all rational thought?"

"No, I'm saying *you* might be like my friend from the coast. You see, he was married to a woman from a very strict family of the island fiber-optic elites. At first, all was smooth. She came to live with him in the city, and only visited the island mansions for ceremonies. He went with her, enjoyed the brilliance of the sunrise holo-festives with people from across the sea—until he realized they were beginning to tolerate his presence more icily with the passing months. His wife began traveling back to those high mansions more often, leaving him to his relatively humble city life. Eventually, she left without word, and when he tried to reach her, she told him she'd been mistaken to think she could go on with a 'secular' or common life, as she'd termed it. He thought to follow her out to the islands, and even rented a small craft to do so, but when he approached the islands, his signal was ignored, and no landing berth extended. He was thrown off course, and in returning to the city, found his life suddenly unbearable. After some weeks, he responded to an obscure ad for the river station, much as I did."

"And then came up on another dead end," Kyra guessed.

"The comparison only goes so far, I admit. But what I found from his story is that you cannot always alter the course of a trajectory that stretches far into the past. The surface of the sea changes, but not the floor far beneath. I'm only wondering if maybe you should break from Eson. Do something else with your life."

Kyra's reaction had the force of a reflexive instinct. "I can't, because all this will vanish! I'll lose the cities within me that I've built with him, and the links with these others who've signed my own deed. The oath would dissolve instantly if I dissolved my bond with him. It's kind of unthinkable, after all we've gone through together. We're closer than anyone might think, and so are the signatures, now that I've bound them to me."

"Why do you have to do this? Why does he have to do these things?"

"I think he's decided he doesn't need to anymore. But I do, at least just this once. I owe the signatures something, seeing how he's… affected their lives."

Struck by a subtle change in the frequency of energy trails, she closed her eyes. The circle of signatures appeared to her as eyes looking out from a midnight forest, curious, wary and waiting. They had all arrived at the fountains.

"They've reached the fountains," she said, opening her eyes and meeting Neriv's. They exchanged a sudden smile of excitement in the dim light of the courtyard. No one was in sight, and the shutters of the windows above them were mostly closed for the night. Their conversation was abandoned for the time being as they hurried over to the fountain.

Kyra laid the parchment face up on the stone edge and gently placed the stone module onto the middle of the page.

As a simple but elegant origami puzzle, she set about folding the parchment over the stone. The parchment could be folded without harm, the ancient text had told her, but if it were to be unfolded, it would require soaking in a rare and unstable plant essence. The paper seemed to give itself over to the reshaping, folding on clean lines and keeping a crisp form. A steady pulse in her subconscious told her the others were aware of the actions being wrought on the parchment. The traces of each identity were being gathered into the packet's minimal form. The signatures themselves, visible through the sheet, had adhered to the stone's surface like a delicate brushstroke pattern.

The finished packet was a simple, smooth shape that called to mind images of an unknowable future, not a distant past. She remembered Eson saying that the technologies of the old world had been coolly advanced, making present-day innovations seem archaic in design. Glancing at her friend, she could see the somehow lucid-seeming object in her hands also impressed Neriv.

A fresh wind set the fountain roses moving again. She stood up and Neriv did as well, looking toward the alcove in the wall above the fountain. Taking the packet gently in both hands, she stepped over into the fountain's edge and began weaving through the roses. *Will they survive if the fountain fills up?* she wondered. The dry, crumbling sound of the fountain's basin sounded louder and crisper in the night air than it had by day. A kind of clarity had settled over everything, monochromatic halftones and clear lines marking out the details in every stone. Reaching the alcove, she placed the stone carefully in a position like that of the prayer offering she'd found at Loken's fountain. Had he chosen the same fountain this night?

She looked up at Neriv and gave a shrug before making her way back to the fountain's edge. At that moment, someone high above looked briefly out of a window before securing it with a solid sound. The two women pretended to have passed through by chance, and went to stand in a shadow where a wall jagged outward. For several moments, nothing happened.

Neriv gestured silently to the alcove, though Kyra was already watching intently. A soft green glow had begun to illuminate it, and a faint rushing sound like a breeze could be heard, growing until it could be felt through the tiles of the ground.

They both stepped forward, drawn in by curiosity, and made bold as they could now pretend they'd only stumbled upon something in progress if anyone appeared and questioned them.

"I wonder if this is happening at all the fountains?" Neriv said.

"I wonder if this is all that's going on at the fountains," she responded, remembering the power outage of the group's earlier attempt. They waited further, both leaning inward over the fountain's edge, though caution advised otherwise.

From the grate system that rested in the wall above the fountain clear water began to flow slowly downward, a green-white river illuminated by the glowing alcove. She and Neriv looked at each other with the glory of successful conspirators—but in that instant she became aware, too, that they were no longer alone in the courtyard.

Three figures stood in shadow midway between them and the opposite wall. All were large enough to be intimidating in the night streets, particularly the central one, who seemed to loom forward. They'd entered silently, and much worse, their energy traces had been completely undetectable to her.

"You just happened upon this by chance, I suppose?" The central figure spoke with a medley of calm authority and cool disbelief.

Neither she nor Neriv answered. The shadows moved forward, slowly but with deliberateness. She and Neriv edged toward one another, while the fountain behind them slowly came to life with water from deep below the city.

In that moment, all three figures broke away from the shadows, and she let out a quiet, "Ah." Sarah was the larger of the two flanking the speaker. The other was an impish-looking man of young to middle years. The man in the middle, at the older edge of young adulthood, gave off an aura of unreadable solidity. Tuning her senses, she surmised that the energy block masking this group was being fashioned by one in hiding in a nearby street. It could only be the gaudy salamander from the casino!

The central figure spoke almost offhandedly. "How many of you are there? I would guess ten, not including your accomplice here."

"There's enough of us," she countered, trying to affect an equal casualness.

"Enough of you to revive all of these fountains. It's exciting work, isn't it?"

The fountain was now a translucent green pool, and she noted with satisfaction that the roses did float, at least for now. Sarah shot her a private look.

"But where do we come in, you are maybe asking yourself. The problem with what you're doing here is simply that the fountains do not belong to you, or to any of your party. They belong to the Unity Energy Conglomerate."

She mustered up her voice. "Do you work for them?"

"No," he replied dismissively. "I'm contracted by them to aid in certain matters. You know about the workings of contracts, obviously. Ours are of a more traditional nature."

"Even with that fellow hiding in the lane?"

"He's different. Ignore him; he isn't here. He only serves to level the field of our sport."

She sensed the field was anything but level. She chose to ask, "And what is the sport in question?"

"Ask yourself that. Why would you, a citizen with no shares in the company, be meddling with energy and water supplies belonging to Unity?" The voice was not one of threat, but of purposeful incitement toward an answer already known.

She hesitated, but felt emboldened by another glance at the fountain. She'd been the one to revive them! But how did this cohort know that they would be in the courtyard at that moment? Were these the people who'd been making life a struggle for Eson?

"We do know of your relationship to Eson, if that clarifies anything for you." The voice was nearly careless in its nonchalance, but the words were too sharp and pointed to be random, or impersonal. She felt a slinking sense of invasion such as she hadn't known since her days in Veridi's service. The speaker's horrid finesse put her unnervingly in mind of the Heiress.

Neriv gave her a look of puzzlement bordering on shock. Kyra placed her hand reassuringly on hers. The fountain radiated an alpine green-white light, and the roses drifted lightly on the water. She was reminded of how she'd associated the roses with honesty when she'd seen them before. She decided to work with basic truths in her account of the situation.

"Sarah, who stands behind you," she said, leaning to the side and looking past the central figure, "Sarah told me about the deep history of these fountains, and guided me along the way to enact what you see tonight. Do you know this?"

Sarah tilted her head to one side and looked to the speaker

with a wry and wise look. Her other companion furrowed his soft brow, clearly only now becoming aware of certain details.

The speaker nodded with contemplative approval. "We may have had a hand in that. In any event, we have something noteworthy here. No one had bothered with these fountains for so long—but here you come along and sign a type of deal with a variety of other persons, agreeing to a division of ownership among yourselves. It would be an unthinkable act of corporate trespass, were it not for your anomalous ability to channel energies."

"Eson could have done this," said Sarah simply, then added, "but he wouldn't have without setting up something irreversible and completely unethical."

"I fit conveniently into someone's plans, then," said Kyra matter-of-factly, perceiving an advantage in cooperation.

"You could say that—but I regret to say you do not own these fountains. Unity will allow your trespass, if only for the novelty of its results."

"Does that mean we won't be rewarded for what we've done here? If that's the case, I'll remove the deed from the fountain myself. I only did this for the benefit of the group."

"You'll each be given a stipend," he said dismissively. "The real oath is between you and Unity. I'm only the link connecting you to them. I know about the other contracts as well, of course, so I was considered a suitable intercessor."

She sensed deliberateness as he let drop his knowledge of the other contracts. Was he implying a tie to Veridi? She felt suddenly cold at the thought.

"So, what must I do?" *And who are you, if you don't work for the Unity Company?* She wanted to ask it but did not, feeling awed by the speaker's stony resolve.

His face broke into a rugged and controlled smile. "You only need to go to this address," he said, smoothly presenting a card with a Unity logo and an address in the Glass City. "Soon," he added, with a note of coercion.

With a nearly rehearsed ease, he turned to the others, and they left the square so rapidly it appeared a trick of the light had enrobed them in invisibility.

She and Neriv watched after them for a moment, taken aback by the encounter, then turned to the fountain, succored by its glow but still held captive by the ominous words of the visitors. Their accomplishment with the ancient watercourses of the city now seemed but a small act in the larger current of the world, pebbles cast into an abyss... but still a success.

That night Jado found himself lying on Eson's living room couch while the low voices of Kyra and Neriv murmured nearby. He'd learned of Eson's retreat to the mountains, and while jolted by the knowledge, had wavered little in his appraisal of Eson. One who has surprised before is likely to do so again, and he had come to expect this of Eson. The north, the mountain house and the springs remained mysterious to him. Eson had disappeared into a place Jado knew only from maps and urban legends.

He finally slept, and woke to the welcome thought of seeing his family that day. Scrawling a short note to the two women, who still slept, he slipped out and hopped a tram to his home neighborhood. The tram released him near the entrance to the lane he'd known since childhood, Glass Spells Out a Name. He entered the lane and moved slowly along its curved length, looking deeply into the glass patterns on the wall before him, drawn into a cyclical sense of time, of future and past melding as he repeated the ritual of finding names in the glass. There were the names of his family, Eson, Kyra, Rael, changing as he saw them, seeming to flow in a two-way river of glass as he moved past. The river led him along the lane as though there were water captured under the glass, and when he came to the end it was as if the river had come to a coastline, an ocean formed by a further curve in the wall.

Looking up at last from the wall, Jado saw before him the figure of Sarah, alone. She was smiling, and he returned the look, glad to see her at last, though there was awkwardness in the notion that he'd helped Eson to attain his wishes while she was polarized against Eson.

"We may at last speak openly," said Sarah in her soothing voice.

Jado nodded. "It's good to be home. I'm sorry I couldn't write again. Eson kept me busy until he returned here a few days ago."

"I know a bit about what you two were up to on the coast. There were others in this city interested in knowing about your coastal works, too. I kept the knowledge to myself though, not to protect Eson, but to protect you. I wanted you to benefit from your involvement with Eson, even though I disagree with his electric scavenger hunts."

"I disagreed with him sometimes, and his—energy pirating, I guess you could call it. He was reckless and changeable, and I never knew on what ground I stood. It's been a great pressure off my mind to be finished with those concerns."

He took Sarah into his confidence as easily as he always had. They walked slowly along the streets of the Niyali community toward his family home. They came to the courtyard called Glass in the Pattern of a Celestial Calendar, and stopped to see the morning light reflecting on the calendar.

"What will you do now?" Sarah asked him, much as an older sibling would.

He swept his arm slowly through the air before the Calendar, as though he were gathering in all the roundness of time that was represented in its colors.

"Right now? I'm going to stay with my family for a while

again before I go back to the coast. I can earn some good money if I work there." He paused, somehow reluctant to tell her about Rael, not wanting Sarah to know everything about his inner life. He told her, instead, of his plans to cross the sea. "Then, I'd like to go to the islands of the Niyali and see for myself what has taken place there, where my family came from."

Looking at the Calendar, he knew this was how he would make his mark in the world of his community, ensuring its future through a pilgrimage to its past. He would gather past and present within him, then bring the past back with him to his family and community here. He felt a sudden pang of sympathy for Eson in that moment, knowing why it was Eson had retreated to the springs, understanding him clearly for the first time.

The underground rivers that supplied the city's fountains also fed green, steam-clouded pools that burrowed soft fissures into the snow of the northern mountains. Through a perfectly transparent sheet of glass, Kyra witnessed the mountain landscape, as though she and her dark train were entering winter. The car around her was nearly empty; the few passengers slept reclined in their mantles, and the svelte metal bones of the train were visible. A steaming dragon with angular chrome sinews ferried the sleepers into winter, dreaming them forward in its protective warmth.

The Unity Energy building had been like a great carapace, winged and fantailed with elevators running from its great center out to the ends of the attenuated wings. She'd been received in a carpeted, low-ceilinged room in the outer wings, and sat on a cushion while an even-voiced and vaguely ceramic-looking representative of the company guided her through a series of translucent and fragile papers. She was designated as a benefactor of the company, and given power to administrate a system of continued compensation to her oath-bound circle. She'd felt relieved, as there was no need, then, to upset any of the signatures with a change in their bargain.

That had been the day after the night at the fountains, and now, on the evening of the day after that, she was on a train traveling into the north. Impressions floated past her of the sleek mercenary who had intercepted the fountain revival, of his chillingly smooth speech that seemed to compress the air with its assuredness.

He, Sarah, the gaudy salamander, and the soft-looking soul who'd stood with them all formed a dangerous alliance. They could wreak confusion over Eson's enchantments—and could possibly even set him under their own collusive will, corralling him under their stronger force! Eson hadn't said these had been the ones to mobilize him out of the city, but she was certain they were. She understood now his action, and would come to him with understanding in her heart instead of the shock she'd felt when he'd told her of his retreat to the north.

The border crossing was easy, the guards almost lax with the sparsely peopled train. They waved her through, knowing of her case in advance. Eson had evidently been able to swing his influence over certain levels of the bureaucracy, at least.

She watched for the first signs of the concealed mountain chateaus, but caught only glimpses of dark glass and wooden beams before the train came to rest at the alpine platform. As she had expected there was a guard, who was neither abrupt nor friendly, waiting to escort her to the house. The wind made low, resonant sounds outside the heated corridors as they ascended.

Two more guards stood motionless before Eson's door. They stepped aside without a word as she entered.

When she'd left the house last, it had stood empty and silent behind her, and only the servant's revenant presence seemed possible. Now there were people and myriad belongings covering every piece of furniture available. The clamor of human voices echoed beneath the distant ceiling, tempering the cool modernity of the décor with life.

She couldn't see Eson in the collage of people, but noticed at a closer look that there were cameras and sound equipment scattered through the room. She recognized some of the faces as those she'd met on her earlier visit—Lida Riso, the filmmaker some years older than Eson, had just noticed her and was coming toward her, disentangling herself from the tableau of visitors.

"You've arrived! Beautiful little Kyra-kara!" She used the northern diminutive, reserved for those toward one feels a closeness or sympathy. She took Kyra under her arm and they walked deeper into the heart of the house. "Eson's out in the springs, and hasn't come out for a while. You should know that before you see him. He's changed. I don't think he even came out of the springs to sleep last night. Most mortals couldn't stay in there that long. He may not be like us anymore."

"You mean he's become more like his ancestors? They lived in devotion to the springs, didn't they?"

"In a way, that may be. But they had technologies to aid in their transformation, I think."

She felt uneasy. "He said he needed to come here and be close to the springs. I didn't know he meant to embark on any kind of transformation."

"I don't think he meant to when he came here. When we arrived, he was surveying his papers and making sure nothing had been disturbed. Over the last few days, though, he's become more and more reclusive. We've all gone into the springs for short periods of time, but no one can outlast him. Maybe you can break through to him."

She was struck wordless. She hadn't thought there would be

a need for breaking through any kind of barrier to speak to him. Maybe he really needed her to be with him, wouldn't respond to any one else.

She changed the subject, suddenly wondering at the large group gathered in the house. "Are you making a movie here?"

"Actually, yes, we *are* shooting some footage here. You see, I'm making a film about Eson's family line, about their history and their present troubles in the political climate of the Steam Territories. We're going to be making a journey to the old world in about a month, to see the valleys where the first ancestors found their power. —But you don't want to hear about that right now. I'll take your case, and you can go out to see Eson."

"Yes, I'd like to see him," she agreed, and handed over her small traveling case. She and Lida clasped hands for a moment, then Kyra wove through the film crew to the sliding door leading to the springs.

Outside the excited murmur of the house, in the intense glow of the rocky enclosure, she was quickly enveloped in the elemental atmosphere of the springs. On the rocks and glass above, the ancient rock bound pine trees held stoic postures, as hands folded in eternal mudras, gestures reverent or meditative over the springs. Along a far edge of the rock wall, water coursed down from the smaller pool above. Eson was alone in the springs, though the litter of shoes and accoutrements on the rock floor attested to earlier company. He looked up when she arrived, watching her through a veil of eternal steam. Though he appeared tired, he seemed flushed with the energy of the springs. Seeing him again, she felt she was again falling over a waterfall's edge.

"Kyra," he said, with an affectionate but melancholic tone, as though he were observing her from a distance.

She placed her hands on the board ledge that rested on the edge of the pool and leaned toward him. Their hands met across the surface of the water, two halves of a floating bridge.

She said simply, "The fountains are running again."

"I could tell. Did you have any trouble, though?" He looked at her with thinly masked concern.

"Trouble with the fountains? No, they ran as easily as if they'd never stopped. Afterward, though, we were surrounded—"

"By who?" Eson interrupted urgently.

"Sarah and that trickster from the casino were there, though the trickster kept hidden in a side street. I'm sure it was him. The other two I didn't recognize; an imposing sort of mercenary who claimed to work with the Unity Energy Company, and a bland-looking fellow I thought I'd seen before."

"You did once, when I met with him in the Glass City and you ran away to dance with your friends. You don't know anything more about the mercenary? Did he have a certain voice about him?"

"Yes, like he could melt metal with his words. Do you know him? Who is he?"

"I was hoping you wouldn't ask, my dear." He hesitated. "You've met Veridi's most recent lover."

Kyra shivered despite the warmth of the steam. Her grip on Eson's hand slackened, and she felt she was being pulled down by magnetic forces in the rocks. Eson gave her a look of understanding and held on to her hand, but did not advance toward her from his place in the springs. "Apparently he has the same effect on you as he does on me," Eson said gently. "I'm afraid of them both, he and Veridi."

Kyra looked up at him. "So am I. Could they really damage you?"

"I don't know. While I was in the city they could, yes, but now that I'm here, no. This is the only safe place for me." He paused, and then said with care, "You should go into the house and get something to eat. This is too much for someone who's just been on a long journey."

"I don't want anything," she said softly, stating a basic acceptance of things. She prepared to enter the springs, piling her clothes on the wooden ledge, and submerged in the pool, letting a shiver of release run through her as the warm waters of the planet surrounded her.

The world around her disappeared, until there was nothing outside the spring: no crowded house or political state, nor any past or future. They were the only people in the universe while unified by the close, dark space of the pool. Yet they were divided from each other, a barrier of vapors and water between them… stationed on opposite sides of a stationary vortex, unable to reach each other through the natural forces of the spring.

"You're divided from me," she said. "You belong to the springs right now."

"Yes, I do. I came here to escape from the outside, but also to develop a new kind of strength. I may stay here for a long time."

She felt a lurch in her heart, the steady surface of the world turning slightly on its side. How could she live if he were to remain walled in with his springs? She couldn't stay here in the ancient waters. She was only mortal, and he was becoming something else. Her body grew weak at the thought, and the force of the springs supported her, keeping her afloat. "How will I love you, if your love is for the springs?"

"It won't be easy for either of us. I don't enjoy that I must be divided from you in order to develop as my ancestors did. With time, I think you could become similar to me, and could join me here, if you wanted."

"But I'm not part of your lineage. I couldn't become like you. I don't have it in me. And it's not what I want, really."

"Of course. I don't know myself if it's possible for someone who is not of our line." He looked thoughtfully at her. "Listen, Kyra. Lida and her crew are traveling to the old world next month, and will stay there for some time. They're going to film in the valleys and ruins of my ancestors, and at the sacred pools of Sarhul. Go with them if you like. You can see another place that's completely different from here. It will alter your perspective on the world. I've told Lida about the orbs you recorded using the vision bird. She'd really like to have you along to assist with filming. Afterward, you could come back."

She suppressed a tumult of resistance and anger. They'd discussed her, and made plans for her without her knowledge. The springs submerged her emotions, and steam veiled her face from Eson. She didn't answer.

"Kyra, I don't want you to be away from me. But I think you should consider it. When you go there and understand what has created all that exists now, you'll be a different person." He looked to her but made no move toward her, and in the dim pool he looked distant and somehow small. But still, the waterfall was there, and as the water of the pool supported her upward, she was also pushed downward by the weight of her emotions.

"Give me time," she said, and turned back to the edge of the pool. She reached for one of the large towels that rested on the wooden ledge, then broke away from the warmth of the water, wrapping herself in the soft material. "Give me time," she repeated, and turned to the sliding door, reinstating the world outside the springs.

Back in the house a few people looked up, but then went back to their discussions of film and lighting, gossip and opinion. Lida called out to her and brought her a plate of food, which she took with murmured gratitude before climbing up to the empty upper rooms of the house. To her relief there was no one in the high bedroom. She curled up once more on Eson's smooth bed, looking at the table where she'd first found the vision bird, and the window beyond. The sky outside was flat with impending snow, the hills white and green, and the windows of other houses reflected the white of the sky.

The rock floor beside the springs represented the last solid ground I would stand on for a long time. I'd only intended to immerse myself in the shelter of the springs, to rebuild my defenses after the ambushes I'd suffered at the high bank and in the casino. Once I'd been immersed for some hours, though, much longer than anyone else could withstand, I understood the springs held a longer sojourn for me.

Now I've hurt Kyra, and may never really have her with me again. I only want her to go with Lida and see the old world, the place of Sarhul's origins, my own origins. It is not such a long time, and when she returns to me here, I'll be ready to be with her again, and perhaps she will be ready to accept the life that I've chosen. She has her freedom. She can go to the city, to the coast, anywhere she likes. I feel she will find a new part of herself if she journeys to the other continent. Kyra has a talent for making movies of her own, as her orb pictures of the Glass City and the steam capital have shown. Though it is not easy for her, she will develop into a strong being, possibly stronger than me. I rely on my inherited powers to attain this state of near immortality, while she was able to revive the fountains using her own newly learned skills!

For my own life, I've concluded it's time to move beyond the perversely acquisitive and delusional exploits in which I've long engaged. That grim panel of judgment was sent to give me a way marker, to tell me that I must change. Veridi's mercenary lover, the Domain Chaoser who drained my energies, Sarah who tracked me and Lonred who led them to me, all synchronized their efforts to move me beyond my limited self. There was nowhere for me to go but back into the mountains, into the springs where I'm now free.

I can still feel the echo of the contracts, so I know Veridi hasn't destroyed them. I've lost them from my domain of control, but I've learned to do without them. They're worth more to Veridi intact than they are if destroyed, because she believes she can exert control over me with them. I won't make an effort to disabuse her of the notion. It provides me with the assurance she will keep them well cared for.

A video communication of Veridi's agent informed me that the contract relating to her personally had been nullified with the help of a special practitioner. This suits me immensely, as I'd as soon have my connections with her dissolved completely.

So I am keeping a long vigil here in the springs. I can sense my ancestors around me, and their protective legacy running through the underground rivers below this pool.

Nothing ever resolves, it only changes. New things are created out of old, but nothing ever really disappears or ends. Within a few days of arriving in the mountains, Kyra decided she would in fact travel to the old world with Lida and her crew. She had a month to prepare for the journey, and planned to go to the coast first with Neriv to see Jado and his new companion, Rael. She spent many hours in the springs, close but never quite completely together with Eson. She always ended up having to step out of the springs to eat or to sleep, while he stayed on with a seemingly tireless, immortal endurance. He spoke of stepping beyond delusion, but at other times lamented it was impossible to do so. She often left him to speak with Lida or to be alone in the other rooms of the house, unable to reconcile Eson's transformation or his isolation with her own emotions.

The fervor of the wanderer awakened in her again and she dreamed increasingly of other countries, places unknown to her heart, as she prepared to make another journey across the meridians of the globe.

Dana Copithorne holds a bachelor's degree in anthropology and has studied Shamanic religions in Siberia, Japanese culture, Zen aesthetics, and Japanese and Buddhist architectural traditions. She has taught the English language in Japan and has been honored by the Czechoslovak Arts and Science Society with the Dr. Josef Hasek Award for her paper, published in the central European journal *Kosmas*, linking socio-political reality in the Czech Republic with Czech science fiction and other literatures. She is also a talented artist in watercolor and pen-and-pencil media, and provided artwork for *The Steam Magnate* drawn from her love of architecture and landscape.

She resides in Vancouver, Canada, where she is currently at work on a sequel.

Find out more about

The Steam Magnate

and author Dana Copithorne
at www.aiopublishing.com

Reviews
Author interview
Write your own review
Direct email link to the author

Order another copy of this book online at
www.aiopublishing.com for free shipping (discounted
shipping for international residents) and fast
fulfillment of your order.

Or to order by mail inside the United States, send a
request and check or money order for $16.00 (South
Carolina residents please add applicable sales tax) to:

Aio Publishing Co., LLC
P. O. Box 30788
Charleston, SC 29417

on**spec**

Please also consider our friends to the north...
OnSpec is the Canadian magazine of the fantastic,
nominated many times over for the Hugo Award (Best
Semi-Pro Magazine). Mention this page
to them and receive a free back issue!